Jaspa's Journey 3:

Jaspa's Waterloo

Rich Meyrick

SPEAKING VOLUMES, LLC
NAPLES, FLORIDA
2017

Jaspa's Journey 3: Jaspa's Waterloo

ISBN 978-1-62815-317-0

For Abi and Henry

*"A man's feet should be planted in his country,
but his eyes should survey the World"*
~ George Santayana

Acknowledgments

Every book takes more than one person's efforts. It's been said many times before, but that's simply because it's true. *Jaspa's Journey* is no exception, so I'd like to thank the following people (in alphabetical order) for their input on all things from storyline, to editing, to artwork: Auriel, Björn, Brad, Bryn, Jamie, Lori, Penny and Tyler. I'd also like to thank François (aka Jiheffe), owner of the *Waterloo 1815* geocache (which has sadly since been archived) for giving me permission to write a story partially based on his cache. Last, but by no means least, I'd like to thank my wife, Sue, the heart and soul of *Jaspa's Journey*.

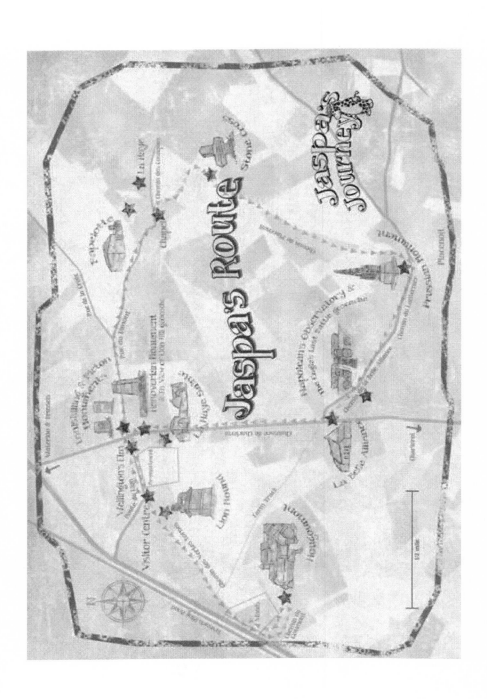

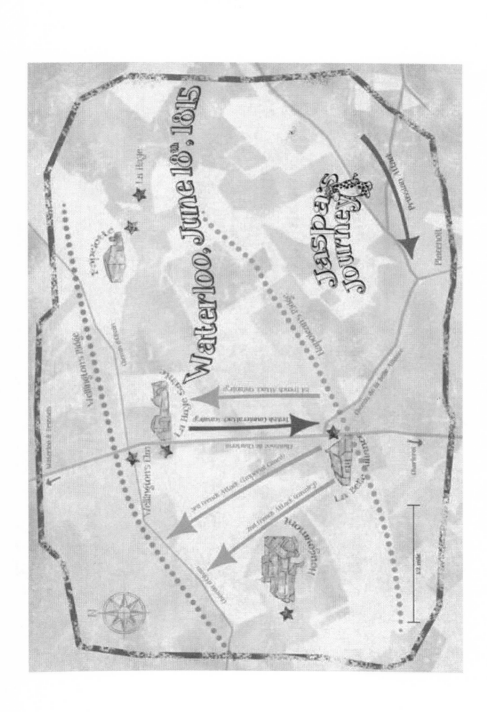

Author's Notes

1. The Real World

Something to bear in mind as you're reading this book: with only one or two small exceptions, everywhere that Jaspa goes and everything he sees is real. Really real. If you're lucky enough you could go there too, and follow in Jaspa's footsteps. In fact the book you're about to read is based around three true stories.

2. Geocaches

The geocaches described in this book were all real and active at the time of writing. For that reason, a (very) few of the details have been altered slightly, so as not to ruin the fun for those who what to go out and find the caches for themselves without too many spoilers.

Sadly, the *Waterloo 1815* geocache upon which much of the story hangs was archived in September 2013

2. Gravee's Glossary

One of the main characters in *Jaspa's Journey* is called Gravee (pronounced Gravy). He's Scottish, and has an accent some people can find a little tricky to grasp at first. If you're not Scottish and you find yourself having a little trouble understanding Gravee, here's a piece of advice... try reading what he says out loud. No honestly, try it. It really does help!

To help the non-Scottish, if you're still having trouble (or just for fun) you can visit Jaspa's website (http://www.jaspasjourney.com/Gravee-s-Glossary-Maps.htm) for a glossary of some of Gravee's more unusual words and pronunciations.

Table of Contents

Prologue

"Now don't forget to look after my smartphone, Ben."

"Aw, Mum!"

"It's nae a toy, ye ken," mutters Gravee under his breath.

"It's not a toy, you know," Mrs McRae informs her son from the driver's seat of the car.

"An' it's only tae be used in emergencies," murmurs Gravee.

Ben treats his friend to a distinctly *un*friendly stare.

"And it's only to be used in emergencies," says Mrs McRae, unaware of Gravee's good-natured mockery.

Sam, Bisckits and Portia put their heads together and whisper in unison, "I mean it, data roaming is expensive abroad."

"I heard that Sam McRae!" declares the children's mother, looking at her daughter in the rear-view mirror. "But it's true. Data roaming is expensive abroad." She wags her left index finger over her shoulder to emphasise her point.

Sam and her accomplices burst into giggles.

Ben just scowls at them.

Jaspa can't help laughing, too. It must be at least the fifth or sixth time Mrs McRae has given her 12-year-old son the same lecture since he got up this morning. And like the others, Jaspa can recite the whole speech practically word-for-word.

***

Mrs McRae parks the car and makes sure her two children haven't left anything behind. Then she leads them around the corner to Edinburgh's Waverley Station.

They enter the main ticket hall of the railway station just after 7 am. The hall is constructed of warm, honey-coloured stone and decorated more like an exterior of a building than an interior. In fact, you could be forgiven for thinking you were standing in an outside courtyard, if not for the ornate ceiling, with its multitude of intricate skylights surrounding a large, grand, circular glass dome in the centre.

The ticket hall is already fairly busy with people rushing to and from trains, most of them presumably on their way to work on this weekday morning in mid June.

***

"There they are!" exclaims Sam. Without waiting for a response, she sprints off towards a small cluster of people gathering by the coffee bar in the middle of the hall, directly beneath the dome.

The group is mostly made up of children and their parents. The adults stand around making small talk, while the kids babble breathlessly to their parents and each other. The children are all members of the Young Adventurers, an increasingly popular association run along similar principles to the Scouts or Guides, but with more of an emphasis on the world around us. Occasionally, like today, this includes travelling to see different places firsthand.

In the centre of the excitement, grinning broadly, are Jimmy and Laurel Williamson, the trip leaders. When not busy organising the Central Edinburgh Branch of the Young Adventurers, the Williamsons run the hiking store near Ben and Sam's home in the city's New Town district. Popular in the local community, Jimmy and Laurel are two of the nicest people you could ever meet.

Unfortunately, the same can't be said for their son, Gobber.

Gobber Williamson (real name Kevin, at least according to his parents) is a bully, plain and simple. He and his mates, Billy and Fergus McIntyre, used to love being known throughout New Town as *the Mob*. In truth, people actually called them *the Bairn Mob* (*bairn* being Scottish slang for *child*), but the Mob conveniently ignored this. Much to his parents' shame, the Gobfather (as Gobber liked to be called) and his cronies revelled in the Mob's small-time notoriety.

Until Ben McRae went and spoiled it all, that is.

***

One cold November evening a couple of years ago, the Mob were knocking around Greyfriars Kirkyard looking for some minor mischief with which to entertain themselves. They began with one of their favourite pastimes: trying to rouse the ghost of Sir George 'Bloody' Mackenzie, a particularly vicious poltergeist believed by many to haunt the Black Mausoleum, the final resting place of the infamous hanging judge. To their disappointment (but not surprise) Bloody Mackenzie once again failed to rise to their tormenting, so they went in search of less supernatural amusements.

To the Mob's delight, Ben McRae chose the wrong time to cut through Greyfriars on his way home. It wasn't long before Gobber and the McIntyre cousins had their prey on the ground, penned in a corner between an ancient tomb and the east wall of the kirkyard.

Then everything went wrong. At least as far as the Gobfather was concerned.

Without warning, the Mob found themselves under attack. One minute they were about to get their hands on McRae's pocket money, the next they were being pelted with a fierce hail of small stones. Even more worrying, the stones seemed to be coming out of thin air.

3

As with bullies everywhere, the Mob much preferred being the ones dishing out the punishment, and didn't like this role-reversal. So when the barrage changed from stones to bits of hardened bird poop, the Mob (who were understandably freaked-out at this point) decided enough was enough and decided to make a run for it.

But none of them got more a couple of steps before they were all unceremoniously hurled to the ground.

Looking like three hog-tied crabs, and in a state of utter panic, the Mob frantically tried to scrabble away, painfully scraping their elbows, hands and knees. Sporting a bloody nose from where he fell over, Gobber (the limited brains of the operation) finally realised that their unseen assailant had somehow managed to knot their shoelaces together. Kicking off their footwear, he and the terrified McIntyres raced for the kirkyard's closest gate as if the hounds of hell were on their heels.

To this day, Billy and Fergus remain convinced that they were attacked by the ghost of Bloody Mackenzie that night. And the effect has been nothing short of miraculous. The cousins are now reformed characters. They no longer pick on other kids, and their school marks have even improved (well, a little, anyway).

Once his initial terror finally subsided, however, Gobber Williamson became increasingly certain that Ben McRae was somehow behind the assault. He still doesn't know how the little runt managed it, but the Gobfather continues to hold Ben personally responsible for what happened that night and, as a consequence, for breaking up the Mob. As such, Gobber never passes up an opportunity to harass or embarrass his sworn enemy.

That being said, Gobber never went back to reclaim his shoes (although he'd never admit it). And hasn't placed a single foot inside Greyfriars Kirkyard since that fateful night.

Not even once!

***

What really happened to the Mob in Greyfriars Kirkyard that chilly November evening is perhaps even more unlikely than being attacked by a blood-thirsty poltergeist. For the thing that came to Ben's rescue that evening wasn't a ghost, but a real, live creature.

A creature called a *Ses*.

A Ses named Gravee.

You've undoubtedly heard or read stories about gnomes, elves, pixies, leprechauns and the like. In fact, there's no end of tales about a whole host of elusive *little people*, which are variously friendly, mischievous, malicious, or out-and-out malevolent.

Now, if any of these miniature human-like beings really existed (which they don't), the Ses (which do) would be the animal world's equivalent. Although without any of that magical nonsense. The vast majority of animals (except humans), from aardvark to chimpanzee, have a Ses counterpart.

Gravee, for example, is a Dogses. A West Highland Dogses, to be precise. As such, he's covered in white fur. And only about three inches tall.

At this point you're probably saying to yourself, *Yeah, right! If Ses are real, how come I've never seen one?*

Well, if you were a Seer you probably would have by now. As for the rest of us, the Ses are able to trick our eyes into basically ignoring them, using an ability they call *blending*.

Now blending isn't magic. As has already been said, there's nothing magical about the Ses. Blending is more of a skill, similar to being able to play the guitar or being good at the long jump. And as with the guitar and long jump, it takes young Ses a lot of practice to master blending. But

5

once they have, a Ses can blend into the background, fooling human eyes into believing they're not even there.

Unless that human is a Seer, of course. Because blending doesn't work on Seers.

And on that momentous night in the kirkyard, Ben McRae discovered he was a Seer.

***

Gravee had lived in Greyfriars Kirkyard since he was a child. Although he'd generally ignored the humans that came and went, he'd often seen the Mob getting up to no good in the cemetery, particularly around the Black Mausoleum of Sir George Mackenzie.

Gravee had also noticed the McRae boy in the kirkyard, usually on his way to or from school. But unlike the Mob, young McRae seemed like a decent child. He was always respectful in the graveyard, and Gravee had even seen him pick up the occasional piece of litter.

On the night in question, Gravee had been minding his own business, as usual. But when he spotted the Mob acting suspiciously near James Harlay's memorial, something had made him take a closer look. The instant he discovered the troublesome trio had the McRae boy trapped, he'd known he couldn't let it pass. Because if there's one thing Gravee can't stand, it's bullies.

So the Dogses had decided to give the Mob a taste of their own medicine, by playing on their obvious fascination with the supposed ghost of Bloody Mackenzie (Gravee doesn't believe in ghosts). Knowing the boys wouldn't be able to see him while he was blending, Gravee had tied the Mob's laces together, before climbing up onto James Harlay's memorial. From there he'd bombarded the confused and alarmed youths with pebbles and pigeon poo.

Although he's not an unkind soul, Gravee had nonetheless taken a great deal of satisfaction from the shock on their faces.

But as the Mob fled, Gravee had got a shock of his own... When the boy in the corner looked him straight in the eye and said, "Thank you. But who are you?"

Now, most Ses grow up believing that Seers are the stuff of legend. Beings invented to frighten Ses children when families gather around the fire at night. But in that instant, Gravee had discovered that wasn't the case, and that Seers really existed.

Ben had made a similar discovery that evening, watching in amazement as Gravee scared off his tormentors. Obviously, he hadn't known what Gravee was at the time (having never seen a Ses before) or even that he was a Seer. Gravee had explained all that later. But Ben had known that his life would never be the same again.

And since that day, Ben and Gravee have been inseparable. Except, of course, for the months Gravee spent lost and alone in Africa.

***

The McRae family travel a lot together, largely to make up for the time that both parents are forced to spend away from home through work. Ben and Sam know they're extremely lucky to have already seen more of the World than most people manage in their entire lifetime. That's why the Young Adventurers is the perfect club for them.

From the moment he and Ben met, it became normal for Gravee to go along with the McRaes on their travels. Although the boy's parents remain completely unaware of this fact to this day, since they're not Seers.

Sam isn't a true Seer either, but she knows all about Gravee. The Dogses had felt an immediate warmth for Ben's likeable little sister, and it wasn't long before he had taken the bold step of revealing himself to her. From that instant, Sam was irreversibly initiated to the incredible world of the Ses.

But during one of the McRae's trips, Gravee had become stranded in the Serengeti National Park, in the East African country of Tanzania. For two months he had hopelessly wandered the Serengeti Plains in search of a way home to Scotland. Then one night, when Gravee was at his lowest ebb, he had stumbled into the camp belonging to Jaspa and his friends. And once again, everything had changed.

***

Jaspa is a Giraffeses. You'd know it from the instant you saw him. And yet he's far from tall and graceful. In fact, Ben thinks of him as being a bit dumpy. And he's only 3½ inches tall.

At the time Jaspa met Gravee, he and his brother, Bisckits, had been in the middle of a rite of passage known simply as *the Journey*, accompanied by their cousin Portia, who had completed the task the previous year. The Journey requires all members of Jaspa's Herd, when they reach a certain age, to complete one whole circuit of the Great Migration—a gruelling 500-mile struggle for survival annually undertaken by over two million wildebeest, zebra and antelope on the Serengeti Plains.

Upon hearing of Gravee's plight, however, Jaspa and Bisckits had abandoned the traditional Journey to help him. Together with Portia and some other Ses friends, they had managed to get the Dogses to Kilimanjaro Airport. There, instead of saying goodbye to Gravee as planned, Jaspa, Bisckits and Portia had unexpectedly found themselves onboard a plane and bound for Edinburgh.

***

Since leaving Africa, the three Giraffeses have trotted the globe with Gravee, Ben and Sam. As a result, Jaspa's Journey has become so much more than anything he could have imagined when he first left home.

And today it's about to continue on a train to Brussels, the unofficial capital of Europe.

***

Part 1

The Battle of Waterloo

Chapter One

Belgium Bound

"Morning, Sam," Laurel greets Ben's little sister. "Are you excited?"

"You bet!" declares Sam, barely able to contain that excitement.

Mrs McRae looks at the Williamsons with mock pity. "You're going to have your hands full this week, aren't you?" she jokes.

"Nah!" Jimmy disagrees, with a smile. "It'll be fun! Besides, Dennis and Diane will keep the wee darlings straight."

Dennis and Diane are students at the University of Edinburgh who regularly help out at Young Adventurer meetings, and who have volunteered to assist on the Brussels trip. The pair stand beside the Williamsons, looking slightly awkward and out of place, grinning self-consciously at Jimmy's compliment.

"Don't worry, Mrs McRae," states Diane, evidently feeling she should say something. "Everything will be fine."

"Aye," agrees Jimmy, winking at Sam. "So long as your two trouble-makers don't misbehave too much."

Mrs McRae laughs. "Well, good luck with that!"

***

Ben wanders over to his two closest friends, Abi and Henry Greaning. Although brother and sister are very close, the Greanings couldn't be more different.

Abi is in Ben's year in school and is almost as tall as he is. She's lean and swift, and loves nothing more than beating the boys at football. Quick to laugh, Abi is popular with the girls, while her straight, shoulder-length red hair and bright smile turn all the boys' heads—including Ben's, although he's careful not to let this show. Abi, for her part, thinks Ben is quite cute, especially his freckles and slightly messy, dark hair, but she likewise keeps this to herself.

Ben takes his mum's smartphone out of his pocket to show the Greanings.

"Wow!" says Henry. "She's really letting you take it?"

Henry is Abi's polar-opposite. He's slightly overweight and a good two inches shorter than his sister, despite being a year older. Unlike Abi, Henry doesn't really enjoy sports, although this is probably due to the disappointment and embarrassment of always being one of the last picked for teams in school.

In many ways, Henry reminds Jaspa of Ernest, their Ratses friend in London. The most obvious similarity is their incredible ability to retain facts and figures, especially when it's something they're interested in. And like Ernest, Henry tends to be a little awkward around other people. In the boy's case, this comes from the fact he's painfully shy, which is a great shame, because among friends he's actually really talkative and has a razor-sharp sense of humour.

"Yep," confirms Ben, with a slightly smug air.

Abi raises a knowing eyebrow.

"Well, alright," Ben concedes, turning slightly red. "I'm only allowed to make calls or use the internet in an emergency. But we can still play the games on it."

"Cool," relents Abi, with a grin.

"What games ha...?" Henry stops mid-word, staring at the ticket hall's main entrance. "I don't believe it!" he groans.

Ben and Abi both turn to follow Henry's gaze.

"What's he doing here?" Ben asks the universe in general. They're not even onboard the train, and already this trip has taken a distinctly unpleasant turn.

Because slouching into the station is the Gobfather.

***

Feeling deflated, Ben rejoins his mother and sister.

"What's wrong?" his mum asks.

"Nothing," Ben lies. Although in truth, the thought of spending almost a week with Gobber has seriously taken some of the shine off the trip.

"Okay everyone," Jimmy Williamson announces. "It's time to go."

Parents say (sometimes tearful) goodbyes, then smile bravely as their children follow Jimmy, Dennis and Diane towards the platform. Every few steps the youngsters turn back to wave energetically at their mums and dads.

Mrs McRae gives both her children a big hug. "Have fun!" she says. "And look after each other."

"We will," they answer together, heading after the others.

"And remember," calls Mrs McRae. "Be careful with that smartphone."

"Interesting," a mocking voice whispers in Ben's ear. "So Baby McRae's got a smartphone, huh?"

Ben and Sam turn to see Gobber's unpleasant smile right behind them.

"Pay nae attention tae th' wee eejit," instructs Gravee. He and Jaspa are perched in their customary place on Ben's shoulder, while Bisckits and Portia are riding in Sam's hood, as usual.

Ben ignores his friend's advice. Instead, with as much scorn as he can muster, he asks, "What do you want, Kevin?" His dig is rewarded with a flare of anger in Gobber's face.

"It's Gobfather to you, McRae," the bully retorts automatically. "But Mr Gobber will do."

13

Gravee rolls his eyes. "Here we go!" he mutters.

Gobber looks slyly behind to make sure his mum, who's bringing up the rear of the group, is out of earshot. "You know what I think?" he hisses at Ben. "I think a phone like that is too much of a responsibility for a baby like you. You should probably let me look after it for you. Just to be on the safe side."

"Go boil your haggis!" suggests Sam sweetly.

"Och!" exclaims Gravee. "Dinnae ye start tae!"

The anger again flares in Gobber's eyes. "You want to be careful, you little brat," he snarls. "Everyone knows how easily smartphones are broken. Or lost."

Jaspa looks at Gravee. "This isn't going to end well," he observes.

"Ye ken, ye huv a reit talent for understatement, pal," the Dogses replies, shaking his head.

***

"*Go boil your haggis?*" chuckles Abi. "Where did that come from?"

"Dunno," shrugs Sam.

The four children face each other across a table—boys on one side, girls on the other—of an intercity train speeding towards the English border. By lunchtime they should be in London. Jaspa, Bisckits, Portia and Gravee are sitting on the table between Ben and Sam, beside the window, although Abi and Henry are totally unaware of them, of course.

"Well, I think it's got potential," says Henry. He puts on his best Hollywood action hero voice, "*Go boil your haggis, punk!*"

"I know Gobber didn't like it much," laughs Ben.

"And you should be more careful, too," asserts Abi, suddenly serious. "Why on Earth would you provoke him by calling him Kevin?"

This time it's Ben's turn to shrug. "It's his name, isn't it?" he replies defensively. "Anyway, he deserves it."

14

"That may be true," Abi admits. "But it's still not smart to annoy a bear with a sore head."

"What's Gobber doing here, anyway?" asks Ben, changing the subject slightly. "He hates the Young Adventurers. And Laurel told me they went on a family holiday through France and Belgium last year, so he's already been to Brussels."

Abi looks around, before leaning forward conspiratorially. The others, including the Ses, follow suit.

"Lily McGregor told me that Gobber was supposed to be staying with his aunt," the younger Greaning whispers.

"Poor aunt," mutters Jaspa to himself.

"Only she changed her mind at the last minute," Abi continues.

"How come?" wonders Henry.

"Well apparently, Gobber fed her dogs some of that laxative chocolate," Abi replies. "Quite a lot, according to Lily."

Sam looks horrified, while Henry and Ben both snigger.

"Dae ye mind!" exclaims Gravee, indignant on behalf of the poor dogs. "That's nae funny." Just for good measure, he punches Ben's forearm, which is resting on the table in front of him.

"Ow!" objects Ben, pulling his arm away and rubbing it. Gravee's pretty strong for his size.

"What's wrong?" asks Abi.

"Nothing," replies Ben, quickly. He gives Gravee a scowl. "Just a pest."

"What's a laxative?" asks Bisckits the Innocent.

"Oh Bisckits!" groans Portia. "A laxative is something that helps you poop, when you can't ...erm ...poop."

"Oh," says her young cousin. Then, "Eeeew!" as the gears of realisation slot into place.

"Lily said Gobber's aunt wouldn't let him stay after that, and Jimmy and Laurel couldn't find anyone else willing to look after him at such short notice."

"I'm not surprised," declares Jaspa.

"I still feel sorry for the dogs," says Sam.

"Aye, lassie," agrees Gravee. "So dae I."

"You should save your sympathy for us," Ben tells his sister. "At least the dogs don't have to put up with his majesty the Gobfather for the next week."

***

The train pulls into London's King's Cross Station just after noon. The Young Adventurers pile out of the carriage and onto the platform, where Jimmy performs a headcount: himself, Laurel, Diane, Dennis, 14 kids... and Gobber. Check. The children are mostly between 11 and 13, with Sam being the youngest, at only nine, and Gobber, who's almost 15, now being the eldest.

Laurel and Jimmy decide they have just enough time for a quick surprise—a very brief stop at what has become perhaps the most-visited location in King's Cross: a mock-up of the famous entrance to Platform 9¾, complete with luggage trolley disappearing into the wall.

Although the McRae children (along with the Ses, naturally) were in London last November, they didn't make it to King's Cross, so they're as eager as everyone else to have their photos taken while pretending to push the trolley through the wall. Bisckits the Harry Potter Fan is equally excited.

From Platform 9¾, the Williamsons lead their charges across the road to the beautifully ornate and newly-renovated St. Pancras Station, from where trains to mainland Europe depart. They pass through the airport-like security into the international departure lounge and board the Euro-star to Brussels.

Almost exactly one hour after arriving at King's Cross, the Young Adventurers pull away from St. Pancras. Once out of the network of tunnels beneath the British capital, the train flashes through the Kent countryside at speeds of almost 190 miles an hour, before diving into the Channel Tunnel at a mere 99 miles an hour.

"It's a good job you've got over your fear of tunnels, Gravee," Bisckits observes, as they rush beneath the English Channel.

"Nae kiddin'," agrees the Dogses.

Just over 20 minutes later they're again racing at top speed through France on their way to Belgium. They arrive at Midi/Zuid Station in the heart of Brussels less than 2¼ hours after leaving London, at just gone 4 o'clock in the afternoon, local time.

***

Chapter Two

Lion's Eye View

Over the next two days, the Central Edinburgh Branch of the Young Adventurers explore the length and breadth of Brussels. Each morning they split into two groups to see the sights, and each evening they come back together to eat and share stories of the day's exploits.

Fortunately, Gobber prefers to waste his time sulking in his room. This means that, although they have to put up with his cutting comments and general unpleasantness in the evenings, everyone (including Jimmy and Laurel) gets to enjoy their days in peace.

The McRaes, Greanings and Ses spend the first day taking in the highlights of central Brussels with Laurel and Diane. Henry in particular enjoys seeing all the old buildings and stuff, which is unsurprising given his fascination with history. (*Something else he has in common with Ernest*, notes Jaspa.) And the entire group is awestruck by the dinosaur exhibit at the Royal Belgian Institute of Natural Sciences.

But if pressed, even Henry would admit that the highlight of their time in the Belgian capital is their visit to the Océade waterpark with Jimmy and Dennis on the second day. They spend most of the afternoon barrelling down the park's waterslides, all the while shrieking, laughing and getting soaked (including the Ses!).

***

Early on the third day, the Young Adventurers find themselves in the Belgian countryside, about 13 miles south of Brussels. They gather around Jimmy at the peak of a towering, grassed, conical heap of earth. Beside them on the summit is a massive stone plinth, supporting an enormous, cast iron lion.

Laurel stands alongside her husband, her hand firmly clamped on Gobber's shoulder to prevent him wandering off and (inevitably) getting into trouble. Dennis and Diane, about whom Portia is starting to have suspicions, talk quietly to each other at the back of the group.

"The artificial hill we've just climbed is called Lion Mound for obvious reasons," Jimmy tells them. "It's roughly 140 feet tall, although everything I read seems to give a slightly different height," he jokes.

Sam knows for a fact that the Mound is precisely 226 steps high—she counted them on the way up here. And she has the sore legs to prove it.

"Ignore the people gathering on the Mound and the stuff down below us for now," Jimmy instructs the group.

Of course, as soon as people are told to ignore something, it immediately becomes fascinating. Unsurprisingly then, the volume of the children's voices increases rapidly as they begin to excitedly debate the possible purpose of the large open square surrounded by temporary grandstands and white tents immediately east of Lion Mound. Unlike the Adventurers, the thousands of people streaming towards the enclosure, and hundreds more already sitting on the steeply-sloping side of the Mound, are clearly in the know.

The Ses can't help wondering about the grandstands' significance too, although to Jaspa it's obvious they form some sort of enormous arena.

Henry grins excitedly to himself. He knows exactly what the grandstands are for, and can barely contain his anticipation.

Jimmy glances ruefully at his wife. The good-natured smile on Laurel's face clearly says, *You said the wrong thing there, didn't you?* She gives her husband a wink of encouragement.

"Okay, okay," says Jimmy over the rising voices. "I want you to stand facing south, the same way as the lion."

The speculation dies away, and there's a moment of shuffling as everyone glances up at the huge metal cat to ensure they've got themselves oriented correctly.

"Can you see that Lion Mound is built on a low ridge, which runs roughly east-west?"

There's a generally positive mutter, as the children look left and right to verify Jimmy's observation.

"And can you also see there's another low ridge, more-or-less parallel to this one, less than a mile away, directly in front of us to the south?"

Again there's that low murmur of confirmation, characteristic of a group of people who are each too self-conscious to be the one who actually opens their mouth to respond properly.

"One final question and then you're off the hook," teases Jimmy with a smile. "Can you see the wide, shallow valley formed between the two ridges?"

"Yes," replies Abi above the familiar mumbling, displaying medal-worthy daring and bravery.

Jaspa nudges Gravee. "Does all this talk of valleys and ridges seem a bit overdramatic to you?" he asks. Despite the fact none of the humans (except Ben and Sam, of course) will hear him, the Giraffeses finds himself whispering the question. "It looks more like a gentle scoop in the ground between a couple of lazy bumps to me."

"Aye, I ken whit ye mean," Gravee quietly agrees.

"I admit it's not the most spectacular valley in the World, geographically speaking," Jimmy concedes, inadvertently addressing Jaspa's concerns. "Although the slopes look a lot steeper when you're down at ground level, as we'll see in a bit."

"But historically, this valley is very important. Because on the 18th of June 1815, it was here that the forces of Napoleon Bonaparte, Emperor of France, clashed with those commanded by Sir Arthur Wellesley, Duke of Wellington, in one of the most famous and bloody battles in history."

"The Battle of Waterloo!" Henry blurts unintentionally. He's been looking forward to coming here more than anything, and for an instant his enthusiasm gets the better of him. But as everyone turns to look at him, Henry's shyness clamps back down. "Sorry," he mutters, turning scarlet.

Jimmy smiles kindly at Abi's brother. "No need to be sorry, Henry," he assures the boy.

"As Henry's rightly said, the battle I'm talking about is Waterloo," Jimmy tells the group. "All afternoon and into the evening, around 140,000 soldiers fought for the right to possess this unexceptional patch of land. And under the moon that night, over 40,000 of them—along with about 10,000 horses—lay dead, dying in agonising pain, or too badly wounded to even move, in the small and otherwise unremarkable valley below us."

"Crivens!" breathes Gravee into the shocked silence.

"Big deal," grunts Gobber under his breath.

***

"Lion Mound didn't exist in 1815. It was built a few years later, to mark the spot where the Prince of Orange, who eventually became King William II of the Netherlands, was wounded during the battle," Jimmy explains, ignoring his son's disrespect.

"But from up here you can see more-or-less the entire battlefield. I think that's a scary thought, when you consider the appalling number of men killed or wounded that day."

The Adventurers' leader pauses to let this sink in. Jaspa shakes his head. He's not the only one struggling to imagine such horror.

"Now, the Duke of Wellington's job was to prevent Napoleon from reaching Brussels. So he arranged his Allied army of British, Belgian,

Dutch and German troops along this ridge, and waited for the enemy to arrive," Jimmy tells his captivated audience.

"The Allies' defensive lines stretched for roughly a mile either side of the main road from Charleroi to Brussels." Jimmy gestures towards the busy highway that still crosses the valley just beyond the temporary arena.

"The lines were anchored at either end by makeshift forts. At the eastern end was the farm of Papelotte..." Jimmy pauses to point out a walled farm, off along the ridge to their left. "While at the western end was Hougoumont Château." He indicates another group of ancient-looking farm buildings surrounded by trees away to their right.

"A third cluster of buildings—the fortified farm of La Haye Sainte—stood just forward of the centre of Wellington's lines, right beside the Brussels road. That's it there on the far side of the grandstands.

"Most of the other buildings you can see today weren't there at the time of the battle. The main exception is La Belle Alliance, the white farm visible on the far ridge, opposite La Haye Sainte. It was Napoleon's headquarters on the battlefield, and also stands on the Brussels road. The road along which an Emperor and his army marched, to bring dread and terror to the Allies."

***

"Hougoumont Château was bombarded by cannon and musket fire almost all day, and La Haye Sainte was also besieged for a good portion of the afternoon," Jimmy continues his gruesome story. "But the three main French attacks were launched at the Allied soldiers strung out in a perilously thin line along this ridge.

"The first of those attacks was a mass infantry assault by tens of thousands of foot soldiers. The second was a series of cavalry charges, pressed home by thousands upon thousands of mounted killers. But Napoleon saved his best for last, releasing the infantry of the undefeated Imperial

Guard in the third attack, to smash whatever was left of Wellington's army to pieces.

"Throughout all of this, the Allies held on in the hope that a third army—the Prussians, led by Field Marshall Gebhard von Blücher—would finally arrive and help save the day."

Laurel looks at her watch and then at her husband. "We should probably be getting to our places soon," she suggests.

Jimmy nods his head in agreement, before turning his attention back to the children. "The first attack took place on the far side of the Brussels road. But the second and third attacks came right up the slope below us, between La Haye Sainte and Hougoumont.

"How about we head down towards those grandstands and see it from the attackers point of view?" he suggests.

This time there's no embarrassed murmuring from the group, just a resounding, "Yeah!"

***

Chapter Three

Confrontations

The Young Adventurers join the rapidly-growing throng of people heading down Route du Lion towards the enclosed area they'd seen from the top of Lion Mound. The Williamsons feel that trying to remain together in one large group increases the risk of someone getting separated and lost in the crowd. Instead they decide to split the children into four smaller, more manageable groups. Diane volunteers to escort the McRaes and Greanings to the arranged meeting point on the far side of the arena.

As they pass the white canvas tents along the northern edge of the temporary enclosure, Ben senses a commotion behind him. He starts to turn around to see what's going on, when he's suddenly and inexplicably wrenched backwards and down. Utterly confused, he finds himself being thrown to the ground by one shoulder.

"What on Earth do you think you're doing?" yells Abi beside him.

At first Ben thinks she's talking to him. He's about to tell her in no uncertain terms that he's not doing anything. But before he can reply someone else speaks up.

"Shut up!" barks an all too familiar voice. And then, "What's in your purse, McRae?"

Still sprawled on the ground, Ben looks up to find Gobber standing over him. The last time they'd seen him, the older boy had been doing something suspicious to a sign near the base of Lion Mound. Now here he is again, complete with the annoying smirk that always appears on his face whenever he's in full-on bully mode.

He dangles Ben's perfectly ordinary—and not at all purse-like—backpack above his victim's head.

That explains why I fell over, thinks Ben. The bag had been slung over his right shoulder. Clearly, Gobber had yanked it off, throwing Ben to the ground in the process.

"Leave him alone," shouts Sam.

"The baby still needs his sister and girlfriend to stand up for him, I see. You should be ashamed of yourself," taunts Gobber as he rummages through the bag. "Where's your mummy's phone then?"

"In my pocket," Ben replies automatically, too bewildered to take offence at his tormentor's jibes. *What girlfriend?* he thinks.

Gobber fumbles around, as if he's wiping his hand on the inside of Ben's backpack. Then he begins twirling the bag around his head, causing the closest members of the crowd to back away quickly, complaining loudly in at least three languages.

"Hand it over," Gobber demands. "Or we'll see how far your purse can fly!"

"Crivens!" moans Gravee. Ben glances down to see his friend lying in the grass beside him, rubbing his head. "Whit happened?"

Before all this excitement began, Ben suddenly remembers, Gravee and Jaspa had been sitting on his shoulder. The same shoulder as the backpack.

Gravee must have fallen when Gobber grabbed my bag, thinks Ben. *So where's...*

"Jaspa!" shrieks Portia. "Hold on!"

Ben looks back up at Gobber. His focus travels to the bag spinning like a helicopter rotor above the bully's head. Then to the loose straps that flick wildly as the backpack rotates. And finally to the tiny figure gripping desperately to one of the straps.

As the bag whirls around Gobber's head, Jaspa bucks like a cowboy on a crazed rodeo bull.

***

As luck would have it, Jaspa had been looking behind—captivated by the ugliest hat he'd ever seen—when Gobber suddenly appeared out of the crowd and seized Ben's bag. Unfortunately, he'd not had enough time to shout a warning to either Ben or Gravee. But in a split-second's realisation of what was happening, Jaspa had instinctively grabbed one of the bag's canvas straps as he tumbled from Ben's shoulder towards the ground.

In hindsight, as he swirls unsteadily at stomach-churning speed around Gobber's unwashed head, Jaspa wishes he hadn't had such quick reactions.

"Jaspa!" shouts Ben, echoing Portia's alarm.

"Come again?" asks Gobber, losing concentration and allowing the bag to slow slightly, much to Jaspa's relief.

"Er... I said... um..." stutters Ben.

"He said *faster*, Kevin!" goads Sam. "See if we care!"

WHAT?! screams Jaspa inside his own head. He's still spinning way too fast to waste effort on actual words. At the moment it's taking all his spare concentration—of which there isn't that much—to keep his breakfast down.

In her defence, Sam hasn't noticed Jaspa flying around on the bag's strap, and so doesn't understand the significance of Portia's frightened outburst. As far as she's concerned, she's just trying to cover-up her brother's Ses-related blunder.

Confusion flashes across Gobber's face. Then he shrugs maliciously. "Have it your way," he gloats, spinning the backpack even faster than before.

"Hold on, Jaspa!" shouts Bisckits, redundantly.

"Oh no!" gasps Sam, finally spotting Jaspa's predicament. Her hand goes to her mouth. "What have I done?"

With Shakespearian irony, at that very moment Jaspa's sweating hands begin to lose grip on the canvas as he whizzes in circles through the air.

They start sliding towards the end of the strap. One inch. Two inches. The speed of the slip increases.

I've had it if I let go, Jaspa thinks. *I'll land somewhere in this crowd and these big, clumsy humans will trample me without even realising it.*

Three inches. Four inches.

He feels his hands reach the very end of the strap... and the rough seam at its tip. He clutches at the seam's edge with all his strength and his fingernails bite into the material. The force of the spin bends his nails painfully, but his grip holds.

For now.

"No!" shouts Ben, swiftly grabbing Gravee and standing up.

"Easy there!" protests the Dogses,

"I said *actor* not *faster*," Ben yells at Gobber, ignoring Gravee's complaints.

The older boy is so mystified he stops spinning the bag completely. "What does that even mean?" he demands, in a slightly higher pitch than he'd intended.

Still gripping tightly to the strap, Jaspa takes a few deep breaths in an attempt to get control of his nerves and breakfast.

"It means... Um... It means you're such an actor," says Ben, trying to sound convincing, while actually making it up as he goes along. "Yeah! Er... You pretend to be all hard and mean. But really you're just lonely and pathetic, because you don't have any friends anymore."

For several long moments Gobber's expression becomes blank and unreadable. Then the malice returns. "Is that so, Dr Phil?" he snarls. "Well, perhaps your purse would be lonely and pathetic if I threw it onto the roof of one of these tents. Let's find out, shall we?" he suggests, already extending his arm backwards in preparation for the throw.

Oh no! thinks Jaspa. *Here we go again!*

***

Gobber accelerates his arm forwards. He puts every ounce of strength into the motion, determined to throw the annoying little brat's bag as high and far as possible. *Who does he think he is, going all trick-cyclist on me?*

But as Gobber's arm reaches the top of its arc, a hand suddenly reaches out and grabs hold of his forearm.

The backpack jerks to a halt, causing the strap to snap like a whip. Jaspa's already burning arms and shoulders are jarred agonisingly. But being a glass-half-full kind of person, he's mostly relieved not to be soaring through the air right now.

Even so, decides Jaspa, *enough is enough*.

With Ben's backpack still suspended above Gobber's head, the little Giraffeses estimates the end of the strap to which he's gripping must be dangling a good four feet above the ground. But all things considered, better to risk the drop from here than wait to be thrown over a tent.

Jaspa takes a deep breath. *Here goes nothing.*

He releases the strap. And drops like a stone.

Well, most of him does. His stomach, not being the brightest of organs, decides to loiter in the air a bit longer, producing that slightly-nauseating sensation familiar to roller coaster riders the World over.

Jaspa has just enough time to regret his decision to let go before he hits the ground. "Ooof!" he grunts, as the wind is knocked out of him.

Fortunately though, this part of Belgium has been hit by a number of big rainstorms in recent weeks, so the turf beside the road is soft and springy. Sam quickly steps forward and scoops him up, to the complete bewilderment of the other humans (except Ben), who have no idea what she's doing.

"Get away from me, you rug rat," says Gobber, directing a poorly aimed kick at Sam.

"That's enough!" Diane declares, still gripping Gobber's forearm.

The bully tries to pull his arm loose, but Diane's grasp is surprisingly strong. "Give the bag back," she insists in a firm tone, looking him straight in the eye.

The two of them stand facing each other, arms and eyes locked in a physical and mental battle.

By chance, Dennis and his group of Adventures suddenly appear out of the crowd. "Diane?" asks the young man. "Is everything okay?"

"I've got it covered, thanks," she replies lightly. Her eyes remain locked on Gobber's.

Gobber, on the other hand, takes the momentary distraction as an excuse to look away. He wrenches his arm again. And stumbles backwards, almost falling over, when Diane simply lets go.

With as much dignity as he can manage, he regains his feet quickly and steps forwards. The pair stand almost nose to nose.

"Give Ben his bag back, Gobber," Diane repeats calmly.

The bully sneers. He looks her up and down slowly. "Or what," he says contemptuously.

Diane treats him to the sweetest of smiles. "Or I'll do this," she says, and stamps hard on his left foot.

"Yeah!" shouts Bisckits.

Gobber squeals like a pig. "That wasn't fair!" he protests, dropping the bag and grabbing hold of his foot.

"You've got to be ready for anything, if you want to play with the big kids," Diane responds. She picks up the backpack and hands it to Ben. "There you go."

"Thanks," he says. "That was awesome!"

Dennis looks equally impressed, but Diane just shrugs as if it's no big thing. "Come on," she replies. "We'd better get going."

As Ben and his friends turn to leave, Gobber directs a baleful stare in their direction. *I'll get you!* he mouths menacingly.

Unfortunately, the overall effect is somewhat spoilt by the fact he's still hopping around on one foot while clutching the other.

Ben and the rest burst out laughing and follow Dennis and Diane into the crowd.

***

"So why *did* you yell *Jaspa*?" asks Abi curiously.

"I didn't," replies Ben, going red yet again. "I said *actor*, like I told Gobber."

"You know, you're a terrible liar, Ben McRae," says his friend. But instead of pushing the issue, Abi turns her attention to Sam. "And what was with you practically throwing yourself at Gobber's feet during all that? You could have got hurt, you know."

"I saw a button fall off Ben's bag," Sam responds, with more composure than her brother.

"If you say so," says Abi, clearly not believing Sam either. "But there's something fishy going on here."

***

Although his arms still ache, Jaspa is none the worse for his ordeal. He and the other Ses get their collective breath back in Sam's hood.

"I was scared stiff," Portia scolds her cousin.

"Well, it was hardly my fault, was it?" Jaspa complains. "I tell you what—in future I'll get your permission before being thrown around on the end of a strap by a deranged bully."

"Good!" replies Portia with a grin. "I think that would be best."

***

30

Chapter Four

Charge!

"Go on!" bellows Gobber. "Kill the lot of 'em!"

His thoughtless and narrow-minded shouts attract stares and mutters of annoyance from almost everyone within earshot, including Jaspa and his friends. Gobber either doesn't notice or doesn't care, and continues his heckling.

The Young Adventurers are gathered on the eastern side of the arena that has been established on the slope beside Lion Mound for today's events. The enclosed area is roughly 250 yards square and surrounded by upwards of 70,000 spectators. Many of the onlookers are seated in the temporary grandstands, but thousands more fill standing areas. A large gap has been left in the southwest corner of the arena, to provide access for the participants.

Those participants, all 3000 of them, are here to re-enact the battle that took place on this very spot 200 years ago, all authentically dressed as soldiers from that time. The Allies are formed up on the north side of the arena, at the top of the slope, almost exactly where they would have been during the actual battle. The French are positioned at the south end of the arena, with their artillery placed in the access gap.

In-keeping with the conditions of June 1815, the unripe crops within the arena have been left standing. 'Soldiers' consequently wade through stalks that are waist-deep in places. When they crouch down, only their heads and the bayonets attached to their musket barrels show above the wheat. The legs of the cavalry horses are also often hidden by the crops, so the animals and their riders seem to float around the enclosure, like strange, giant ducks on a green sea.

To Jaspa the whole scene seems totally chaotic. A mass of French infantry marches up the hill, but is seemingly repelled by their British counterparts at the top, in what Jaspa supposes is the first attack Jimmy had mentioned at the top of Lion Mound. Meanwhile, cavalry gallops back and forth, and there seems to be a whole lot of milling around. There are even people running about with stretchers, collecting the 'wounded'.

Male voices on a PA system provide some idea of what's going on, describing the unfolding battle in English, French and Dutch. But the commentary is obscured by the loud, incessant crackle of musket fire, frequently punctuated by the deeper bangs of cannons. And somewhere amongst the cacophony are the sounds of drums, trumpets and pipes.

Not long into the display, the ominous grey clouds hanging above the field release a brief shower of rain. Like time-lapse footage of mushrooms sprouting from the Earth, a crop of gaudy umbrellas instantly appears above the crowd. Fortunately, the rain doesn't last very long.

Umbrellas aside, Jaspa is surprised at how colourful the 'battle' is. He knows that modern combat is all about camouflage, the closest humans come to blending. But Napoleonic uniforms seem to have been more geared to standing out than hiding. There are jackets of red, of black, of white and seemingly every shade of blue, green and grey. There are hats and helmets of every size, shape and colour, sporting a rainbow of different plumes. There are flags, banners and pennants combining red, blue, white and yellow, not forgetting the French Tricolour and British Union Flag.

***

The Williamsons and their charges occupy the middle part of the front three rows of one of the eastern grandstands. It's situated halfway down the slope, less than 100 yards from the historic buildings of La Haye Sainte, one of the fortified farms garrisoned by the Allies during the battle.

Since Sam and Henry are two of the shortest Adventurers, the McRaes and Greanings have been given places in the front row, providing them an unobstructed view of the action.

"Let the bloomin' Frenchies have it!" yells Gobber again.

This time, the focus of Gobber's 'encouragement' is a group British infantry about to be swamped by a ragged mass of French cavalry charging up the hill, led by a man wearing a blue jacket and white breeches, riding a grey horse.

The French reach the top of the slope, but to Ben's surprise they fail to actually attack the clusters of vulnerable-looking foot soldiers. Instead they aimlessly circle the defending infantry, being harassed and tormented the whole time by Allied horsemen. After a while, the French abruptly break off their offensive and gallop back down the slope.

***

"Hey," exclaims Jaspa suddenly. "Look at that!"

"What?" Portia asks.

"At first I thought it was a bird," replies her cousin. "But there's something about the way it's flying... I'm sure it's a Ses."

Portia shades her eyes with her left hand, which is missing two fingers thanks to a misadventure with a snake during her own Journey. "Where?"

"There," Jaspa points to spot in mid-air. "Above those horsemen galloping down the slope."

"Ye've better eyes than me, laddie," admits Gravee. "I cannae see a thin'."

"I see it! From the speed it's flying, I'd guess it's some kind of Falconses," declares Bisckits the Ornithologist.

"You might be right," agrees Portia, finally spying the swooping Ses.

Gravee shrugs in frustration. "If yers say so."

Bisckits guess is pretty good, since they've in fact spotted a Peregrine Falconses. In a special dive known as a *stoop*, actual Peregrines can reach speeds of over 200 miles an hour, making them the fastest animals on or above the planet. No contest! That said, the Falconses Jaspa and his friends are currently watching could clearly give a real Peregrine a run— or perhaps that should be *a flight*—for its money.

Bisckits the Aviator stares, breathless and envious. "That looks like so much fun."

Jaspa isn't so sure. He has a recurring dream about the time they flew across the Serengeti on the backs of vultures. It usually ends with him waking up in a cold sweat.

The Falconses, however, appears to be of the same mind as Bisckits. It rolls between the cavalry, brushing the top of the crops, the merest flick of its wings instantly changing its direction. On extended wings it shoots high into the sky. Then it folds those wings tight into its body and plummets back Earthwards. It climbs, dives and wheels through the air, around and between the French horses, unmistakably caught up with the joy of life on the wing.

"I wish I could do that," Bisckits whispers, his voice choked with longing.

***

"Don't just stand there, shoot them!" screams Gobber.

Abi looks over her shoulder and treats him to a hard stare. Not that it does any good.

Laurel leans forward from her seat, which is directly behind Abi's. "Just ignore him," she sighs, with a long-suffering smile and an exaggerated eye roll.

"Kevin never seems to grasp that re-enactments like this aren't just a bunch of people running about, playing soldiers," Laurel confides, shaking her head. "I know they're fun and entertaining, but they also help keep alive the events of the past and remind us how unbelievably horrible war is. They're definitely not supposed to open old wounds between people, or provide opportunities to look like a fool."

Jimmy puts a comfortingly arm around his wife's shoulders. "So have you guys figured out what's going on at the moment?" he asks, indicating the action on the field with his free hand.

As Laurel has been speaking, the French cavalry have regrouped. A blare of trumpets now signals another charge.

"Erm... It's the second French attack, isn't it?" replies Henry, cautiously. "The cavalry charges."

"Correct!" confirms Jimmy. "Did you all know that?"

Abi glances at Ben and Sam's blank faces before answering. "Not a chance!" she laughs. "Henry's our resident expert."

"So can you tell us anything about the second attack, Henry?" prompts Laurel.

"Well..." he says hesitantly. "It took place at about 4 o'clock, on this part of the battlefield."

"Anything else?" she encourages.

"Er... well... something like 10,000 French cavalry took part all together."

"That's right," Jimmy agrees. "The first charge alone was about 500 horses wide and 12 deep. That's roughly twice the total number of people taking part in today's entire re-enactment, and probably 100 times the number of cavalry currently galloping up that hillside."

"Wow!" says Ben.

"I read that the front of the attack was so wide that its ends were in firing range of both Hougoumont and La Haye Sainte, just behind us," adds Henry, his enthusiasm conquering his shyness. "The horsemen on

the outsides squeezed so much towards the centre—to protect themselves—that those in the middle told stories of riding up the slope with
their own horses' hooves not even touching the ground."

"Really?" gasps Sam.

"So they claimed," Jimmy confirms. He turns back to Henry, "Here's
another question for you: Do you know who lead the French cavalry
charges?"

"Marshal Michel Ney," replies Henry without a moment's hesitation.
"Napoleon nicknamed him the *Bravest of the Brave*."

"He did indeed. In case you hadn't realised, that's supposed to be him
out in front, there," Jimmy gestures at the rider in the blue jacket on the
grey horse. "I hope that guy's horse has better luck than those of the real
Ney, though. Between the battles at Waterloo and Quatre Bras—which
happened two days earlier—four or five of his horses were killed while he
was riding them, including one during these very cavalry charges."

"But he still carried on fighting," Henry points out.

"Yes he did," agrees Gobber's dad, with a nod. "You really know your
stuff, don't you? I'm impressed."

"Thanks," replies Henry, bashfully.

A thought occurs to Jimmy. "Did you notice the round building at the
base of Lion Mound?" he asks Henry

"The big white one?"

"That's the one," confirms Jimmy. "That's the Waterloo Panorama.
On the inside wall is an incredible circular mural, 360 feet long and 40 feet
high. It's meant to give a 360° view of just this point in the battle. It's very
impressive. You'd like it."

"It sounds neat," Henry replies.

Jimmy turns his attention to Ben, Sam and Abi. "As Henry could no
doubt tell you, the French cavalry dashed themselves against the impreg-
nable Allied infantry formations at least half a dozen times. Many of the
horsemen died, but it was ultimately all for nothing."

***

Jaspa finds everything that Jimmy, Henry and the others have been discussing very sad. To his knowledge, there's never been a battle between Ses, let alone a whole war. That's not to say that all Ses are sweetness and light. Anyone who's met Crispin, the former leader of London's *Pride*, knows that's just wishful thinking. But still, the idea of Ses going into ba…

"Something's wrong!" calls Bisckits.

The panic in his brother's voice derails Jaspa's train of thought.

"Whit's th' problem?" asks Gravee.

"The Falconses," replies Bisckits. "It's gone."

"Aye well, it probably flew away hame," the Dogses speculates. "It's tired, nae doot."

"No!" insists Bisckits. "You don't understand. It was right there, and then it was gone."

"Slow down," says Jaspa, trying to calm his brother. "Start at the beginning. Tell us exactly what happened."

"Well, the Falconses was flying around like before," Bisckits begins. "Then, as it was diving close to the ground, a whole bunch of muskets fired right in its path. It flew straight into the smoke, like I've seen it do several times before. But this time it didn't come out the other side."

"Goodness!" exclaims Portia. "You don't think it got hit by a musket ball, do you?"

"Dinnae be daft, lassie," scoffs Gravee. "Ye dinnae think these bampots are usin' real ammunition, dae ye?"

"I suppose not," says Portia, sounding slightly embarrassed. "So what happened to it?"

"I don't know, but we've got to find out," Bisckits declares. "It could be in trouble."

37

"But how would we even find it out there among those crops?" objects Jaspa.

"It went down over near that burning pile of straw on the other side of the arena," replies Bisckits the Determined. "I'll start there. You don't have to come with me."

Jaspa, Portia and Gravee briefly exchange glances.

"Hold ye Horseses, ye wee eejit," sighs the Dogses. "O' coorse, we're comin' wi' ye."

***

Chapter Five

Into Battle

While Jimmy continues to tell the story of the battle (now with Henry's help), the four Ses slip away without bothering Ben or Sam. Waiting for an opportunity to tell the siblings discretely will just waste valuable time, they reason. Plus, the young McRaes won't have to worry about them if they don't know what they're up to. And anyway, the children will just make a fuss.

As soon as they're out of the grandstand and down among the wheat, they all—even Bisckits the Unshakable—begin to wonder whether this is such a smart idea. Noble, certainly. But smart?

Still, there's a Ses out there who might need their help. And anyway, they're committed now.

"We should be bloomin' committed," mutters Gravee to himself.

On the plus side, the pile of burning hay near which Bisckits saw—or rather, didn't see—the Falconses disappear is directly in front of them, across the slope from where they've been sitting. On the minus side, it's located near the far end of the arena, perhaps 200 yards away.

On the flat, the average human adult could easily walk 200 yards in two or three minutes without exerting themselves. But given that Portia is the tallest of the four friends and still fails to reach four inches in height, 200 yards is a much bigger challenge for the Ses. Under ideal conditions, they could probably walk it in a little less than 25 minutes. But these are far from ideal conditions. Especially with a bunch of would-be soldiers tearing around the arena on foot and horseback.

Fortunately, all Ses learn to *shift* at an early age—to move rapidly from one point to another, without having to resort to running. As with blending, shifting isn't magical, but a skill that takes a lot of practice for a young Ses to master. Unfortunately, it's also extremely tiring and so can only be used for short bursts, which is why Ses generally reserve it for emergencies.

The current situation definitely falls under that category.

Perhaps surprisingly, the wheat has no real effect on the speed Jaspa and his friends are able to move. Three feet above the soil, the unripe ears form a dense, swaying carpet. But down here at ground level, the stalks are relatively widely-spaced—particularly when compared to the closely-packed grasses of the Serengeti's Long Grass Plain—and the Ses are able to pass between them quickly and unhampered.

The bigger problem for the four friends is how to navigate such a long distance through vegetation that's 10 times their height, and so obscures everything more than a few inches away. Fortunately, Portia rapidly comes up with a solution.

"The fire is more-or-less the same height up the slope as we started," she tells the others. "So as long as we don't go up or down, we should be heading in roughly the right direction."

"Good thinkin', lassie," Gravee concurs. "An' when we get a bit closer, mah nose will be able tae guide us th' rest o' th' way."

***

Through a combination of shifting and walking, shifting and walking, within just five minutes they reach a wide swath where the wheat has been pounded flat by the passage of French infantry up and down the slope. Rather than making progress easier for the Ses, however, it actually makes the going more difficult, since they have to clamber over heaps of flattened wheat instead of simply walking between the standing stalks.

On the other hand, the open ground does give them a chance to assess their progress. They're thrilled to find they're already at least halfway to their target. The fire in the pile of straw towards which they're heading is almost out, but it still produces enough thin grey smoke to show them the way.

Jaspa and his friends plough back into the standing crop on the far side of the trampled track. In amongst the wheat, the noise of battle once again becomes distorted and reflected in strange ways, as if heard through a layer of cotton wool, making it impossible to identify the distance and direction from which sounds originate.

They've only gone a few yards when Bisckits feels, rather than hears, a distant rumbling. "What's on Earth is that?" he asks, looking uncharacteristically wide-eyed.

Jaspa senses it a moment later, through the soles of his feet. The sensation grows rapidly as the seconds creep past, joined by a concussive hammering in his ears. It's as if all the thunder that ever was has been trapped underground and is now trying to escape.

"I guess the French cavalry are heading our way," Jaspa replies, attempting—but failing—to sound calm. "So unless we want to be pounded into a sticky mess by horses hooves, I suggest we get a shift on."

"Reit ye are," agrees Gravee. "An' I just got a whiff o' that burning straw, so follow me!"

***

The intensity of the rumbling swells to a crescendo, like a thousand bass drums rolling down a steep, uneven hillside. It physically shakes the ground beneath the Ses.

Jaspa looks around wildly, wondering whether he'll even see the hoof that's sure to mark his gooey end.

41

Then, almost as quickly as it built, the noise of confined underground thunder begins to fade away, without any of them seeing so much as a single horseshoe.

A couple of minutes later they step out into the open once more, this time beside the damply-smouldering pile of straw. Gravee's nose has done them proud. An occasional tongue of flame leaps briefly into life and climbs toward the sky, but these die back as quick as they appear, as the pockets of unburnt straw are rapidly consumed.

"Reit then, we're here," announces Gravee, a little unnecessarily. "Whit noo?"

All heads turn to Bisckits, who shrugs uncertainly. "We look around, I guess," he says.

"Where about did you last see the Falconses?" asks Portia, taking charge. "Relative to the fire, I mean."

"On the arena side," replies her cousin. "And a little higher up the slope. But not far away."

"Good. We should start in that direction, then," suggests Portia. "And it'll probably be faster if we split up."

"Definitely," Jaspa agrees.

"But don't go too far," Portia instructs them in a business-like tone. "And if you can't find your way back, sit down and wait for the rest of us to come and find you."

***

The Adventurers watch as the French troops assemble at the bottom of the slope in preparation to re-enact the third attack: the final assault by Napoleon's invincible Imperial Guard.

A whole company of infantry raise their muskets to their shoulders. At a signal from an officer, they fire a volley in unison. And instantly disappear in a cloud of smoke. A few seconds later the company beside them is also given the order to fire. They comply in a more piecemeal fashion, however, so the puffs of smoke ripple up and down the front of the formation, like white keys beneath a pianist's fingers.

Company after company lend their musket fire to the overall effect. The smoke from the constantly discharging weapons accumulates, thickens and drifts across the battlefield, like a heavy evening mist on a lonely floodplain.

"That's a lot of smoke," Sam observes. "I can hardly see the soldiers anymore."

"Just imagine what it must have been like during the real battle, then," says Jimmy. "Picture the dreadful amount of smoke produced by hundreds of cannons and tens of thousands of muskets being fired repeatedly hour after hour. Soldiers frequently couldn't see more than a few yards in any direction, and often followed the progress of a battle by sound more than sight."

"That's scary," says Sam.

"No more scary than anything else to do with this battle," Abi comments.

Everyone nods their heads in mute agreement.

Ben watches as the French infantry climb the arena's slope. Every so often they pause to direct a volley of musket fire at the waiting Allies. Even in the slightly murky light, the golden eagles of their standards shine brightly above them.

***

Ten or so minutes after separating from the others, Jaspa returns to the bonfire to find Gravee, Portia and Bisckits already waiting for him.

"We were aboot tae send oot a search party," Gravee jokes nervously.

Jaspa directs a small smile at his friend, then states the obvious. "I guess nobody found anything."

"Nah," replies Bisckits. "Portia found a small patch of fresh blood, just over there." He points northwards, out into the field. "But it could just as easily have been from a mouse, or a crow, or even one of these humans. There's no sign of any Ses."

"So what do we do now?" asks Jaspa, turning to look at Portia.

As if on cue, a stuttering volley of cannon fire echoes across the battlefield. At least six distinct detonations, one after another.

"That disnae sound good," observes Gravee.

The Ses look south towards the sound, which originated from the arena's access gap. Although the tall crop prevents them seeing the French guns themselves, six clouds of white smoke indicate the cannons' positions. The plumes thin, combine and drift southwards, as a light breeze carries them across peaceful fields that were once the scene of such misery.

"I don't think there's much more we can do here," Portia answers her cousin's question. "I say we get back to Ben and Sam as quickly as possible."

All attention now turns to Bisckits.

"We gave it our best shot," Jaspa tells his brother.

"I know," agrees the youngest Giraffeses, with a quick, nervous nod of his head. "Let's get out of here."

***

This time, Gravee is the first to detect the all-too-familiar rumbling within the Earth. "I dinnae like th' soond o' that," he calls over his shoulder without slowing down.

The pounding through the ground grows stronger. All four Ses recognise a subtle difference in the sensation this time around. As if each contributing footfall is less intense than last time, but there are far more of them.

Upslope from the Ses, the third French attack has been repulsed by the Allies. From the comfort of their grandstand, the McRaes and Greaning watch enthralled, as the Emperor's infantry flees down the hill.

Although the panicked retreat is simply for the benefit of the spectators, down among the wheat stalks, the re-enactment seems all too real. A leather-clad, human foot strikes the ground so close to Bisckits' face that he shifts straight into it at full speed. He comes to an instant, undignified and painful stop, with a sound like a wet towel hitting a tile floor.

"Owww!" the little Giraffeses protests, dropping to the floor and clutching his bloody nose. The offending boot disappears southwards through the crop, unaware of the trouble it's caused.

In moments, Bisckits' friends are at his side. Gravee and Jaspa each grab an arm and haul him back to his feet.

"Owww!" repeats Bisckits.

"Sorry," apologises Jaspa.

Gravee is more business-like. "C'mon, laddie," he says. "This is nae time tae be restin'."

"But I wasn't res..." begins Bisckits.

"Look out!" warns Portia.

A multitude of fleeing French fugitives suddenly materialises, as if out of nowhere, crossing the path of the Ses from left to right. The press of their feet smashes down the wheat as they go, flicking stalks forwards and downward to slash at Jaspa and the others like whips.

The Ses stagger on, trying to reach the edge of the arena and safety, while desperately dodging through a seemingly endless procession of feet.

Some soldiers march steadily in formation. Others hurtle downhill as fast as they can. All are oblivious that one wrong step on their part could turn Jaspa, Gravee, Bisckits or Portia into a jam-like stain in the wheat. The fact that the danger is unintentional, and the retreat is only an act, won't make the consequences any less deadly.

The tiny companions weave around like drunks in their efforts to avoid being squished. To make matters worse, the flattened stalks create an ever changing barrier, which they must also scale. And the ranks of retreating soldiers just keep on coming.

Then, just when it seems there's no end to the escaping Frenchmen, there's a lull in the parade of crushing boots.

By unspoken agreement, the four exhausted Ses pause in their headlong dash. Jaspa leans forward, trying to catch his breath, and Bisckits drops to the ground on his back.

"Nae time fur that," pants Gravee. "There could be mair of the greit galoots any second."

"He's right," says Portia between clenched teeth. "We've got to keep going."

Jaspa helps Bisckits back to his feet and they set off again. Shifting, running, shifting, running...

***

Jaspa and Bisckits crash out of the wheat beside the eastern grandstands, close on the heels of Gravee and Portia. Realising they've escaped the immediate danger, this time all four of them collapse to the ground, gasping heavily.

After a minute or two, Portia recovers enough to take in her surroundings. In the stand directly in front of them, people are getting to their feet and shuffling along rows towards the already-packed steps. Only then does it dawn on her... there's no more sound of musket or cannon fire. The Battle of Waterloo is over once again.

Feeling a different type of panic begin to rise in her chest, Portia looks frantically around for the McRaes. She's actually quite shocked to spot them still sitting in their seats, less than 15 yards away to her left.

"Come on, you three," Portia says. The relief in her voice is clear. "The show's over. We'd best get back to Ben and Sam before they leave without us."

Her friends are all still too breathless to even comment. They haul each other to their feet and plod along the edge of the crop until they're directly opposite Ben and Sam. Then they use the last of their energy to dart through the milling crowd to the bottom of the children's grandstand.

Ben sees them almost immediately. He 'accidentally' knocks his bag off the front of the stand. "Oops! I've knocked my bag over," he says, in a display of Oscar-worthy theatrics (Not!). "I better crouch down and pick it up."

While doing just that, he rests his hand on the ground and allows the Ses to climb aboard. "Where've you been?" he enquires quietly, lifting them up. "I didn't even know you'd gone."

"Aye, well," replies Gravee. "We fancied a wee bit o' a stroll, ye ken."

The boy looks at him suspiciously. Then he notices the dried blood on Bisckits' nose. "Oh no!" says Ben, suddenly concerned. "What happened to your face?"

"It got the boot," Jaspa answers with a grin.

***

Chapter Six

Banerminated

"That was well cool!" enthuses Ben.

"It was interesting," agrees Abi, before adding, "Even though all the gunfire, and the smoke, and the men and horses running all over the place sometimes made it a bit confusing."

"*Interesting?*" exclaims Gravee with a grin. "*Confusing?* The lassie disnae ken th' half o' it."

"Ha!" laughs Jaspa. "I for one never expected to be taking part in a battle today, that's for sure."

Still talking animatedly about the re-enactment, the Adventurers walk east along Route du Lion, away from the temporary arena and the small hamlet of buildings at the base of Lion Mound. Just ahead, the street they're on ends at the main Brussels road, which nowadays is called Chaussée de Charleroi.

"I think the whole thing is fascinating, in a horrible kind of way," says Henry thoughtfully. "I mean, isn't it incredible that three guys—from France, Britain and Prussia—ended up fighting one of the most famous battles in history here in Belgium?"

"I suppose," admits Ben. "I hadn't really thought about it."

"I think it's fascinating," Henry repeats.

"You're such a nerd, Greaning!" taunts Gobber, appearing unannounced once more.

"Oh no," breathes Jaspa. "Here we go again."

Sam and Abi look at each other. "Go boil your haggis, Kevin," they chorus before bursting into giggles.

A vein in Gobber's temple starts to pulse noticeably. "You're as bad as McRae, Greaning," he snorts. "Needing girls to stand up for you. You should learn how to fight your own battles before worrying about one that happened centuries ago."

Henry looks at his feet and says nothing. Gobber smiles nastily at the other boy's discomfort.

"Leave him alone," demands Ben.

Gobber sneers as he makes a big show of looking around. "Or what, McRae? Are you going to run and tell your babysitter Diane on me? Hide behind another girl?"

"She's not my babysitter," growls Ben.

"Whatever," says Gobber infuriatingly. He makes a half-hearted attempt to snatch Ben's bag again, but the younger boy quickly steps backwards out of his grasp.

"Your babysitter was lucky earlier," claims Gobber, goading Ben once more. "But she'd better not get in my way again."

"What's wrong with you?" yells Bisckits.

"He can't hear you, Bizzee," says Portia kindly, using the nickname she gave Bisckits when they were children.

"I know. But he's such a cretin," protests the little Giraffeses.

"Don't let him get to you," Jaspa advises.

Bisckits is too busy plotting to hear him. "You know, I could make him see and hear me," he muses slowly. "That'd give him the shock of his life!"

"Don't you dare!" declares Portia firmly. "The last thing we need is people like him finding out about the Ses. Gravee's stunt when he met Ben was risky enough."

"Hey!" objects the Dogses. "Dinnae brin' me intae this!"

As the Ses talk, Jimmy appears. "Everything alright here?" he asks brightly.

Gobber gives his father a disdainful look and melts away.

Jimmy puts a encouraging hand on Henry's shoulder. "You know, there's nothing nerdy about a battle that killed or wounded over 40,000 men," he says, making it clear he'd heard everything his son had said. "In fact, if you really want to learn more about it, Laurel's got a book back at the hotel you might not have seen. I'm sure she'll lend it to you, if you like."

"That'd be great," replies Henry, cheering up.

"Where are we going now?" wonders Abi out loud.

"Well, we're going to go and have our lunch..."

"Great," says Ben. "I'm starving."

"...And then Laurel has a surprise for you."

"A surprise?" asks Sam excitedly. "What kind of surprise?"

"Ah-ha," responds Jimmy, tapping the side of his nose with his index finger in a manner that says *You'll have to wait and see.*

***

On the far side of Chaussée de Charleroi, Route du Lion becomes Rue du Dimont. While Route du Lion is easily wide enough for two-way traffic, with ample space for pedestrians to walk on either side, Rue du Dimont is barely wide enough for a single car.

Near the southeast corner of the crossroads is a picnic area with three sets of tables and benches, two of which are beneath a permanent, roofed structure. Since there's been no more rain since the brief shower just after the start of the re-enactment, the McRaes and Greanings are happy to grab one end of the third table, out in the open. They're quickly joined by Callum McGinnis and his foster brother, Davy Fletcher.

"Mind if we sit here?" asks Diane, as she and Dennis approach.

Without a word, Callum and Davy shuffle up towards Ben and Henry, giving up their end of the table.

"Cheers," says Dennis in friendly tone. "Appreciate it."

"Let's see what the hotel gave us for lunch," says Abi, taking a brown paper bag out of her backpack.

Sam pulls a length of French bread from of her own bag. "*Sandwich au Jambon*," she says.

"Huh?" says Ben.

"It's French for *ham sandwich*," Sam informs him. "It's what I've got for lunch."

Ben shakes his head, while Bisckits looks on enviously. The Giraffeses' stomach grumbles as if on cue.

"Are ye a wee bit peckish there, laddie?" laughs Gravee. "Dinnae worry, I'm sure Sammie will share her piece wi' ye, if ye ask nicely."

Unable to answer properly because of the other humans at the table, Sam winks at Bisckits and secretly hands him a corner from her sandwich.

***

"I've got a ham sandwich too," says Callum. "With a banana and a carton of orange juice."

A chorus of agreement around the table indicates that they all have the same.

Great, thinks Ben reaching into his own paper bag. *I hate bananas.* To his disgust, his hand is greeted by a slimy sensation. He jerks it out to find his fingers covered with pale yellow mush.

"Good Grief!" declares Abi, sounding horrified. "What's that?" Her hand moves involuntarily to her mouth, as if she might throw-up.

Ben gingerly sniffs his hand. "Banana," he says, screwing up his nose.

"Here," says Davy, handing him a paper napkin.

"Thanks," replies Ben, accepting the napkin and wiping his hand.

Ben takes the paper bag containing his lunch and carefully tears it open. Inside are the mangled remains of his meal. It looks like someone has squeezed the banana and sandwich together in their fist. The banana's peel has burst along one of the seams and the flesh from inside has been mashed into the bread of the sandwich. Even the orange juice carton is smeared with banana innards.

"Gobber," says Jaspa.

"Gobber," says Henry. "He must have done it while he was searching for your mum's phone."

Ben looks across at the other tables to find his nemesis already staring back in expectation, a sly grin on his face. The bully takes a large bite out of his own sandwich and mimes a big show of how tasty it is.

"Dinnae dae anythin' rash," says Gravee.

Abi picks up the remnants of the fruit by its stalk. "It's been banerminated," she says, trying to lighten the situation.

One look at Ben's face, however, tells Abi this is no time for jokes. "Sorry," she apologises. "You can share my lunch if you like."

"No thanks. I'm not hungry," Ben lies, wrapping up his entire meal in the torn paper bag and stuffing it back inside his backpack.

"But before you said you were... ow!" says Henry. "What did you do that for?" This last question is directed at his sister, who has just kicked him hard in the ankle.

"What?" she asks innocently.

"Did Gobber do that?" enquires Diane from the far end of the table.

"Yes," replies Sam, before Ben can stop her.

"I've had it with that kid," declares Diane, rising to her feet. "He's going to get a piece of my mind!"

"No!" shouts Ben, louder and angrier than he'd intended.

Shocked by Ben's outburst, Diane stops in the process of getting up. Several of the other tables' occupants turn to see what the commotion is.

"You'll only make things worse," says Ben, in a more level tone.

"But he shouldn't get away with this stuff," states Diane, once more standing up.

"I don't need a babysitter," Ben snarls, the anger flaring up again.

"Ben!" exclaims Portia, horrified at her friend's behaviour. "She's just trying to help you."

"I don't need a babysitter," repeats Ben, flatly.

Diane's eyes start to well up, making Ben instantly regret his harsh words. She looks so upset, and Ben is about to apologise.

But before he can find the right words, Dennis takes Diane by the hand and pulls her gently back onto the bench. "Forget the ungrateful little wretch," he says, continuing to hold Diane's hand. In return, she rewards him with a smile that is at once shy, grateful and rueful.

Ben groans inwardly. Trust Gobber to spoil everything, as usual.

***

A couple of minutes after Ben's outburst, the Ses huddle together at the end of the table, talking quietly among themselves.

Gravee glances up at his young Seer pal. The boy looks like all the weight of the World is currently resting on his 12-year-old shoulders. "I hate seein' him like this, yers ken."

"Diane's right about one thing," says Jaspa. "This can't go on."

"So what are we going to do about it?" asks Bisckits.

"There's nothing we can do," sighs Portia. "Except give him our support and just be here for him if he needs us."

Abi gives her brother a gentle nudge with her foot under the table, to get his attention. She looks meaningfully at Ben and then jerks her head sideways, while raising her eyebrows.

Henry catches on immediately. "There's something I want to look at over there," he says to Ben. "Are you coming?"

His friend shrugs, but starts to get up anyway.

"I reckon me an' Jaspa should tag along," Gravee suggests.

"Good idea," says Portia. "Bisckits and I'll stay here with Sam."

Bisckits, who has just stuffed another large piece of Sam's sandwich into his mouth, can only manage a thumbs up.

***

Henry leads Ben to the other side of the bike path that runs along the eastern edge of the picnic area, parallel to the Brussels road. He stops next to a roughly-squared stone resembling a grave's headstone, with a metal plaque on it.

"I thought Picton's Memorial should be around here somewhere," Henry declares after reading the inscription. "I remember seeing it on one of my maps."

Ben says nothing.

Gravee and Jaspa exchange glances, concerned by Ben's uncharacteristic gloom.

"This is the spot where Lieutenant General Sir Thomas Picton was killed," Henry continues, as if having a normal conversation instead of basically talking to himself.

Ben just stares blankly at the stone in front of them without saying a word.

"He was shot in the head by a lead musket ball."

"Ouch," winces Ben, as if coming out of a daydream.

"Exactly," agrees Henry. "That musket ball gave Picton the dubious honour of being the highest-ranking soldier to die at Waterloo."

Although sympathetic to poor General Picton's untimely end, Jaspa and Gravee both feel a wave of relief, happy to hear Ben talking again.

***

Chapter Seven

In View of Lion Hill

"I spoke to Diane while you were over with Henry," Abi tells Ben when he returns to the table. "She's still a bit upset—and I don't blame her, to be honest—but she understands how much Gobber is getting to you."

"Thanks," replies Ben, awkwardly.

"Dennis still seems pretty annoyed, though," Abi adds.

"Okay, listen up!" calls Laurel, cutting off any further discussion.

Jimmy leans over to Sam. "Here's the surprise," he whispers.

"I want to introduce you to a hobby Jimmy, Kevin and I enjoy doing together," Laurel announces.

"Hah!" snorts Gravee. "Whitever it is, I dinnae reckon wee Gobber enjoys it as much as his maw thinks!"

Jaspa glances over at the bully. Sure enough, Gobber's sneer seems to express something more than the usual irritation at his parents' continued use of his real name.

"It's called *geocaching*."

"That sounds familiar," says Portia.

"Aye, it does," agrees Gravee. "Although I cannae put mah finger on where I've heard th' name afore."

"Geocaching is like a worldwide, high-tech, treasure hunt," Laurel explains. "I've heard it described as *using multi-billion dollar military satellites to find Tupperware hidden in the woods*."

As Laurel had hoped, phrases like *high-tech*, *multi-billion dollar* and *military satellites* are guaranteed to grab the Adventurers' attention. "How many of your parents have GPS devices in their cars?" she asks.

At least half the children raise their hands.

"Well, this is a handheld version," she says, holding up what looks like a really chunky cell phone.

"Sweet!" says Bisckits the Navigator.

"One of the things it can be used for is geocaching," continues Laurel. "The idea is pretty straightforward. Someone hides something, using one of these to record the latitude and longitude of where they place it," she flourishes the GPS unit again. "When they get home, they upload those coordinates to a website, together with a description of what they've hidden, how difficult it is to find, how strenuous the terrain is... stuff like that. Then someone else downloads that information and goes out to try and find the cache, as it's called."

All the children sit up a little straighter, their attention a little more focused. "People hide cash?" asks one of the other boys, sounding slightly amazed, voicing the question on all their lips.

Laurel grins, as if she's been waiting for this. "No, Tommy. This is *cache* ending in *c-h-e*, not *cash* ending in *s-h*. It means a hoard or collection."

"Oh!" says Tommy in a disappointed tone. "So what's the point?"

"There is no point," grumbles Gobber.

Laurel gives her son a quick but harsh stare before answering herself. "In some ways, Kevin's right. There's no prize or anything. Most people just do it for the challenge of the hunt and the satisfaction of finding the cache.

"But geocaching also gets you out and about, and can take you to places you might not otherwise visit, or even know exist. Our family's seen all sorts of wonderful things we would've otherwise missed, if not for geocaches hidden by complete strangers."

"So what happens once you've found a cache?" asks Callum.

"Good question," replies Laurel. "Most caches have a logbook in them, which you sign to prove you were there. Then when you get home—or even while you're still out, if you have a smartphone—you post an online log to the cache's webpage. In your online log you can tell the story of how you found the cache, or give advice to people looking for it in the future. You can even upload your photos, if you want. Sometimes they can provide the best hints of all, even if that isn't what the person uploading them originally intended."

***

"I've got it!" declares Portia.

"I dinnae want it!" Gravee jokes.

"I remember where we heard about geocaching before," says Portia, ignoring him. "Mad mentioned it when we were helping Ernest with *the Path* in London last year. I think it was when we found the clue in Covent Garden. The one stuck to the pipe with a magnet."

"Oh yeah," agrees Jaspa. "I remember thinking it sounded like fun at the time."

"That's it!" exclaims Bisckits, clearly remembering something of his own. "The Path!"

"What about it?" asks his brother.

"I knew the Duke of Wellington was familiar," Bisckits replies.

"Other than fur 'is boots, ye mean," laughs Gravee, on a roll.

"It's been bugging me all day," continues Bisckits, also ignoring the Dogses. "But Portia mentioning the Path just reminded me why I know his name. It was when we were trying to solve the puzzle in St Paul's Cathedral. Ernest and I ended up in the crypt, where we saw Wellington's tomb. It was really impressive—all huge and carved out of stone."

***

"You'd be amazed how many caches there are hidden around the World," Laurel tells them. "Last time I checked there were over three million, and that number is growing all the time."

There's a chorus of *Wow!* from the group (including the Ses).

"And it just so happens that one of them—called *In View of Lion Hill*—is..." she makes a big show of looking at the screen of the GPS unit in her hand "...less than a hundred yards from where I stand."

Laurel holds the GPS out in front of her, as if offering it to the children. "So which table wants to be the first to try and find it?"

A couple of the kids look less than impressed, but Sam springs up like a rocket-powered jack-in-the-box. "Can we go first?" she begs. "Please!"

Jimmy and Laurel share a satisfied smile. They love it when the kids show such enthusiasm. In fact, both agree that it's moments like this that make running the Central Edinburgh Branch of the Young Adventures so rewarding and worthwhile.

***

Laurel spends several minutes showing the six children—Ben, Sam, Henry, Abi, Callum and Davy—(and unknowingly, the four Ses) how to work the GPS. Finally she selects the navigation screen and hands the device to Sam.

"Just follow the big red arrow," says Jimmy encouragingly.

Sam nervously takes the GPS, pauses, then hesitantly takes a few steps forward. As she does so, the arrow swings right.

"You need to go that way," instructs Bisckits the Navigator from her shoulder, pointing in the direction of the arrow.

"I know!" snaps Sam. Then, catching the suspicious look from Abi, she declares. "I know I can do this."

Like a formation of migrating geese, the others follow Sam, as she in turn follows the arrow on the GPS's display screen. Laurel and Jimmy stay with the rest of the group, but Diane tags along with Sam and her friends, just to be on the safe side.

With one eye firmly fixed on the arrow, Sam leads them south along the cycle path that runs down into the valley. Almost immediately they enter a small clump of trees, situated between Chaussée de Charleroi and the field where the first French attack took place two centuries ago. As the path starts to curve back towards the road, between raised banks on both sides, the arrow once again begins to swing to the right.

Sam stops abruptly, and the others gather round. The arrow points at right angles to the path, straight at the western bank. The digital display in the top right-hand corner of the screen indicates they're just 24 yards from their destination.

"What do we do now?" asks Davy uncertainly.

"Climb the bank, I guess," suggests Abi.

***

With Sam again in front, they scale the steep bank, using the trees and bushes to haul themselves upwards.

"Twenty yards...," the youngest McRae counts them down as they go. "Fifteen..."

"You need to go that way a bit," says Bisckits into her ear.

Sam sighs, but nonetheless angles slightly to the left, guided by the arrow and Bisckits' 'help'. "Ten yards...," she says.

Not far ahead through the leaves, they can see a grey stone monolith, perhaps 15 or 20 feet high. In some ways it reminds Jaspa a little of photos he's seen of Egyptian temples. A neatly-trimmed hedge, coupled with an abandoned-looking fence, bars their path to the monument.

"Six... ow!" Sam's gaze is so focused on the screen, she doesn't pay proper attention to where she's walking and trips over a wayward root.

With impressively-fast reactions, Bisckits and Portia quickly grip hold of her jacket, to save being thrown to the ground.

"Are you alright?" Ben asks, reaching out to help his sister.

"Yep," she replies, instinctively looking down at the passengers on her shoulder.

"We're fine, too," Portia assures the children.

Ben lets go of Sam's arm and she resumes her countdown, pushing her way through some bushes. "Five yards... four... three... four... five... Hey, something's gone wrong with this thing!"

"You must have gone past it," says Callum.

"But it never got any closer than three yards," Sam argues.

"That's probably to do with the accuracy of the GPS," guesses Abi.

He looks at Diane for confirmation, but she just shrugs her shoulders. "Don't ask me," she laughs. "I just work here!"

Her returning good-humour fills Ben with a sense of relief.

"Maybe Sam's just forgotten how to count," grins Bisckits.

Sam presses her lips together, but doesn't reply.

***

"So how big is this geocache-thingy, do you reckon?" asks Davy, looking at the hedge. "And what's it look like."

"Dunno," admits Ben, after everyone one else fails to answer.

"I think they can be just about any size," offers Abi. "Jimmy told me the biggest one he's ever found was an actual treasure chest, in the Geo-caching World Headquarters in Seattle, and the smallest was a tiny magnetic button thing, about the size of an M&M."

"So you're saying it can look like anything and be just about any size," observes Davy dryly. "That's not much help, is it?"

Abi shrugs an apology.

"Isn't there something on the GPS that tells you about the cache?" Portia asks Sam.

"Hold on a second," she replies, pressing icons on the screen like Laurel had shown them. After several wrong turns—including ending up in the settings menu three frustrating times—Sam finally locates the correct page.

"Okay... *In View of Lion Hill*," she reads aloud in her best public-speaking voice. "It shows 1½ out of five stars coloured in for *difficulty*."

"That means it should be fairly easy to find," translates Abi, who had been paying the most attention to Laurel's instructions.

"And *terrain* has 1½ stars out of five coloured in, too."

"That means it shouldn't be too hard to get to," supplies Abi. "So it probably isn't up a tree or anything."

"Okay," says Callum. "That narrows things down a bit, I suppose. Does it say how big it is?"

"Er, I think so," mutters Sam. "Oh, here it is... It says, *cache size: regular*."

"I'm guessing that means it's not a treasure chest or an M&M, then," says Henry.

"So, we've got a medium-sized container, that's easy to get to and easy to find once you get there," Ben recaps. "So what are we missing?"

"I think you just need a bit of experience," says Diane encouragingly. "I'm sure you'll get your eye in after you've found a couple."

Ben is happy that Diane is talking to him again—then something else occurs to him. "You know where it is, don't you?" he asks suspiciously.

"Maybe," chuckles the young woman. She raises her right eyebrow in a way that clearly says that *maybe* means *yes*.

"What about in that stump?" suggests Jaspa, indicating a tree trunk that's been cleanly sawn through a couple of feet above the ground. "The rock in the top of it looks a bit out of place."

Ben takes two paces to his right and crouches down beside Jaspa's stump. It's a little over a foot in diameter.

"I've found a hint," Sam announces, as her brother lifts out the rock that's nestled in the hollow top of the stump. "It says, *Walk up behind the monument between the railing and the hedge, look in one of the tree stumps.*"

"Like this stump, you mean?" asks Ben with a grin, as he removes a clear plastic box from the hole.

***

The geocache is about the size of a fat paperback book. It's the sort of plastic container they have at home to keep leftovers in the fridge. Someone has used a black marker pen to write *IN VIEW OF LION HILL. GEOCACHING. HARMLESS* in capitals on the lid. Inside the box they find a blue notebook, a pen, a couple of Pokémon cards and a shiny American quarter.

"What do we do now?" wonders Davy.

"We write our names in the book," answers Abi.

"Okay," says Ben, taking the notebook out of the box. He opens the book, and discovers that quite a few other people have already signed it. Flipping to an empty page, Ben picks up the pen and begins to write.

He gets as far as *Ben Mc*, before Abi stops him. "You're not supposed to use your real name. You're supposed to come up with a nickname, one especially for geocaching."

"Like what?" asks Ben, the tip of the pen still on the paper.

"I dunno," admits Abi.

"What names have other people used?" asks Henry. "That might give us some ideas."

Ben turns to the last log in the notebook. "It was found on Wednesday by someone called *Kleine welp.*"

"That means *Small Cub* in Dutch," Diane informs them.

"Hmmm," says Abi, impressed at Diane's linguistic skills.

Ben flips back a few pages, scanning the names signed in the book. "Someone called *Papau* found it last month. And here's someone called *CEPI* a couple of months before that."

"Are there any English-sounding names?" asks Davy.

"Erm... What about *Robby992*?" says Ben, stopping randomly. "Or *Big Family*? Or *JKL*?"

"It says here that the cache was hidden by *Wilkinsons*," Sam tells them. "That's an English name."

"Maybe you could come up with names together?" Diane suggests. "But we need to be quick about it."

Taking Diane's advice, the six children split into pairs to consider possible geocaching names—Ben with Sam, Abi with Henry, and Davy with Callum.

"What about something like *Mighty McRaes*?" Sam says quietly to her brother.

"I don't know," Ben replies. "I reckon it sounds a bit big-headed."

"How about *Edinburgh Geocachers*?" Sam tries again.

"Too dull," her brother responds immediately.

"*Moray Place Adventurers*?" Moray Place is the name of the square where the McRaes live back in Edinburgh.

"Nah!"

"Well you come up with something then," says Sam, getting annoyed.

"Hey!" objects Bisckits. "Don't we get a say?"

"That's not a bad idea," replies Ben. "How about a name for all of us? Like the *Ses and the Seers*?"

Sam's face falls. "But I'm not really a Seer," she says glumly.

"Never ye mind," Gravee tries to console her.

"You know, it was Jaspa who spotted where the cache was hidden," chuckles Portia. "Maybe we should reward him by naming our geocaching team after him?"

"What?!" cries Jaspa. "No!"

"Yeah," cheers Bisckits. "That's a great idea!"

"No," repeats Jaspa. "It's a terrible idea."

"C'mon," calls Diane. "We need to give the others time to find the cache too, you know."

Ben looks at his sister. "What do you think?"

"Actually, I was joking," admits Portia nervously.

Sam shrugs. Then smiles. "Well, we haven't come up with anything better."

"Ye'll be famous yet, laddie!" laughs Gravee.

"This is a bad idea," complains Jaspa. But no one is listening to him.

***

"So what names have you come up with?" asks Diane.

"Davy and I are both huge Hearts fans," Callum explains. Hearts—short for Heart of Midlothian—is one of the two big football clubs in Edinburgh. "So we're going to call ourselves *HMFC Forever!*"

"Me and Henry still couldn't come up with anything good, so we're just going to use *HenAb*," Abi apologises.

"They both sounds like a perfectly good names to me," says Diane cheerfully. "And what about you guys?" she asks Ben and Sam.

"We're going to call ourselves *Jaspa's Journeyers*," declares Sam proudly.

Sam's proclamation is met by a kind of stunned silence.

"What sort of a name is that?" blurts Davy after a few moments, speaking for all the others. "And who on Earth is Jaspa?"

"I said this was a bad idea," mutters Jaspa, shaking his head.

Ben suddenly understands the implications of the name they've chosen. And realises Jaspa was right, it *was* a bad idea. But it's too late now. "Er... Well... We got the name from Abi earlier," he tries to bluff. "When

64

I said *faster* and she thought I said *Jaspa*. We decided it sounded like a cool name, so we figured we'd use it."

Davy and Callum both look bemused, while the Greanings look at their friends with curious expressions. Abi purses her lips suspiciously, but says nothing.

***

Chapter Eight

Gobber's Dare

The friends return to their table and are quickly joined by Jimmy. "So what do you think of geocaching, then?" he asks, as the second group heads out in search of the cache.

"It was alright...," replies begins Davy.

"...But not as much fun as playing footie," finishes Callum.

"Well, the rest of us thought it was great," declares Ben.

"I'm glad," Jimmy says, with an appreciative nod of his head. "Like Laurel said earlier, it's taken us to some really cool places over the five or so years we've been doing it."

"What's your geocaching name?" wonders Abi.

"JKL," Jimmy replies.

"That's you?" asks Abi excitedly. "We saw your name in the logbook of the cache we just found."

"Excellent," says Jimmy. "Originally JKL was for our whole family..."

"That's clever," comments Portia. "It's a chunk of the alphabet with all their initials."

"...But not long after we started, Kevin decided he wanted his own geocaching name."

"Gobber's got his own geocaching name?!" blurts Ben, incredulously.

"Oh yeah," confirms Jimmy. "Despite what he says now, Kevin used to love geocaching. Although admittedly he doesn't do it much anymore."

"So what's Kevin's geocaching name?" asks Henry.

Jimmy suppressed a grin. "Anakev Skywalker," he replies, with an almost straight face.

"No! Really?!" gawps Abi. "That's priceless!"

Jimmy doesn't need to reply. The twinkle in his eyes and the smile twitching around the corners of his mouth say it all.

The entire table dissolves into hoots of laughter. Bisckits rolls on his back, while Ben slaps the tabletop beside the Ses with a the flat of his palm.

"Hey!" objects Gravee, tears of mirth still pouring down his face to soak the fur. "Watch where ye're thumpin'!"

"So if Gobber used to be Anakev Skywalker..." observes Henry, his breaths shallow as he attempts to control his laughter, "... Does that now make him Darth Kevin?"

The whole table, Ses and human alike, erupt into renewed floods of hilarity.

***

"We'd really like to try and find some more geocaches," says Sam, as the laugher finally begins to subside.

"As it happens, we found a particularly good one here last summer, called *Waterloo 1815*," Jimmy confides. "It's a special type of geocache called a multicache. That's where you have to visit several different locations—called waypoints—before you can find the cache itself."

"That sounds cool," says Abi.

"They are," agrees Laurel's husband. "The one here takes you around pretty much the entire battlefield. In fact, in many ways it was the inspiration for bringing you all here this week."

"Can we try it?" asks Sam excitedly.

"I'd love to say yes," admits Jimmy. "But it takes several hours to complete. And I'm afraid we just don't have enough time today."

***

67

Dennis has produced a mini football from somewhere, and Callum, Davy and a couple of the other kids not currently looking for the geocache are kicking it about energetically. The McRaes and Greanings huddle together at their picnic table.

"I wish we could do that multicache," sighs Sam. "I think it would be fun."

"Yeah," agrees Henry. "And I'd really like to see some more of the battlefield."

"But you heard what Jimmy said," Abi puts in. "It takes too long to do it today."

"Just as well," says Gobber, slinking up to their table and sitting down beside Sam. "There's no way a bunch of losers like you would be able to do it, anyway. Not without help. Come to think of it, I bet Diane had to show you where the cache you just did was, didn't she?" He smirks at Ben. "By the way, how was your lunch, McRae?" he asks slyly.

"Och, I really should huv thrown bigger rocks at th' wee scunner back in Greyfriars Kirkyard," says Gravee between clenched teeth. "Mebbe it wud huv knocked some sense intae that thick heid o' his."

"What do you want, Gobber?" asks Abi quietly, diplomatically deciding not to make matters worse by tormenting him with his proper name.

"Just a friendly visit, Greaning. Just a friendly visit," Gobber smiles, nudging Sam with his shoulder. "We're all mates here, aren't we Sammie?"

"I could bite his earlobe," suggests Bisckits thoughtfully. "That might shut him up."

"Or make him squeal like th' wee jessie he is," adds Gravee.

Sam giggles, causing a characteristic pulse of anger to distort the bully's features.

"You'll do no such thing, Bizzee!" declares Portia, rolling her eyes as if silently begging the universe for help, or strength, or both. But then she adds, "Even if he does deserve it."

Gobber composes himself. "Yeah, it's a shame you can't try *Waterloo 1815*. It's a lot of fun. But probably too challenging for you lot." He shakes his head in pretend regret. "Unless you had a grown up—or someone who thinks they are—to hold your hands through it." His scowls as his glance drifts briefly towards Diane, who is laughing at something Dennis has just said.

"What?" demands Ben. "Like your mum and dad did for you, Anakev?"

A look like thunder crosses Gobber's face. "Ha! Is that the best you've got?" he snorts. "Say what you like, McRae. The fact is that I've found it and you haven't. And never will!"

"We could do it!" Ben insists. "And without any help from grown ups, too!"

"I bet you couldn't!"

"I bet we could!"

"Interesting," says Gobber. He rubs his chin with the thumb and forefinger of his left hand for a moment. "I bet you £20 you couldn't."

"Careful, Ben," says Jaspa. "He's up to something."

But Ben's already retorting, "I bet you £50 we could!"

"Really?" smiles Gobber viciously. "Prove it!"

"What?"

"Are you deaf now, too?" sneers the older boy. "I said, *prove it!* Prove you're so bloomin' clever and find the cache."

"You know we can't," Abi steps in. "Your dad has already said we don't have enough time."

"Not today," Gobber concedes. "So come back and find it tomorrow, then."

"But we're going to..." Ben begins, but the bully cuts him off.

"I knew it!" he scoffs, standing up suddenly. "You're all talk, McRae! You know as well as I do that tomorrow you and your stupid Adventurers get to choose what you want to do. So choose to come back here and do

69

the cache. I dare you!" He looks down his nose at the four of them, then turns to walk away. "Unless you want everyone to know what a bunch of chickens you all are," comes the parting shot over his shoulder.

***

"So, what do you think?" Ben asks his friends.

"About what?" replies Abi.

"About coming back here tomorrow to do the cache."

"You're not serious!" declares Henry.

"Why not?" demands Ben

"Because we're going to Bruges for the day tomorrow," Abi reminds him.

"Yeah, but Gobber was right about one thing," Ben points out. "We can choose what we do tomorrow. Perhaps it's not too late to change."

"I still think that boy's up to something," says Jaspa.

"Aye," agrees Gravee. "An' ye can bet it isnae anythin' good."

But Ben's in no mood to listen to the Ses's good advice. "So who's in?" he asks his human companions.

"I am!" declares his sister immediately.

"I knew I could depend on you, Sammie," says Ben with a grin. "Henry?"

"I guess," replies the eldest of the group, uncertainly.

"Abi?"

Henry's sister doesn't answer for several seconds, but finally nods her head in agreement. "Alright," she says. "Go ahead and ask Laurel and Jimmy if it would be alright. But I can't help thinking Gobber is playing us somehow."

"Can the lassie hear us, or whit?" wonders Gravee out loud.

***

Ben returns from speaking with the Williamsons, looking troubled.

"They said no, didn't they?" groans Sam.

"Thank goodness for that," breathes Portia. "I think Jaspa and Gravee are right. Gobber's much too eager to get you to try and find this geo-cache."

"It's probably for the best," says Abi, echoing Portia's words. "I don't trust Gobber."

"Are yers sure she cannae hear us?" enquires Gravee.

"That's not it at all," Ben answers his sister's question. "Actually, they said with a bit of rearranging they can probably make it work."

"That's great!" declares Sam happily.

"But...?" prompts Abi.

"But we can't do it alone. There has to be an adult with us."

"Great!" says Henry. "Gobber's going to have a field day with that!"

***

Part 2

Waterloo 1815

Chapter Nine

Deception

"I don't need a babysitter!" Ben almost screams. "Just leave us alone!"

"Ben!" exclaim Portia and Abi in horrified unison.

Gravee looks suspiciously at the girl.

Jaspa shakes his head. *This isn't going to end well*, he thinks.

"Why you little brat!" snarls Dennis.

A range of emotions compete for the use of Diane's face. In other circumstances, the battle might have been quite comical. Except the feelings Diane's features are trying to express are things like shock, disbelief, anger and hurt. Finally, they give up and settle on tight nothingness.

Gobber sits in the back of the minibus, grinning fit to burst.

***

As Ben had predicted the previous afternoon, the Williamsons have indeed arranged things so he and his friends can spend the day attempting the *Waterloo 1815* geocache. Frustratingly, but also as expected, they've been absolutely unmovable in their insistence that Diane tag along.

Throughout yesterday evening, Ben, Sam, Abi and Henry all took turns at trying to convince Laurel and Jimmy to change their minds. But none of their pleas or arguments had any effect.

Gobber's tormenting had been relentless.

And in his desperation, unknown to the others, Ben hatched a reckless plan.

***

Ben's scheme is simple: make Diane so mad at him, she'll actually refuse to go with them. Even Ben can see this plan has holes in it big enough to fly an airliner through. Not least of these is what will happen afterwards, even if the deception works?

The fact of the matter is that Ben and his friends—especially Abi— would gladly have Diane accompany them. She's fun to be around and doesn't treat them like they're dim-witted, just because they're younger than she is.

But Gobber's stupid dare makes it an impossibility. If Diane comes along, Ben and his friends have lost, even before they begin.

So Ben finds himself hurting the sweet-tempered young woman once again. This time on purpose. And he feels utterly rotten about it.

Fortunately—or unfortunately, depending on how you look at it— Ben's hare-brained scheme actually seems to be working.

Perhaps working a little too well.

And Gobber is loving it!

***

"Forget the ungrateful vermin," Dennis advises. "He and his mates aren't worth the agro. Come to the waterpark with us instead."

Dennis has been charged with taking Gobber and two of the younger Adventurers back to the Océade waterpark.

"Don't worry," says Diane quietly, her face unreadable. "I intend to."

"But...!" begins Abi.

Ben shoots his friend a sharp look, that instantly silences her.

Diane climbs back into the minibus and slams the door closed. Jaspa sees her lips mouth *Let's go* to Dennis, and the vehicle pulls away.

Four humans and four Ses stand on the path outside the battlefield's visitor centre, watching the van leave. They're all feeling slightly shell-shocked at what just happened.

Through the back window they can see Gobber practically crying with laughter.

"I hope you're proud of yourself!" Abi rounds on Ben, as the minibus turns the corner.

"Of course I'm not!" Ben shouts back. "But what choice did I have? You know as well as me, we have to do this alone."

Abi stops short. "You mean you did all that on purpose?" she asks quietly.

The McRae boy lowers his head and sighs. "I couldn't see any other way," he admits in barely a whisper.

"Oh Ben," groans Abi, feeling a little foolish. "I'm sorry. I didn't realise."

***

The silence drags on until Gravee breaks it as gently as he can. "I ken this is difficult," he tells Ben kindly. "But since ye've gone tae such trouble tae be here alone, mebbe we should be gettin' on wi' this geocache of yers."

Ben nods his head, almost imperceptibly, and tries to shake off the gloom he feels. He puts his hand in his pocket, takes out the GPS unit, and presses the button on the side. The device makes a beeping sound and the screen flickers into life.

"I suppose we should get on with this," says Ben for the benefit of the Greanings. He hands the GPS receiver to Abi. "I think you'd better have this for now. You seemed to be able to work it better than the rest of us yesterday."

Abi accepts the GPS without comment. She impatiently waits the 15 seconds or so it takes the unit to lock on to enough satellites to identify its position. Once the device knows where it is, Abi presses a short sequence of icons on the touchscreen, setting the geocache *Waterloo 1815* as their destination, before selecting the compass screen. She takes a few steps to allow the arrow to settle down.

"That direction, about 155 yards," she says, pointing towards Lion Mound through the narrow gap between the visitor centre and the Panorama next door. "It looks like it's probably at the top."

"Not again!" exclaims Sam.

"It's not that high, Sammie," Ben consoles her.

"Not to you, maybe," his sister complains. "But my legs are shorter than yours."

"They're not shorter than ours!" laughs Bisckits.

"Hold on a minute," says Abi, interrupting the McRaes' discussion. "It looks like these coordinates are just for Lion Mound."

While Sam and Ben have been debating the height of the artificial hill, Abi has been reading the cache description. "Yes. It says, *At the entrance, outside the Centre du Visiteur building, find the following information...*"

"The *Centre du Visiteur*?" repeats Portia.

"That's French for *visitor centre*," says Sam knowledgably.

Abi gives the younger girl a grin. "Quite right," she says, thinking Sam's statement is a direct response to what she herself had just said.

"I could have guessed that," insists Portia, a little defensively.

"Which means we're already where we need to be," observes Jaspa.

***

"So, we're in the right place," says Ben. "What do we need to find out?"

"We need... er..." begins Abi. "Here it is! We're looking for the *number of European countries engaged in the battle* and the *number of men engaged in the battle.*"

The children and Ses start to scan the various signs in front of the visitor centre. Almost straight away Henry spots the answers they need on a large sign written in several different languages. "It says here," he reads aloud, "That *300,000 men from seven nations faced one another.*"

"He probably knew that already," notes Bisckits.

"Good," says Abi. "Now we have to do a bit of maths, to work out the values of *A*, *B* and *C*."

"Really?" groans Sam.

"Don't worry, it's nothing difficult," smiles Abi. "In fact, *A* is simply the number of countries."

"So *A* equals seven," supplies Ben.

"Thank you, Einstein! Next we need the number of men divided by 100,000 times two."

"Six," says Jaspa without even pausing to think. Everyone (apart from the Greaning siblings, obviously) looks at him in surprise. "What?!" he asks defensively.

"Since when have you been so good with numbers?" demands Bisckits accusingly.

"I dunno," admits his brother. "I realised just recently, I guess."

"Well, you never told me!"

"Nor me," agrees Portia.

"So a Ses being good at maths is a crime now, is it?" asks Jaspa, feeling unnecessarily put upon. "It's not like I just admitted to pulling the wings off baby birds for fun!"

"Crivens!" exclaims Gravee, sounding horrified. "Why on Earth wud ye want tae dae that tae puir wee birdies?"

"That's not what I..." begins Jaspa.

But Gravee can't keep a straight face and bursts out laughing at his own joke.

Jaspa scowls, clearly indicating he doesn't find the Dogses' sense of humour very funny.

"Right, so we've got 300,000... divided by 100,000... times two... erm," mutters Abi again, this time to herself. She bites her lower lip, concentrating on the numbers swimming in her mind. "*B* equals six," she says after a few moments, answering her own question.

"And finally, *C* is *A* plus one."

"Eight," declares Sam, firmly.

"See, I told you the maths wasn't hard," Abi smiles at Sam again. "Which all means that *ABC* is... um... 768.

"Now, if I use this to modify the coordinates according to the instructions..." She presses another sequence of buttons on the touchscreen, each one accompanied by a beep. "...It means our next waypoint is..." Abi takes a few steps towards the Panorama to settle the GPS down once again, before turning a full 180° back towards her friends. "It means our next stop is down near the main road."

"Let's go then!" declares Henry, already moving.

***

"It's warm in this sun," observes Ben.

As he walks, Ben does a curious, almost dance-like manoeuvre. He shrugs his backpack onto one shoulder in order to slip his opposite arm out of his jacket, then he reverses the process to remove his other arm. As has become traditional, Jaspa and Gravee ride on Ben's right shoulder. But they're as well practiced as Ben at this particular operation, and shuffle out of the way at the appropriate moment.

Much of the sky above them is a perfect blue and it is, as Ben just commented, pleasantly warm in the patches of sunshine. That said, there are also quite a few heavy-looking cumulous clouds with ominously dark edges floating about, particularly to the west. Beneath these clouds the temperature drops noticeably.

Humans and Ses lapse into silence as they walk (or ride, in the Ses's case). They all now understand the reasons for Ben's earlier actions, yet they're still a bit stunned by them, Ben included. Although she's trying not to show it, Abi remains particularly upset, since she's become quite friendly with Diane during this trip.

The group heads east down Route du Lion, past the arena used for yesterday's re-enactment. The tents and grandstands are well on the way to being dismantled.

"These days there are laws protecting the battlefield because of its historical importance," says Henry, breaking the silence. "So most of the valley looks pretty much the same as it would have appeared to Wellington and Napoleon. The big exception is this part of the Allies' ridge, between Lion Mound and the Brussels road."

"How so?" wonders Abi.

"Well, the earth from this area was scraped together to build Lion Mound. As a result, it's estimated that this part of the ridge crest is five or six feet lower than it was in 1815," her brother answers. He chuckles, "Apparently Wellington wasn't too happy about it. When he came back a few years later and saw what they'd done, he said, *They have spoiled my battlefield.*"

"So when the French attacked Wellington's soldiers," says Ben, after a few moments consideration, "They were actually fighting above where our heads are now."

"I suppose so," muses Henry. "But only along this section of the ridge."

***

"I wonder what it was like being a soldier at Waterloo," muses Sam.

"Pretty bloomin' 'orrible, nae doot," observes Gravee, succinctly.

"Nae doot," agrees Jaspa, in a passable imitation of his friend's accent.

"Well Sam, pretend you're a soldier in Wellington's army on the morning of June 18th, 1815," Henry instructs. "Many of the older soldiers around you are full of confidence, in themselves and Wellington, thanks to many years of battle and victory. But like half the Duke's troops, you're a raw recruit—a rookie, if you like. Today is going to be your first major battle. And possibly your last."

Sam gawps at the implication of Henry's words, her mouth forming a wide 'O' in shock.

Ben and Abi exchange a glance, grinning at the younger girl's reaction.

"Just think! You've no real idea what to expect, although you're sure it's not going to be good. Imagine how scared you are, knowing you might not live to see the sunset. Especially when the majority of the enemy soldiers are veterans of the Emperor's previous wars and so, unlike you, know how to fight.

"On top of all that, you've heard that most Belgians consider themselves to be French, and actually want Napoleon to win! In fact, many of the Belgian troops supposedly on your side used to be in the French army. There are rumours that only two days earlier, at the Battle of Quatre Bras, many of them refused to fight. So you're a bit worried about their loyalties, to say the least. What if they do the same today? Or, worse still, what if they actually change sides mid-battle?!

"To make matters worse," Henry goes on, "A thunderstorm struck during the retreat from Quatre Bras yesterday afternoon, bringing with it torrential rain that lasted well into the night.

"Like most of the army, you were forced to spend last night outdoors in a muddy field of trampled rye. This morning you were woken with the dawn, at about 4 o'clock—assuming you'd actually managed to fall asleep in the first place—and ordered to your appointed position, to wait for the terror that will inevitably follow.

"But as the morning drags on, the French seem in no hurry to get things started. In fact, you can't even see them, since they're camped out of sight, just over the far ridge. All you can see is the smoke from their cooking fires."

Sam, Jaspa and the others involuntarily look through the bare bones of the arena's stands, down the slope, and across the valley. So powerful is Henry's storytelling, they almost expect to still see the smoke of French campfires hanging over the opposite ridge.

"Imagine how your thoughts wander in bone-chilling terror at what today will bring. Then, just as you're beginning to hope that Napoleon has decided not to fight after all, the Emperor himself appears on the French ridge, riding a white horse, to watch his army parade into position.

"Regiment after regiment march into view up the Brussels road before turning either left or right to line up along the far ridge. Thousands upon thousands of veteran French soldiers—infantry, cavalry and artillery. All glorious in their gleaming dress uniforms, accompanied by drums and trumpets, as if on a parade ground instead of a battlefield. All cheering *Vive l'Empereur*—Long Live the Emperor—as they march past Napoleon himself. All projecting absolute confidence across the valley. The whole intimidating display screams, *Beware! We are the might of France! And we cannot lose!*

"And then there's you; soaking wet, exhausted and covered in mud. You're unsure how you and your fellow new recruits will fare against the French veterans parading on the far ridge. You don't even know whether your Dutch-Belgian comrades will stay to help once the fighting begins. I suspect you're feeling utterly miserable and understandably sorry for yourself."

They all listen spellbound as Henry paints his bleak picture of what it must have been like for an inexperienced British soldier that morning. Appalled, Jaspa tries to visualise it in his mind's eye. It doesn't make for pleasant viewing.

"Then, a little before noon, your vain hopes of a peaceful afternoon are shattered..." Henry claps his hands together suddenly. Sam isn't the only one to jump. "...By the massive boom of cannon fire. The entire opposite ridge disappears in a bank of smoke, as nearly 250 French guns hurl a wall of sound at you, followed closely by a hail of metal. Almost instantly, your cannons respond, thickening the smoke.

"The guns' cold barrels cause the first few volleys to fall short. But all too soon cannonballs and shells start to fall among your ranks. Officers tell you to lie down behind the crest of the ridge, where the French can't see you.

"But the enemy gunners have followed Napoleon across most of Europe and know how to do their grisly job well. And so the horror begins."

Sam stares wide-eyed at Henry.

"Crivens!" breathes Gravee.

Jaspa is once again inclined to agree.

***

Chapter Ten

The First Attack

"It looks like the coordinates we calculated outside the visitor centre should take us to something called the Picton Memorial," says Abi, reading the next part of the cache description. "Where Sir Thomas Picton was apparently killed not long after the battle started."

"Huh!" exclaims Ben. "We already know where that is. If we'd read ahead, we could have skipped stage one completely!"

"I guess not everyone doing this cache would know where Picton was killed before they started," muses Henry.

"I still don't," complains Sam.

"Don't worry, Sammie," Abi consoles the younger girl. "I wouldn't know either, if the GPS wasn't pointing me straight at it."

"Oh, sorry," Henry apologises. "Picton was shot near the picnic area where we had lunch yesterday."

"Och!" exclaims Gravee. "It wis reit thoughtful for them tae provide a wee picnic area for all the puir soldiers."

Portia shakes her head, making Gravee chuckle.

"Ben and I saw his memorial while you were smoothing things over with Diane," adds Henry in the meantime.

His sister gives Ben a troubled look. "Fine lot of good that did in the end," she sighs.

Ben stares off into space.

"Yeah, well, erm..." says Henry, trying to remove his foot from his mouth. "Perhaps we'll need the values we found at the visitor centre again later on."

"I suppose," admits Ben a bit grumpily. His tone suggests he's not convinced.

***

A few minutes later they reach the end of Route du Lion, where it hits Chaussée de Charleroi. Henry leads the others to the southwest corner of the intersection, clears his throat, and briefly picks up his story of the battle.

"For the longest time, Chaussée de Charleroi was the main road between Brussels and Charleroi, which is down towards the border with France. So it provided Napoleon and his army the fastest route to Brussels.

"Since the road ran through the middle of the battlefield chosen by Wellington, both commanders located their headquarters beside it. If you remember, Jimmy mentioned La Belle Alliance yesterday, the farm that Napoleon used as his headquarters on the battlefield."

While he's been talking, Henry has slowly walked over to a medium-sized tree, the trunk of which he now slaps with his hand. "Well, this elm tree was planted to replace another one that stood on this spot during the battle, which Wellington used as his command post," he tells them.

"Wait a minute," objects Sam. "So Napoleon gets a whole farm and Wellington only gets a tree?"

"A farm doesn't sound that great a command post to me, either!" declares Ben.

"I guess not," laughs Henry. "But 200 years ago, farms were more than just a farmhouse, a barn and a few sheds. You can see La Haye Sainte just down the slope here, for example. The individual buildings are made of stone with massive walls and are really sturdy. And they all face a central courtyard, so the farm really is like a mini fort.

"In any case, neither headquarters was actually used for defence. They were more like rallying points in the centre of the respective lines."

"Wellington's tree must have taken quite a pounding from French cannon and musket balls," says Abi.

"It suffered a worse fate a few years after the battle," Henry grimaces. "When it was chopped down and made into souvenirs."

***

They cross Chaussée de Charleroi and carry on though the picnic area. Up ahead Jaspa can see Picton's Memorial, looking like a lonely gravestone beside Rue du Dimont. Opposite it, on the other side of the narrow road, he can make out a another roughly-carved stone of similar size and shape.

"*To the gallant memory of Lt. General Sir Thomas Picton,*" reads Abi sombrely, as they gather around his monument. "*Commander of the 5th Division and the left wing of the Army at the battle of Waterloo. Born 1758. Died near this spot in the early afternoon of 18th June 1815 leading his men against Count Drouet d'Erlon's advance.*"

"So the Prince of Orange gets wounded and they build Lion Mound, but General Picton is killed and all he gets is this little stone," says Bisckits. "That doesn't seem very fair."

"Most men who died here got nothing at all," Portia observes.

Her younger cousin nods his head, acknowledging this sad truth.

"So, *Count d'Erlon's advance* mentioned on this plaque, is what Jimmy called the first French attack, right?" Abi asks her brother.

"That's right," Henry replies. He makes an expansive gesture with both arms, taking in everything to the east—the ridge, the road, the slope and the valley below. "And this is where it happened."

"Wow!" say Sam and Bisckits.

Jaspa notices the field draping southward down the slope, into the bottom of the valley. He observes how the single-track Rue du Dimont follows the line of the ridge. And from this angle it's also easy to see the landscape starting to dip down to the north, on the road's far side.

"Imagine again you're a British soldier positioned on this part of the ridge," says Henry, returning to storyteller-mode (which he's clearly beginning to enjoy). "Perhaps even in one of the Scottish regiments that fought here so bravely."

Out of the corner of his eye, Jaspa notices Gravee's chest swell slightly with Scottish pride.

"You're sheltering on the back slope of the ridge, behind the crest on the other side of the lane. At the time of the battle it would probably have been a sunken dirt track—and there were definitely hedges along it—but otherwise it looked much the same as it does now.

"So, there you are, lying in the mud to present less of a target to the French gunners, who for the last half hour have inflicted a brutal bombardment of cannonballs and shells on you.

"Suddenly, at about 2 o'clock in the afternoon, the barrage stops. For a moment all you feel is relief. Relief that the shelling has stopped. Relief that you're still alive and unhurt.

"Then you realise that the quiet is also a sure sign that a big attack is imminent.

"The infantry along this part of the ridge, which includes you, is command by Sir Thomas Picton, a Welshman. He now orders you forward, to join your fellow soldiers already 'sheltering' behind the hedges along the road. With the cannons now silent, you can hear the sound of marching feet coming up the slope, encouraged onward by drums and great shouts of *Vive l'Empereur!*

"But the French aren't having a fun time of it either. The slope is steeper than it looks from up here. And don't forget, it's been raining cats and dogs for much of the last 24 hours, so the ground beneath the increasingly trampled crops is a muddy mess.

"Finally, Picton gives you the order to stand. And what do you see?" Henry pauses dramatically.

"What?" asks Sam, breathlessly.

"You see thousands of French infantrymen only 40 yards away, marching up the slope towards you," replies Henry. "Supported behind by artillery and cavalry."

Good grief! thinks Jaspa. *It must have been terrifying.*

"*Fire!* commands Picton. You pull your trigger, as does every other infantryman along this part of the Allies' ridge, sending thousands of small lead balls screaming at the approaching enemy. You hear Picton's voice again, *Charge! Hurrah! Hurrah!*, and you're pushing your way through the hedge to rush the French with your bayonet.

"On the other side of the smoke produced by your massive volley, you discover the French have been stopped dead in their tracks, in many cases literally. But General Picton also lies dead, shot in the temple."

***

"What's next then?" enquires Sam, pulling the group's attention back to the geocache.

"*On the Inniskilling Regiment Memorial nearby, find the total number of officers and men who joined the battle,*" Abi reads from the screen.

Jaspa taps Ben on the shoulder. He points at the second stone, across the road behind them. "Could that be it?" he asks.

"Maybe," whispers Ben, turning around and crossing the road. The stone stands on the narrow grass verge between the road and the adjacent field. On this side facing them is a cast metal plaque. The shape of the plaque reminds Ben of houses scribbled by young children. He crouches down in front of the stone and begins to scan the inscription.

"Found something?" asks Sam, as she and the others join him.

Ben's eye is drawn to a line near the bottom of the text, which reads *The Royal Irish Rangers* in letters larger than the rest. Unsurprising then, he's about to say this isn't the right memorial. Then he spots the word *Inniskilling*. "Yeah, I think so," he answers instead.

Peering over Ben's shoulder, Abi reads aloud the passage on the commemorative plate. "*In memory of the heroic stand by the 27th (Inniskilling) Regiment of Foot at the Battle of Waterloo on 18th June 1815 when, of the 747 officers and men of the regiment who joined battle, 493 were killed or wounded. A noble record of stubborn endurance.*"

"*Stubborn endurance?!*" exclaims Jaspa. "That's almost exactly two thirds of the regiment either dead or injured." This time no one thinks to mention the speed of his calculations.

"*Of them the Duke of Wellington said, 'Ah, they saved the centre of my line'. Erected by their successors, the Royal Irish Rangers,*" Abi concludes.

"Good grief!" breathes Ben after a few seconds. "That's heavy stuff."

"Yeah," agrees Henry. "Makes me glad we didn't live back then."

"I've forgotten what we needed to find out," admits Sam, bringing them back to the present once again.

Abi re-examines the cache description on the GPS. "*DEF is the number of men who joined battle.*"

"So that's 747," states Ben's little sister.

"Just like a Jumbo Jet," Bisckits observes happily.

Gravee looks bemused. "Whit are ye talkin' aboot, laddie?"

"A *Jumbo Jet!*" answers Bisckits the Aviation Expert. Then seeing that the Dogses still isn't getting his point, he adds, "It's the nickname of a Boeing 747 airliner."

"If ye say so," retorts Gravee. "At least ye've stopped callin' them *hairyplanes.*"

***

Chapter Eleven

An Emperor's Eagle

Abi again inputs the new coordinates into the GPS, but this time hands the device to the youngest member of the party. "Here you are, Sammie," she says. "Just keep us going along the road. We're looking for an old chapel of some sort."

Sam proudly accepts the GPS from Abi and marches off down the lane, heading more-or-less eastwards. The others smile at each other and set off in pursuit.

Rue du Dimont is barely 10 feet wide and rustically paved with roughly-squared cobblestones the approximate size and shape of house bricks. The centre of the road is slightly domed, although it still doesn't reach the level of the fields through which the lane passes.

On either side of the street, between the cobbled surface and raised grass verges, are narrow, muddy, pothole-filled shoulders, although Jaspa can see these fade out up ahead. Water has gathered in the potholes, and occasionally in spots where the cobbles have subsided slightly, proof that it rained here again during the night.

"So unlike on the other side of the main road, this part of Wellington's ridge hasn't changed much in the last 200 years," Henry tells Ben and Abi.

"Makes you think, doesn't it?" his sister says.

"Back then, this lane was called the Ohain Road," Henry expands. "Apparently, it was just a dirt track at that time, like most roads in the area, and it had hedges on both sides."

He pauses and looks down the slope to the right of the road, south across the valley and up the other side to Napoleon's ridge. Abi and Ben also stop and follow the older boy's gaze, as do Gravee and Jaspa.

"Can you imaging being right here during the battle?" Henry asks no one in particular. "Sheltering from cannonballs behind nothing but a couple of hedges, watching thousands of French soldiers climbing the hill, all wanting to kill you?"

"No," says Ben. "Not really."

Henry breathes out heavily. "Me neither!"

"Thankfully!" adds Abi sincerely, with a shake of her head.

***

"I've been wondering," Ben says to Henry. "What happened after the first French attack was stopped? Did they just turn around and march back down the hill?"

"Not quite," Henry replies. "They were strongly encouraged to leave by the British heavy cavalry, including the Royal Scots Greys."

"Why were they called the Scots Greys?" Abi interrupts.

"Erm... because they were Scottish and all rode grey horses," grins her brother.

"Really?"

"Honest!" Henry laughs briefly, before becoming serious once more. "The British cavalry sent the French infantry packing in the most terrifying way possible! The French formations were torn apart and slaughtered. So many men were taken prisoner that most of them ended up escaping again, because the Allies simply didn't have enough spare men to guard them."

"Blimey," says Abi.

"But that wasn't the end of it," says Henry. "You've heard of a regiment's *Colours*, right?"

"That's like their banner or flag, isn't it?" Ben answers.

"Often it is," agrees Henry. "The Colours are extremely precious to a regiment. They represent its heart and soul. Soldiers will fight viciously,

90

even to the death, to protect or capture them. During Napoleon's time, each French regiment was presented a gilded golden Eagle by the Emperor himself. Capturing one was every British soldier's dream, as it almost always brought instant glory and promotion.

"And as they crushed the first French attack, the British cavalry took not just one, but two Regimental Eagles. One of these was captured by Sergeant – soon to become Ensign – Charles Ewart of the Scots Greys."

"I know that name," says Ben slowly, tapping his top lip with his right index finger.

"Aye," says Gravee. "Ye've passed his grave a hundred times, on th' Esplanade ootside th' castle."

"Well, you've seen his grave outside the main gate of Edinburgh Castle," Henry echoes Gravee's comment.

"That's it," Ben quickly confirms.

"But we also saw Ewart's Eagle when your granddad took us to Edinburgh Castle last summer," Henry tells Ben. "It's on permanent display in the Greys' museum inside the castle."

"That's right," agrees Sam's brother. "I remember now."

"The capturing of a French Eagle was such a big deal it became the cap badge of the Scots Greys," Henry adds. "That's how they got their nickname, *The Bird Catchers*."

Jaspa is startled by a loud sniff beside him. He turns to Gravee in time to see a single large tear detach from the Dogses' eye and disappear into the white fur of his cheek.

"What's wrong?" asks Jaspa. "I thought you'd be proud that a Scotsman did something so heroic."

"I am proud, o' coorse," replies Gravee. "But I cannae get mah heid aroond th' idea that so many people died here. An' all for th' ambition o' one man. It's a terrible waste, reit enough."

***

"Unfortunately, glory is about to turn to disaster for the British cavalry," Henry goes on, unconsciously reverting to his storytelling-style. "They should chase off the beaten enemy infantry and return in good order to their own lines. That way they'll be ready for whatever comes next.

"Except the horsemen are drunk on victory and blood. With incredible but misplaced bravery, they take off on an undisciplined counter attack, charging the far ridge. It's as if they've already defeated all of France and nothing and no one can ever stop them or hurt them. But they're about to find out just how wrong they are.

"As they gallop up the other side of the valley, the British cavalry ride straight into the clutches of Napoleon's cannons, muskets and swords. First they're blasted by artillery and infantry fire from the waiting French lines. And then come the French cavalry.

"By this point, the British horses are worn out from galloping across the valley. But the French cavalry have fresh mounts and fall mercilessly upon their British counterparts, taking revenge for what has just been done to their infantry.

"Within moments, the glorious British heavy cavalry goes from invincible hunters to helpless prey. Only half of them manage to escape the French and get back to the Allies' lines. And even they are so exhausted, they take no more part in the rest of the battle."

"Whoa!" exclaims Ben.

"That's awful!" says Jaspa.

"That's jist whit I wis sayin'," responds Gravee. "A terrible waste."

***

Ben stops and stares quizzically at Henry.

"What?" demands his friend, uncomfortably.

92

"When did you learn so much about the Battle of Waterloo?" the younger boy wonders.

"You really have to ask?" exclaims Abi, in disbelief. "I've lost count of the number of books, documentaries and movies he's buried himself in since last summer. Ever since the pair of you saw that bloomin' Eagle up at the castle. How could you not have noticed?!"

"I find it interesting, that's all," declares Henry, squirming slightly.

"To be fair, I think you're getting really good at this storytelling," Abi compliments her brother. "I've never really thought much about Waterloo. But seeing the battlefield myself and the way you talk about it makes me think perhaps I should read one of your books when we get home."

"Oh, you should!" enthuses Henry. "There's one that..."

"I said *perhaps*," laughs Abi. "Don't push it."

"I reckon you sound more and more like Jimmy," observes Ben as they trudge along the road. "Although he's even more over-the-top than you are. I mean, with all that *dying in agonising pain* and *dread and terror* stuff."

"His stories frighten me a little," Abi confesses with an involuntary shiver. She looks at her brother, "But so do your descriptions of the battle, if I'm honest."

"I know what you mean," Ben sympathises. "But I think that's the point. I think they're just trying to remind us what war's really like for the people doing the actual fighting."

"And dying," adds Abi.

"I don't do it on purpose, but I suppose you're both right," agrees Henry. "Movies and video games make war look cool and fun. And sometimes real footage looks less believable than the fake Hollywood stuff. I mean, when you see a clip of a bridge or something blowing up, sometimes it's hard to tell whether you're watching images from a movie, a game or from the nose of an actual missile. But real war..."

"Real war is real people getting hurt and killed," Abi finishes his sentence.

"And in many ways, war was even more brutal at battles like Waterloo," Henry adds. "It was certainly a lot more personal back then."

"What do you mean?" enquires Ben.

"Well, think about it..." his friend replies. "There were no planes, or missiles, or tanks, or machine guns at Waterloo. Most of the fighting was done with muskets—which were notoriously inaccurate—bayonets, swords and cannons. Which meant a lot of the time you had to look your enemy in the eye as you tried to kill each other."

"That's horrible!" exclaims Abi.

"I know," Henry shrugs. "But that's the way it was."

***

"Who said, *Those who cannot remember the past are doomed to repeat it?*" wonders Abi aloud.

No one has said anything for a couple of minutes and her question takes Ben and Henry a little by surprise. They both look at her with blank faces.

"Dunno," admits Ben after a moment. "But it kinda makes sense. If people remembered how bad war is—I mean, really remembered—I guess they'd think twice before starting another one."

"But clearly people don't remember," observes Henry. "Not properly. If they did, we wouldn't have any more wars. Or terrorism. And yet there's dozens of conflicts going on all over the World right now."

"I guess some people just don't care," says Ben, with a frown.

"That's a gloomy thought," observes Abi.

"You know, when he saw all the dead and wounded after the battle, Wellington apparently said, *A victory is the greatest tragedy in the World, except a defeat*," Henry tells them.

"Another gloomy thought," sighs Abi.

"George Santayana," says Gravee.

"George Santayana?" blurts Ben.

"George who?" enquires Henry.

Ben mentally kicks himself. He hadn't meant to speak so loudly, but (not for the first time) he'd been surprised by Gravee's knowledge of human history and culture. "Um..."

Gravee rolls his eyes. "George Santayana," he prompts.

"George Santayana," repeats Ben, for the benefit of the others.

"What about him?" asks Henry.

"Erm... He's the bloke that said that thing about people who don't remember the past being doomed to repeat it," says Ben uncomfortably, following Gravee's prompts.

"Actually, he said *condemned* not *doomed*," the Dogses corrects him.

"If you say so," declares Abi, in response to Ben, not Gravee, of course.

"But you were the one who asked who said it," objects her friend.

"Doesn't mean I know the answer," Abi points out. "I just remember it sounding smart. Anyway, I thought you said you didn't know who said it either."

"Look who knows all sorts of stuff now," laughs Henry.

Ben blushes bright red. He feels like a complete fraud. Especially since he's also never heard of George Santayana.

"I'm impressed, in any case," says Abi, nudging Ben with her elbow. "So who is George Santa-wotsit anyhow?"

"Some guy," stammers Ben, trying to discourage further questions.

"He wis a philosopher an' author, actually," supplies Gravee. "He also said *History is a pack o' lies aboot events that never happened told by people who werenae there*, as well as *Only dead men huv seen th' end o' war.*"

"He must have been a barrel of laughs at parties," notes Jaspa dryly.

***

Chapter Twelve

Air Attack

The sun is out, the sky is blue (mostly), the stages of the cache have been easy so far and there's no Gobber to bother them (although Jaspa suspects he's probably off terrorising some other poor souls at the waterpark). Despite the morning's traumatic beginning, life feels good and even Abi is relaxed. She and Henry stop to take off their jackets and so drop back a little.

Ben carries on, not wanting his sister to get too far ahead. He and his two Ses passengers can clearly hear Bisckits the Navigator 'helping' Sam, even though all she really has to do is follow the road.

"The wee laddie's got a real taste for this 'ere geocachin', hasn't he?" notes Gravee.

"Of course!" remarks Jaspa, rolling his eyes. "Don't you remember how he went on and on about it after we got back from London last year?" Then he smiles warmly. "But at least you can't say he's unenthusiastic! Portia says you could power half of Scotland if you could harness his energy."

"Perhaps we can convince Mum and Dad to get a GPS when we get home," suggests Ben quietly. "They'd probably love us having a new outdoor hobby."

"I'm sure they would!" laughs Henry. The Greanings have caught up quicker than Ben expected.

"Who are you talking to this time?" asks Abi, poking her friend playfully in the ribs.

"Just myself," mutters Ben.

"What again?" replies Henry, still laughing. "You know, our Dad says that talking to yourself is the first sign of..." He draws circles in the air beside his right temple with his index finger.

"Yeah, but he also says that these days people just assume you're on the phone," adds Abi.

"Who knew?" observes Gravee. "Mobile phones cure insanity!"

"It's a medical marvel," agrees Jaspa with a broad grin.

"It willnae be long afore doctors are handin' them oot instead o' pills," the Dogses chuckles. "Feelin' a wee bit wacky, Mr Smith? Take two cell phones an' call me in th' mornin'."

***

"*Vive l'Empereur!*"

The shout seems to come from above and slightly behind.

"Good grief!" exclaims Ben, as something whistles past his right ear at an incredible speed, narrowly missing the Ses perched on his shoulder. Abi and Henry gawp at him in bewilderment.

Ben, Jaspa and Gravee stare at the sky, but can see no sign of whatever just shot past them.

"Whit wis that?" cries Gravee, gripping tightly to Ben's sweater.

"No idea," replies Jaspa, sounding equally alarmed.

Then Jaspa spies something directly ahead of them. A dark, shrinking speck, close to the ground. It suddenly arches steeply into the sky, rocketing vertically into the heavens. Eventually the speck comes to a halt in mid-air, high above them. Now Gravee sees it too.

"Can ye tell whit it is yet?" asks the Dogses, regaining some of his composure.

"No," admits Jaspa bluntly, craning his head back as he stares up at the miniscule spot. "Bisckits would perhaps be able to make it out, but my eyes aren't as good as his."

"Whose are?" remarks Gravee distractedly, trying to focus on the hovering speck way overhead.

But frustratingly, Bisckits is with Sam and Portia, totally oblivious to what just happened.

"The good news—or perhaps the bad news—is that I don't think we're going to have to wait long to find out what it is," Jaspa announces.

Because whatever the speck is, it's begun to grow once again.

Which means it isn't hovering, after all.

It's dropping straight back towards them!

***

Ben is infuriated at not being able to join in the conversation, but he daren't say anything with the Greanings standing right beside him. He's made enough blunders already in the last couple of days, which is completely out of character. He's usually so careful when interacting with the Ses around other humans. But more annoying at the moment, is that he still can't see the object Gravee and Jaspa are talking about.

To be fair, the Ses aren't much better off. Although in the last couple of seconds, the swiftly approaching speck has grown into a dot, and is by now a blotch.

"Ye ken, it's movin' at a heck o' a speed," notes Gravee, with forced casualness.

Yet they still can't make out what it is. It remains little more than a blurred shape, silhouetted against the sky. Just an indistinct blotch. But a blotch plummeting swiftly towards them, and with a definite aura of purpose.

And at the speed it's travelling, it doesn't remain a blotch for long.

Before long, even Ben can see it.

***

Jaspa and Gravee are both briefly reminded of the time they stood by the runway at Kilimanjaro International Airport back in Africa, not long after they'd met, watching Bisckits' *hairyplane* appear out of the heat haze. On that occasion, first the fuselage and then the wings had seemed to solidify, as the aircraft approached through the shimmering air.

Today, the general impression is quite similar. Except the winged shape is in a high-speed dive straight at them from above, instead of slowly sinking Earthwards at a gentle angle. And this time, the thing rapidly approaching is also very much alive.

The bird—or rather, Birdses—hurtles out of the sky, its body buffeted by the air. The creature compensates using only the slightest movements of its wings, which are folded close to its body. Its head is rock solid. Unwavering. With the hook of its razor-sharp beak locked on a direct path to its target, guided by piercing black eyes rimmed with yellow. Gravee finds it an awe-inspiring sight.

Even though the intended target is clearly him!

As if realising that its prey can finally see it properly, the Falconses suddenly begins hurling abuse at the Dogses. Unfortunately for the attacker, the speed of its descent whips the words away from their intended recipient. But in some ways the effect is all the more frightening for it.

Gravee doesn't need to know what the aggressor is actually shouting. The look of hate in those cold eyes, and the silent but frenzied screams plainly issuing from the beak between them, is quite enough, *thank ye very much.*

***

The final few seconds of the Falconses' dive seem to play out in both slow motion and fast forward at the same time.

On the one hand, Jaspa and Gravee see every twitch of the Birdses' wings as it finalises the trajectory to its prey. They see it flare its wings and lower its legs in one smooth movement, bringing its taloned feet forward, so they will be the first thing to strike its victim. They also notice the ugly cut above the Falconses' right eye, where crusted red blood is turning black.

Yet all this is registered in a split second, as the living, breathing missile is suddenly upon them, arriving at terrifying speed.

Gravee attempts to dodge out of the path of the crazed Raptorses, shifting as fast as he can to his left. But all his years of practice aren't enough. A subtle movement of a half-folded wing easily compensates for his futile attempt to escape.

Fortunately for the Dogses, he's not the only one to have spotted that—for whatever unfathomable reason—Gravee is the focus of the Falconses' fury. What's more, Jaspa has also realised that there's no way his friend is going to be able to get out of the way in time. So he does the only thing he can think of...

He shoves the Dogses away from him with all the strength he can muster.

Jaspa's unexpected push drops Gravee to his knees, slamming him into Ben's neck. The Dogses feels a whoosh of wind, as clawed feet rip uncomfortable close to his right ear. The rush of air is accompanied by a strange shout, sounding almost like a battle cry, which rises and falls as the attacker roars past.

"...Pour la gloire de la France!..."

Gravee breathes a sigh of relief. *That was too close!* he thinks.

But his celebration is cut short, literally, by a searing pain in his right ear. Gravee cups the affected ear in his hand, which he then brings back down to inspect. The tiniest amount of blood is visible on his paw.

The tip of a single talon must have made contact with skin, resulting in a scratch no worse than—but just as painful as—a paper cut.

That really was too close!!

***

As every schoolchild learns, thanks to Sir Isaac Newton, *every action has an equal and opposite reaction*. So, by shoving Gravee in one direction, and having no time to set his feet and balance properly beforehand, Jaspa effectively pushes himself the opposite way.

The Giraffeses staggers backwards, arms whirling like adrenaline-boosted windmills. His heels trip over a ridge in Ben's sweater, and for the second time in less than 24 hours, Jaspa feels himself beginning to fall.

Again? he thinks. *Really?*

But luck is on his side once more.

In response to the second near miss between the Kamikaze Falconses and his head, Ben instinctively jerks forward. If the Birdses had been truly trying to hit him, the boy's reaction speed would have been laughably slow. But fortunately, Ben's automatic movement is just quick enough, and in exactly the right direction, to keep his shoulder in contact with Jaspa, as the little Giraffeses flails for balance and a handhold.

Jaspa grips Ben's sweater tightly, dangling by his arms above the ground. He takes a deep, calming breath. Then begins to haul himself, hand over hand, up towards the top of Ben's shoulder. Suddenly, a white furred paw grips him by the wrist and hauls him the rest of the way.

"Thanks!" breathes Jaspa, as he and Gravee collapse back on Ben's shoulder, their pulses racing.

"Reit back at ye."

After a few seconds the Giraffeses recovers enough to glance across at his friend. "Looks like you cut yourself," he says, pointing at his Gravee's ear.

"Och, it's jist a wee flesh wound," his friend grins.

"So what did you do to upset this Falconses so much?" asks Jaspa.

101

"I huvnae got a Scooby," replies Gravee. "I've nae even seen him afore."

"Well, he seems to know you."

"Honest," insists the Dogses. "I dinnae ken th' bampot. Th' first time I..."

But Gravee never gets to finish his sentence. Because at that moment, Ben starts flapping his arms about like a maniac.

***

"Gerroff!" yells Ben, swiping wildly at the air.

The Falconses, it appears, has decided on a new plan of attack. He hovers directly in front of Ben, occasionally making swift darting motions towards the two Ses sitting on the boy's shoulder.

The three friends can finally get a good view of their aggressor. The first thing they notice is that he's smaller than they first thought, although nowhere near as tiny as their Ratses pal, Ernest, from London, or Jaspa's Elephantses friend, Oripot, back in the Serengeti.

The Birdses' plumage is quite spectacular. Dark grey feathers cover his head, back and the upper sides of his wings. In contrast, his belly, underwings, upper legs and cheeks are rusty-white with dark brown flecks. His throat is the same colour as his underside, but without the patterning, while his tail is striped, above and below. Exposed, bright yellow skin covers his unfeathered lower legs, and also encircles his eyes and beak. The hooked beak itself is dark-grey, as are the vicious-looking talons.

The Birdses continues to flit this way and that, looking for an opening. All the while he screams insults at Gravee.

"'Ow dare you show your filthy faces 'ere!" he cries. "Eet eez an insult to zee Great Napoleon!"

"Look pal, I dinnae ken whit yer problem is, but..."

"I am not zee one wiz zee problem!" the incensed character shouts back. "Eet eez you wiz zee problem. Can you not see, you are not welcome 'ere?"

"Aye," mutters Gravee to himself. "I'm beginnin' tae get that impression."

The Raptorses zips forwards again, then retreats just as quickly, effortlessly avoiding another swat from Ben. He returns to his original position, hovering just out of the boy's reach.

"Why eez eet you are riding on zis human?" he demands. "An' 'ow can eet see me?"

"He's oor friend," Gravee answers. "And he's a Seer."

"What nonsense eez zis?!" the Birdses bellows. "You Rosbifs are all zee same. You are all liars!"

"Whit did ye call me?" Gravee shouts back.

But the odd creature just continues his rant. "You will not bee so insolent when zee soldiers of France crush your puny armée!"

"Whit army?" asks Gravee, getting more confused by the instant.

Once again the Falconses shoots forwards, and once again Ben tries to smack it away. But all he succeeds in doing is throwing himself off balance. Luckily, as he stumbles forwards, he accidentally moves his friends out of harm's way, as they struggle to keep their footing.

"By zee end of zee day," their opponent continues, "Your so-called Duke of Wellington will bee begging zee mighty Napoleon for zee mercy!"

"But Wellington's been deid for over 150 years, ye greit galoot!" yells Gravee, trying to make sense of the situation. "An' Napoleon's been deid even longer!"

"**SILENCE!**" the Raptorses screams. "Why do you continue to tell such reediculous lies! Napoleon Bonaparte, *l'Empereur de la France*, stands upon zee 'ill before you wiz 'is Grande Armée! Soon zey will cross zees vallée and crush you Rosbifs like zee bugs you trulee are!"

Yet again, the befuddled individual makes a dart at Gravee. But whether because of anger, complacency, or sheer bad luck, this attack is not as well-timed as the previous ones. And Ben manages to catch him with a fingertip as he dives.

It's just a glancing blow. No more than a brush, really. But given tiny size of the Falconses, that's all it takes to send it spinning through the air.

The attacker recovers almost immediately, coming back to the hover, although he keeps a noticeably greater distance from Ben this time. The Birdses hangs there for a few seconds, almost motionless, apart from the beating of his wings. Then he seems to reach a decision.

"Zees eez not over," he declares, beginning to rise into the air.

Ben, Jaspa and Gravee watch as the Falconses climbs rapidly into the blue sky, getting smaller and smaller. He continues to hurl a string of curses and insults behind him as he goes, until he eventually disappears with a final, "*Vive l'Empereur!*"

"I don't think he's very well," observes Jaspa.

"Ye reckon?!" exclaims Gravee. "He needs a whole truck full o' cell phones, that one. Intravenously!"

***

With the Falconses gone, Ben finally notices Abi and Henry looking at him with concern. Like he might need a nice lie down. Or perhaps a cell phone or two of his own.

"What's with all the arm waving?" asks Henry, waggling his own arms around in a half-hearted imitation of his friend's recent activity.

"Er... It was a wasp," replies Ben lamely.

"I didn't see any wasp," Henry counters.

"It was a very small one."

"Really?" demands Abi. "Is that what you're going with?" She stares at Ben for a moment. Then she shakes her head and storms off after Sam.

"I tell yers," says Gravee. "That lassie's on tae us."

***

Chapter Thirteen

Chapels and Crosses

Perhaps a third of a mile east of the main Brussels-Charleroi road, the street splits to pass either side of a white building with a red tile roof. The left fork continues to follow the line of the old Ohain Road—although this part is called Rue de la Croix these days—along the crest of the ridge. Ben and his friends, however, remain on Rue du Dimont, which hugs the right side of the house and then begins to angle gently downhill.

"I expected there to be more people about today," notes Jaspa.

Apart from a couple of cars, they haven't encountered a single soul since they left the memorial to the Inniskillings—not including the deranged Falconses, of course. At the moment, the only person visible is someone (most probably a woman, is Jaspa's impression) in a dark blue jacket with the hood up, about a quarter mile behind them.

"I ken whit ye mean," Gravee replies. "Especially when ye think hoo many folk were here yesterday."

"Perhaps they all went home after the re-enactment," Jaspa speculates.

Gravee shrugs noncommittally.

Rue du Dimont gradually curves to the right as it crosses the slope. So by the time the cobbled road reaches the valley bottom, about half a mile further on, it ends in a 'T' junction with a marginally wider, asphalted street.

"Chemin des Cosaques," Abi reads the name of road at which they've just arrived. "Way of the Cossacks," she translates.

Sam makes a fairly sharp left turn onto this newest street, aiming them eastwards once more. "The next stop should be roughly 150 yards straight in front of us," she announces.

From his perch on Ben's shoulder, Jaspa can see a dark-coloured roof up ahead, poking above the high hedge on the left-hand side of the road. "I bet that's it," he says to Gravee.

"Aye," the Dogses agrees. "Most likely."

***

The gang arrive at a crossroads where Chemin des Cosaques meets Chemin de la Papelotte.

"We're here!" declares Sam.

About a hundred yards up the hill to their left is a large building with high walls and an octagonal tower above the gate. "That's Papelotte farm," Henry tells them. "It formed the eastern end of Allies' line during the battle. From here you can really see how the buildings surrounding the central courtyard made it like another small fortress."

"I like the tower," says Sam.

"I think I read the tower has been added since the battle," Henry informs her. "But I agree, it is very cool. Actually Papelotte..."

"Wow, how do you remember so much stuff?" laughs Ben.

"I'm just interested in it," replies Henry, a little defensively.

"Me too," grins Sam.

Encouraged, Henry picks up from where Ben had interrupted, "Papelotte wasn't the only fortification here on Wellington's left flank. During the battle there were also Allied soldiers in that other farm up ahead." He points to another cluster of buildings, a hundred yards further along Chemin des Cosaques. "It's called La Haye."

"Wait a minute," objects Ben. "I thought La Haye was the farm on the main road, down the hill from Wellington's elm tree."

"Ah, no. You're talking about *La Haye Sainte*," Henry corrects him. "This is just *La Haye*."

"Well, at least that's not really confusing then," complains Ben.

***

"This business about farms and fortresses is all very fascinating," Abi interjects, putting her jacket back on. "But I'm getting cold just standing around. What are we looking for again, Sammie?"

"It's something to do with this shrine, isn't it?" asks Portia, referring to a small roadside chapel situated at the northwest corner of the intersection.

"Hold on, I'll check," the younger McRae says to both of them, dabbing at the GPS's touchscreen with a finger.

Sure enough, Portia's chapel supports the roof Jaspa had spotted as they'd approached. Its red brick walls are pierced by an arched entrance at the front and similarly arched windows on either side. The windows are guarded by wrought metal grills, which match the gate that bars the entrance. Through this gate they can see an ornate altar of creamy-white marble with golden highlights. The entrance, windows and corners of the structure are outlined in a creamy-coloured sandstone. Above the entrance is a marble plaque.

"Got it," declares Sam. She begins to read aloud. "*At the chapel, you have arrived at the extreme left side of the battlefield (seen from allied point of view), the Papelotte farm.*"

"That's just what you said, Henry," remarks Ben.

"*From here, the road continues to Lasne, Wavre etc... This is how the Russian troops arrived from Wavre on the battlefield late in the afternoon, forcing the defeat of Napoleon.*"

"Actually, that should say *Prussian* troops," Henry corrects her. "With a *P*."

Sam squints at GPS screen. "You're right, it does," she confirms. "I thought it was a spelling mistake."

"Sounds like I made a similar mistake yesterday," admits Ben. "Jimmy mentioned the Prussians briefly, but I assumed I'd misheard him, and he'd actually said Russians."

"It's not a spelling mistake, and you didn't mishear," says Henry, facing first Sam then Ben. "Prussia doesn't exist anymore, but it used to include most of the northern areas of modern day Germany and Poland. We haven't said much about the Prussians yet, but I'm sure we will before the day is out."

"Huh!" exclaims Abi, thoughtfully. "I'd never heard of Prussia either."

"Ye still huvnae told us whit we need tae find oot 'ere," Gravee reminds Sam.

"Oh yeah," she mutters. Then louder she reads, "*Write down the date you'll see on the frontispiece of the chapel (GHIJ).*"

"What's a frontiswhatsit?" wonders Bisckits.

"I guess they must mean the plaque on the front there," Abi suggests, inadvertantly answering Bisckits' question.

The short inscription on the plaque is in French: *Chapelle batie a l'honneur de S. Roch par Lucie Plasman epouse de Joseph Mathieu.*

Jaspa assumes (correctly) that *chapelle* means *chapel* and *l'honneur* means *honour*, and so guesses the basic meaning of the message is something like: *This is a chapel built in honour of a particular saint by someone in memory of someone else.* Which is close enough, although Abi could inform him that *epouse* actually means *wife.*

In any case, the important piece of information is clear to them all, since the inscription is followed by a year: 1867. Or, as the cache description calls it, *GHIJ.*

***

"Okay," says Abi, programming the frantically beeping GPS unit. "This time the numbers we've found are used to calculate two intermediate way-points, which will guide us towards our next proper destination."

"I don't get it," admits Sam.

"Don't worry, Sammie," laughs Abi. "You'll see what I mean."

The older girl turns her back on the chapel and the fortified farm of Papelotte. "We start by going this way," she says, leading them south down Chemin de la Papelotte, which is little more than a muddy track in this direction.

Almost immediately, they find themselves walking between high earthen banks, reaching at least 10 feet tall on both sides. The banks are thick with trees, bushes and abundant undergrowth, which curves above them to all but block out the sky overhead. Unsurprisingly, the lane rapidly develops a rich, earthy smell. It also becomes noticeably cooler, so that Sam, Ben and Henry follow Abi's lead and put their jackets back on.

Jaspa feels as though they've entered a tunnel made of soil and vegetation. He's suddenly grateful that Gravee conquered his fear of enclosed spaces during their time with Ernest and Mad in London.

"Wow!" breathes Henry as they make their way along the strange, almost subterranean passageway. "This is what the sunken lane must have been like."

"The what?" asks Abi.

"Do you remember earlier how I told you that the top of the Allied ridge to the west of Wellington's elm was scraped together to build Lion Mound?"

"Uh-huh."

"Well, before the earth was removed, the part of the Ohain Road following that stretch of the ridge crest was below the level of the surrounding land, like this road here. So was the crossroads where it met the main road, beside where the picnic area is now.

110

"The French cavalry galloping up that part of the slope during the second attack must have got quite a shock when they discovered a chasm like this—but without the trees and bushes to give it away, I'm guessing— unexpectedly blocking their path. And the French attacking up the Brussels road past La Haye Sainte must have been equally freaked when they realised the banks were suddenly rising up on both sides, and British infantry were shooting at them from the top."

"It must have been pretty frightening, either way," agrees Abi.

"I bet they felt like rats in a barrel," observes her brother.

***

After only 150 yards, and still within the sunken way, they come to a split in the road. "This is the first waypoint," Abi informs them.

"So what do we need to find here?" asks Sam, looking around.

"Nothing," answers Abi. "This waypoint just helps guide us in the right direction."

Sam looks blank.

"You've done join the dots puzzles, right? Where you draw a line from dot to dot to make a picture."

"Of course," nods Sam. "They're one of my favourite."

"Think of this as a kind of giant join the dots game, with the waypoints as the dots, and us as the pencil. At some of the dots we have to search for information..."

"Like at the chapel," supplies Sam.

"That's right," confirms Abi. "But other dots are just points we have to pass along the way."

"Is that why they're called *waypoints*?" asks the youngest member of the team.

"I suppose it is," agrees Abi, with a chuckle.

111

"Ye cannae fool that wee lassie," declares Gravee, with a touch of pride.

"Anyway, the next dot is in that direction," says Abi, pointing down Rue de Babeau, the left-hand fork. She hands the GPS back to Sam. "I'm sure you can take it from here."

Sam accepts the device with a serious nod and once again starts off along the lane. "The next waypoint is about 300 yards away," she announces.

Ben and Abi again share a broad grin.

***

The lane climbs slightly as they follow Sam southeast, and the banks gradually decrease in height. Before they're even halfway to the next waypoint, they emerge from the shadows of the trees, back into open fields and warm sunshine.

A couple of hundred yards later they come to a crossroads. "We're here," states Sam again.

"So what do we do next?" asks Ben.

"Er..."

"What does the cache description say?" Abi prompts her.

"Oh yeah..."

There's a short pause while Sam brings up the required information. *"At the crossroads, take to your right. You are now at the extreme right wing of the French troops, seen from French point of view."*

They all find themselves looking back over their left shoulders towards the farm buildings of Papelotte and La Haye, less than 500 yards away.

"It's hard tae believe that two huge armies could stand so close together, waitin' tae be told tae kill each other, isnae it?" Gravee says to Jaspa and Ben.

112

"The whole idea of war is hard to believe," replies the Giraffeses.

Ben nods in agreement, but doesn't say anything. He just stares across the bottom of the valley towards the farms that became fortresses for a day, 200 years ago.

"I guess we go this way, then," says Sam, breaking the spell. She points down a track – grandly named Chemin de Plancenoit – that leads south across the fields, deeper into what had been French territory during the battle.

"Sounds about right," agrees Henry, indicating with a flourish of his arm that Sam should lead the way.

Instead the little girl offers the GPS unit to her brother. "Wanna go?" she asks.

"Sure," Ben replies. "Thanks, Sammie."

***

"Looks like we've got a bit of a walk ahead of us," announces Ben.

With a little guidance from Abi and his sister (and Bisckits the Geocacher/Navigator), he's brought up the cache information on the GPS. "*Follow the path for about 1.6 km, until you arrive at the Prussian Monument,*" he reads.

"Ah-ha!" exclaims Henry triumphantly. "I told you it wouldn't be long before the Prussians were mentioned!"

"How far is 1.6 kilometres in miles?" wonders Sam.

"Er... Roughly a mile, I'd say," supplies Abi.

"Do we have a waypoint?" enquires Henry.

"Not yet," replies Ben, scowling slightly. "It says we have to keep an eye out for a stone cross along the side of the road. The inscription on the cross is supposed to give us the information we need to calculate co-ordinates for the monument."

"How far is it to the cross?" asks Portia.

Sam quickly repeats the Giraffeses' question, for Henry and Abi's benefit.

"Don't know. It doesn't say," answers Ben. He grins, "Less than 1.6 kilometres, I hope!"

"Dae ye reckon?" says Gravee, rolling his eyes.

***

Fortunately, they've gone less than 200 yards when Bisckits spots what they're looking for in the weeds beside the track on the left.

"I found the cross," declares Sam, again for the sake of the Greanings.

The light-grey limestone cross stands at a slightly crooked angle, partially hidden by tall grasses and nettles. Its upper and left arms end in blunt points, but the tip of its right arm has been broken off sometime in the past. Luckily, none of the words carved into the stone appear to be missing. They remain legible despite years of dark staining and lichen growth on the surface of the cross.

"*A la mémoire de François Désiré van Espen, mort malheureusement en chasse, le 17 novembre 1840, à l'âge de 21 ans. Passants priez pour lui,*" reads Abi, in a convincing French accent.

"Impressive," says Ben. "But do you know what it means?"

"I think so," replies Abi. "*In memory of François Désiré van Espen,*" she begins, a little hesitantly, "*Dead unfortunately in the chase,*" she translates word-for word. "Erm... No wait, we'd say something more like: *Unfortunately killed while hunting. The 17th November, 1840, at the age of 21 years. Passers pray for him.*"

"That's really impressive," Ben congratulates her.

"Thanks," she replies, obviously feeling a bit self-conscious.

"She's always been good at languages," says Henry with evident pride. "She also dabbles in German, Spanish and even Italian," he adds, even though he knows Ben and Sam are totally aware of the fact.

"*Ciao! Bella!*" says Ben.

"*Perbacco, non pensavo tu sapessi parlare italiano!*" declares Abi.

"Huh?"

"I said, *Wow, I didn't know you spoke Italian.*"

"I don't like to boast," says Ben with mock-modestly. "*Pizza ai funghi!*" he says in a terrible Italian accent, while gesturing dramatically with his hands. "*Leonardo da Vinci! Venizia! A.C. Milan! Spaghetti carbona...!*"

"You don't really speak any Italian, do you?" interrupts Abi. "I didn't think you did."

"*Ferrari?*" replies Ben, with a grin. "*Leonardo DiCaprio?*"

They all burst out laughing, Ses and human alike.

***

"Sorry, but just standing still is making me feel chilly again," admits Abi, getting them back down to business. "What information do we need off the cross?"

Ben studies the GPS screen, seeking the answer to Abi's question.

Jaspa stares at the cross while they wait. "You know, it's amazing how peoples' idea of what's important changes over time," he comments, mostly to himself.

"Whit dae ye mean?" asks Gravee

"I mean, in 1815 this was a battlefield where over 40,000 men were killed or wounded. Many of them died horribly, often while performing incredible acts of bravery, to stop a dictator conquering Europe and changing the course of World history. And yet most of their names are forgotten," the Giraffeses explains.

"Aye," agrees his friend. "It disnae seem quite reit, does it?"

"But here on that same battlefield is a memorial erected just 25 years later, to a single young man who died while hunting, which was an every-day activity back then."

"I suppose life goes on, nae matter whit has come afore."

Jaspa and Gravee's discussion of the strangeness of life is cut short when Ben announces that he's discovered the information they need to calculate the next waypoint. "It says here, that *KL* is the age at which the person on the cross died, plus four," he informs the others.

"Twenty-five," mutters Jaspa under his breath. Gravee gives him a look.

"You said he was 21 when he died, didn't you?" Sam asks Abi.

"That's right," the older girl confirms.

"So KL equals 25!"

At Sam's request— (quote): *in case all of Abi's fingers fall off and she isn't able to do it herself* (unquote) —Henry's sister gives her friends a recap on how to input a new waypoint.

Once they're all happy with how to program the GPS, Henry takes a turn at leading. "The Prussian Monument should be about point nine of a mile down this track," he tells the others. "Let's step it out a little, shall we? It'll help warm us up again."

***

Chapter Fourteen

Ses Down!

Chemin de Plancenoit turns out to be no more than a compacted dirt ribbon, just seven or eight feet wide, wandering across the farmland. It's really more a path than a road. Along much of its length, gravel has been concentrated in the lines left by vehicle tyres, to form two distinct, parallel stripes. These stripes are sometimes so well defined that grass grows in a slightly raised area between them. Once in a while, a field exit joins the main track, like a stunted tributary meeting a stream.

The farm track has a few kinks in it, but heads roughly southwest across the fields towards the village of Plancenoit. The landscape rolls gently, so that in places grass banks line one or other side of the lane, and occasionally both. Sometimes these banks are topped by trees or bushes. But for the most part, track and crops are separated by nothing more than a narrow grass verge, dense with wild flowers and weeds.

A skin of sticky, heavy, dark-brown mud coats much of the lane's surface. From time to time, this thickens to form treacherously deep and slippery patches, often beneath puddles of brown-stained rainwater. In these spots, the children are forced up onto the damp verges, in an attempt to avoid the worst of the muck. Jaspa and the other Ses are extremely grateful they're not having to make their own way through the cloying mud.

"That person's still back there," notes Sam.

"Which person, Sammie?" enquires Abi, glancing over her shoulder.

"The lady that was behind us on the way to the chapel."

Abi and the others look back along the track the way they've come. Sure enough, what appears to be a slender woman, in a dark blue jacket with the hood pulled up, has just appeared at the crossroads beyond the stone cross.

As if conscious of their gazes, the person comes to a sudden halt. After a moment, they resume their advance up the lane towards the group of children, although slowly, as if they're looking for something.

"I bet she's doing the geocache, too," reasons Sam. "She's probably looking for the stone cross."

"You might be right," agrees Henry.

Sam cups her hands to mouth and shouts. "It's in front of you! On the left! In about 200 yards!"

"Sam!" objects Ben. "You don't really know it's a woman. And you definitely don't know if they're doing the cache. And anyway, even if they are, they might not even speak English."

Just then, the person waves an arm. Although it's impossible to tell exactly what the wave means at this distance, Sam takes it as a sign that her brother is wrong. As usual.

***

To the Ses, the sunshine feels warm and pleasant, and before long Jaspa, Gravee and Portia begin to get sleepy. One by one they gently fall into a relaxed doze, while the ever excitable Bisckits chatters constantly in Sam's ear.

For the human members of the party, it's one of those days when it's a bit too warm to wear your jacket, but a little too cold without it. Less than five minutes down the track from the stone cross, the discomfort becomes too much for Henry. He shrugs his coat off his shoulders with a sigh of relief, and lets it slide down his arms, catching it in his hand before it hits the muddy road. Ben follows suit almost immediately. Abi gives an involuntary shiver and shakes her head at them.

Two minutes later both boys have their coats back on. *Told you so*, thinks Abi to herself.

Yet before long Ben and Henry are jacketless again.

So it goes on. Every few minutes the boys take off their jackets, or put them back on again. And all the while they draw ever closer to Plancenoit and the monument to the Prussian soldiers who fought and died there.

***

Despite the mud, the group makes pretty good time on the whole. Sometimes they walk in silence, but the majority of the time they talk animatedly, about all sorts of things, both meaningful and trivial.

Maybe half an hour after leaving the cross, they reach the outskirts of Plancenoit village. Chemin de Plancenoit makes a sharp right, and shortly thereafter ends at Chemin de Camuselle. Less than 50 yards further on, an ancient red brick wall rears up on the right side of the road.

The wall is topped with black iron railings. Behind these, within a copse of mature deciduous trees, they can see a pointy, black obelisk-like object. A sign on the wall confirms (in French) that they've found their next goal: the Prussian Monument.

Henry, Abi and Sam begin congratulating each other. Then Ben shocks them all to silence by emitting a soul-tearing moan full of pain and loss.

The young boy stumbles to the wall and slumps down to the ground with his back against the bricks and his knees pulled in tight to his body. He puts his chin on his chest and clasps his head in his hands, so that his elbows and knees are touching and his forearms are covering his face.

"What on Earth's the matter?" asks Abi, her voice on the edge of panic.

Her friend doesn't answer. He just begins rocking backwards and forwards, mewling like a newborn kitten.

Sam rushes over and crouches down beside her brother. "What is it?"

"Oh my goodness!" Portia suddenly gasps. "Where's Jaspa, Ben?" she almost begs. "Where's Gravee?"

***

"Oh no!" exclaims Sam, squeezing her face in her hands, pursing her mouth into a tight 'o', like that of a goldfish. "What have you done?!" she demands of her brother in an angry hiss.

Ben doesn't react or respond in any way.

Unfortunately, it doesn't take a genius to figure out the answer to Sam's question. The warmth of the sun and the rhythm of Ben's walking lulled Jaspa and Gravee off to sleep. Then, with the boy constantly taking his coat off and on, at some point the two Ses were knocked unnoticed to the ground.

"That's not helping, Sam," declares Bisckits, sounding uncharacteristically mature and composed. "But we have to go back. Right now!"

Sam instantly realises that the little Giraffeses is correct on both counts. They do have to go back, and getting mad isn't helping. She tries to calm herself. But there's an obvious problem.

"Abi and Henry will want to know why we need to backtrack all of a sudden," she whispers to the two remaining Ses. "They'll already be wondering what's wrong with Ben."

Sam's brother is still frozen with guilt and terror. In his mind's eye, he replays flashbacks of what it was like during the months that Gravee was lost in Africa.

Despite being close to panic herself, Portia quickly comes up with a plan. "Tell them that Ben has dropped your mum's smartphone," she instructs Sam. "That'll go some way to explaining why he's so upset and why we have to head back as fast as we can."

"Brilliant!" says Bisckits.

Sam quickly supplies the Greaning siblings with Portia's invented reason for what's come over Ben and the urgent need to retrace their steps. Neither of the children questions Sam's explanation for a second.

"Do you think he's up to it?" asks Henry dubiously. He looks down at Ben, who is still hunched against the wall.

"He has to be," replies Abi. "Mrs McRae will be furious if we can't find that phone. Here... give me a hand," she says, bending down and gently taking Ben's left arm.

Henry grasps Ben's other arm, and they haul the stricken boy to his feet.

***

With Sam scampering off ahead, Henry and Abi guide their stumbling friend back to Chemin de Plancenoit, and then out among the fields once again.

They've gone less than 200 yards along the muddy track when they hear the faint sound of music.

"Hey!" exclaims Henry. "Isn't that...?"

"Yep," confirms Abi, a wave of relief flooding through her. "*Yellow* by Coldplay."

"Hey! Sam! You can come back!" yells Henry. "The panic's over!"

Straight away, Sam turns around starts hurrying back towards them.

Abi treats Ben to a huge smile. "It's alright," she reassures him, shaking his arm encouragingly. "There's no need to worry anymore."

Because Coldplay is Mrs McRae's favourite band.

And *Yellow* is the song she uses as the ringtone on her phone.

***

Abi and Henry are utterly baffled. The sound of Mrs McRae's phone ringing somewhere in the depths of Ben's backpack should surely have lifted their friend out of his stunned state. Why then does he look more distressed than ever?

And even more confusing is that Sam seems genuinely upset that the missing phone isn't missing after all.

"There's something weird going on here," whispers Abi.

"No kidding," agrees Henry.

With Ben still in shock, Sam answers the phone. "Hi Mum," she says in an overly-bright voice.

In the quiet of the countryside, the Greanings can clearly hear Mrs McRae on the other end of the phone. "Hi Sammie. Is everything alright? Where's your brother?"

"Er... he's up a tree. We're geocaching."

"That's nice, dear. Listen, I can't speak long, but since you're coming home tomorrow, I just wanted to remind you to bring some Belgian chocolates back for Dad."

"We've already bought them," replies Sam, truthfully.

"Oh good. I knew I could rely on you both," says Mrs McRae. "Well, enjoy the rest of your day and have a safe trip home."

"We will."

"Give my love to Ben, and I'll see you tomorrow."

"Okay."

"Love you."

"Love you too, Mum."

The phone goes dead as Mrs McRae ends the call.

***

"C'mon, Ben. Snap out of it, mate!" Henry encourages the younger boy with forced cheerfulness. "The disaster's been averted and your mum's none the wiser."

In all fairness, Ben seems to have recovered a little. For one thing, he no longer needs the Greanings help to stand up. And he's stopped making that pitiful moaning sound too, thank goodness.

But he's clearly still not totally with it, and Abi's face and voice are full of concern as she suggests, "Let's head back towards the monument."

"No!" exclaims Sam. "We can't!"

"Why not?" asks Henry. "We found the phone."

"Because..." Sam stammers. "Because we've lost something else, too."

"What?" demands Henry, more forcefully than he intends. "What else have you lost? And what aren't you telling us, Sam?"

In a new and disturbing turn of events, rather than answering Henry's questions, Sam begins talking to her shoulder. "What do we do now?"

And to make matters worse—if that's even possible—it's clear that Sam believes her shoulder is answering.

"Really? Are you positive?" the girl asks of nobody.

Abi and Henry exchange yet another worried glance. How could they have been so unaware of Ben and Sam's obviously enormous mental issues and frailty?

"I know we have to go back," continues Sam, still talking to thin air. Then after a moment, as if waiting for someone to respond, she adds, "No, I can't think of another way, either."

Sam nods her head, evidently agreeing with something. "Okay. If you're sure."

Ben's sister turns back to the Greanings. "Henry's right," she says. "There's something we've not told you."

123

"You think?" mutters Henry under his breath.

"The thing is..." Sam pauses, then sighs heavily. "The thing is, Ben and I have some friends you don't know about. Friends that are here with us right now."

"Yeah, about that..." says Abi, her voice tight with worry. "We should probably use your mum's phone to call Jimmy and Laurel. We need them to come pick us up as soon as possible. I think we need to go visit the hospital."

"No! Just wait," pleads Sam. "I know what you're thinking, but what you're about to see will explain everything."

"Look Sammie..." begins Henry.

"Just look right here," Sam forcefully interrupts, pointing at her shoulder. "And brace yourselves... this may come as a bit of a shock."

Despite the absurdity of the situation, the Greanings' eyes automatically track to the spot Sam is indicating with her finger.

"Look Sam," Henry tries again. "I know you think...WHAT THE...?!"

Abi barely stifles a scream, as she and her brother both stagger back a pace.

Because out of nowhere, two small creatures have just appeared on Sam's shoulder.

"Seeing your first Ses is quite a surprise, isn't it?" laughs Sam, despite the gravity of their situation. "I know I nearly jumped out of my skin when Ben introduced me to Gravee."

***

Chapter Fifteen

Can Open, Ses Everywhere!

Seeing no alternative available to them, Bisckits and Portia decide drastic action is called for, and reveal themselves to the shocked siblings. The result is pretty much as they expected: initial astonishment and fright, followed by a torrent of questions.

With help from Sam, the two Giraffeses hurriedly cover the essentials. They provide a quick background on the Ses, blending and Seers. But their friends could be in danger, and time is pressing.

"The thing is," says Bisckits. "We're happy to tell you anything you want. But the reason we've let you see us—and the reason Ben's so upset—is because my brother, Jaspa, and our friend, Gravee, are missing."

"There are more of you?" gasps Abi. The last few minutes have been tough to process.

"Yes," replies Bisckits, bluntly. "And they're lost somewhere along this track. We have to go back and find them before something bad happens."

"Of course!" agrees Henry. "Let's go."

"I just hope we're not already too late," frets Portia. She catches herself directing a brief accusatory glance in Ben's direction, then scolds herself for being unfair. *It's not like he did this on purpose, is it? And he clearly feels worse than terrible. But still, how could anyone be so careless?!*

Fortunately, Sam's brother sees none of the internal battle being played out on Portia's face.

***

With Ben now rapidly coming back to his senses, they continue retracing their steps along Chemin de Plancenoit towards Papelotte. They travel as swiftly as possible, moving almost at a jog. All the while they scan the ground ahead of them, desperately seeking any hint of Gravee and Jaspa.

"Hold on a minute," puffs Abi, as they pass one of the tracks coming in from a neighbouring field. "If your friends are still blending, will Henry and I even be able to see them?"

"That's a good question," agrees Ben, without slowing down. These are the first words he's spoken since his meltdown at the monument and everyone is relieved to hear them, including Portia.

"You should be able to," Portia answers Abi's question, glad of anything that distracts her from worrying about Jaspa and Gravee. "After one Ses reveals themselves to a human, blending usually stops working on that person, no matter which Ses is doing it. It's as if the person's eyes learn the trick of seeing past the blending."

"It doesn't always work that way, though, does it?" Bisckits puts in. "Remember that bicycle messenger we got a ride with in London? What was his name?... John?... Jack?..."

"It was Jim," supplies Portia.

"Jim! Of course," agrees Bisckits. "Didn't Harjantee tell us he sometimes transports the Ses looking after the animals in London Zoo around the city? But he can't even see those Ses that have already revealed themselves to him, let alone others. And his mum's a Seer!"

"You're right," admits Portia. "But the way I understand it, Jim's case is quite unusual." She turns back to Abi, "Which means that if a Ses reveals themselves to the wrong type of human, it potentially puts all Ses in danger. So you see, we've taken a big risk—and not just for ourselves— by letting you see us."

"It's okay," Abi replies earnestly. "You can trust us."

"We wouldn't have revealed ourselves if we didn't believe that," says Portia. "Although you didn't know it, we've spent quite a bit of time around you and your brother. So we know what kind of people you are."

"That'd be really creepy," laughs Henry. "If all this wasn't so cool."

Portia tries to join in with Henry's mirth, but all she can manage is a weak smile. Her cousin and friend are still missing, after all. And as much as she tries, she can't shake being annoyed at Ben.

***

Less than a third of a mile from the Prussian Monument, Bisckits' sharp eyes spot a commotion up ahead. "I see something!" he hollers. "Get a move on, Sam! Can't you go any faster?"

"I'm going... as fast... as I can!" gasps Sam, sounding frustrated.

Ben tries to sprint off ahead, but instead skids theatrically on the slick surface of the track. For a moment he looks like an actor from a 1930s black and white slapstick comedy.

Luckily for Ben, Henry has quicker reactions than you'd expect. As the younger boy begins to slide on the mud, his friend's arm shoots out and grabs him, saving him from a nasty—or at the very least, messy—fall.

"Thanks!" breathes Ben sincerely, his heart racing.

"No problem," replies Henry. He massages his shoulder, which feels like he may have pulled something. "And welcome back, by the way."

Ben gives him a small lopsided grin in response.

"C'mon ladies!" Abi yells at them. "You can hug later!"

***

They hurry towards the disturbance Bisckits has spotted. Unfortunately, the treacherous mud slows them down considerably.

"It looks like some type of Birdses attacking a bush," observes Portia.

127

"I think it might be a Falconses," Bisckits tells them, shading his eyes with both hands and squinting in an attempt to see better. "I wonder if it's the same one we saw during the re-enactment yesterday."

"I don't know about that," says Ben. "But we were attacked by a Falconses earlier. On the way from the Inniskilling memorial to the chapel."

"Why on Earth didn't you say something before," snaps Portia, her annoyance rising once more.

"It was kind of difficult," replies Ben defensively. "At the time I was trying not to arouse Henry and Abi's suspicions."

"And how's that been going for you?" Abi teases him.

Ben looks sheepish.

"Not that we had any idea what was really going on," Henry confesses.

Abi makes a wry face, expressing agreement with her brother.

"To be fair, Jaspa and Gravee had just as much opportunity to tell us," Bisckits the Mediator points out to his cousin.

"Hmmm," mumbles Portia, clearly unconvinced.

Abi's brow furrows as something else occurs to her. "Is that what all your arm-waving was about?" she asks Ben.

"Uh-huh," he confirms, glad of a slight change in subject. "I was trying to shoo the Falconses away."

"Why don't you tell us exactly what happened?" suggests Portia, trying to regain her patience.

"Well, it just appeared out of nowhere and started having a go at us. Actually, we're pretty sure it was after Gravee," Ben admits. "We think Jaspa and I were just in the way."

"But what could a Falconses from Belgium possibly have against Gravee?" Portia persists.

"Well, around here they prefer mayonnaise on their chips, don't they?" jokes Henry. "Sorry!" he adds quickly, in response to the baffled stares he receives from the others. "Bad timing."

"I don't know," Ben continues, ignoring Henry and instead answering Portia's question. "But it was raving about Napoleon and stuff. Like it thought the battle hadn't happened yet."

"Great!" declares Bisckits, his mature façade slipping for a moment. "So on top of everything else, we're dealing with a crazy, homicidal Falconses with a grudge against Gravee. That's just brilliant!"

Abi turns to her brother. "Is it just me, or does this keep getting weirder?!"

***

Before long even the human members of the group can see—and hear—the Falconses. It appears to be dive-bombing a small clump of bushes beside a shallow cutting through which the track passes. The strange Birdses shrieks incessantly, and none of them have any doubt about who is the focus of its assault.

"You 'ave no right beeing 'ere!" the Falconses screams, as it makes yet another pass. "An' yet 'ere you are, acting like you own zis place!"

"We're jist goin' for a walk, laddie," comes the yelled reply from within the shrubbery. "I'm reit sorry if that causes ye offence, but dinnae ye think yer overreactin' a wee bit?"

Ben's knees buckle slightly at the sound of Gravee's voice. *We've found them*, he thinks, his eyes welling up.

Bisckits, Sam and Portia are no less relieved.

The Birdses comes to a hover above the bushes. "We will see who eez overreacting when zee Mighty Napoleon crushes you all into zee mud!" it retaliates with a manic laugh.

"What's your problem, eh?" demands another voice from the undergrowth.

It doesn't belong to Jaspa.

***

A handful of steps further and the rescue party finally spy their friends, sheltering beneath a bush. Both of them look in desperate need of a bath, but otherwise appear none the worse for their most recent misadventure.

Surprisingly, it turns out that Jaspa and Gravee aren't facing this latest unprovoked attack alone. With them is a another Ses. One the others have never seen before.

The three Ses beneath the bush stand facing outwards, their backs to the stem and each other, covering all potential directions of attack. In their hands they hold sticks, which they've clearly been using as makeshift clubs to keep their foe at bay.

The humans move in to cluster around the shrub where Jaspa, Gravee and the mystery Ses are weathering the storm of the Falconses' inexplicable wrath. The Birdses is once again forced to abandon its offensive and flies off, screaming all the while.

"Zees eez not zee end!" it screeches, mirroring what it said at the end of their last confrontation. "I shall bee watching as zee *Armée de la France* crushes you!"

"An' a Merry Christmas tae ye, tae!" Gravee calls after it.

***

Sam sets Bisckits and Portia on the ground, and they rush over to enfold Jaspa and Gravee in a group hug.

"Are you all right?" demands Portia. "We've been so worried!"

"We're fine," replies Jaspa. "Just a bit muddy, is all."

"I'm really sorry!" declares Ben, his voice cracking as the guilt rushes back in. "What happened?" he asks, and then answers his own question.

"I knocked you off my shoulder when I was taking my jacket on and off, didn't I?"

"Och, dinnae worry. It wis jist an accident, laddie," Gravee tries to comfort the boy. "An' we should huv bin payin' mair attention instead o' sleepin'."

Gravee's unconditional forgiveness fills Portia (and to a lesser extent, Sam) with regret over her treatment of Ben. Now she knows her friends are safe, Portia's anger at the boy evaporates. Of course Ben didn't knock them off on purpose, and of course he's been just as upset and frightened as her.

And did I really lose my temper, leaving Bisckits to be the mature and sensible one? Portia cringes with shame at the thought. *What's the World coming to?*

"But why didn't you call out after you fell?" Ben asks Gravee and Jaspa. Although everyone else may have forgiven him, he's not quite ready to forgive himself just yet.

"Well, if ye must know, I banged mah heid on a rock when I hit th' groond," the Dogses admits. "Went oot like a light!"

Jaspa nods in agreement. "And I landed face-first in the mud, as you can probably tell," he grins, gesturing with both hands at his dirt-smeared snout. "By the time I managed to pull myself out, you were too far away to hear me shouting. I would have shifted after you, but I didn't want to leave Gravee unconscious in the middle of the road."

Ben face turns white yet again.

"Ach, dinnae worry yerself, bairn," Gravee repeats. "Ye found us, didn't ye? Nae harm done, except a wee bump on th' heid and a bit o' mud." He raps his skull with his knuckles. "Besides, this noggin o' mine's as hard as nails. An' Jaspa could do wi' gettin' a bit mucky noo an' again!"

"That's what I always say," agrees Bisckits.

"I think they've got a point, Waver," laughs Portia, now mostly trying to help lighten the mood for Ben's sake.

"Hey!" objects Jaspa, his grin widening.

***

With the initial relief of finding Jaspa and Gravee safe and well starting to subside, all attention now turns to their new companion.

The unknown Ses is perhaps half an inch taller than either of her comrades-in-arms, although not quite as tall as Portia. Her face is round and friendly, bearing a broad smile despite the seriousness of the situation they were in just moments before. Instead of fur, the newcomer has emerald green skin, and Bisckits spots that her hands and feet are partially webbed.

"This is Phyllis," Jaspa introduces her. "She's a Frogses from Canada."

"Canada?" blurts Sam in surprise. "What are you doing here?" Then, remembering her manners, she adds, "If you don't mind me asking."

"Of course not," replies Phyllis.

Although the Frogses' tone is friendly enough, it seems to Jaspa that something briefly crosses her face. Like a cloud scudding across the sun.

"Fact is, I've been *backpacking around Europe*, as they say, for the last five or six months."

Now that they hear her speak more than a few words, Phyllis's North American accent is clearly noticeable.

"Are you on your own?" asks Portia.

"For the moment, yes."

"Isn't it lonely? Wandering around Europe by yourself, I mean."

"No way!" the Frogses replies. "It's fun to travel by yourself, eh. And anyway, you're always crossing paths with all sorts of interesting Ses from all over the World. Sometimes you stick together for a while, but eventually you go off in your separate directions, to see different stuff or perhaps head home."

"It sounds a lot like the Journey," observes Jaspa. He briefly describes his tribes' tradition and its purpose.

"Seems like your Journey and mine do have a lot in common, eh," agrees Phyllis. "I know I've seen all sorts of stuff—good and bad—that's really opened my eyes. The difference is that no one said I had to do mine, I just chose to."

"But why come here?" wonders Portia. "I mean, wouldn't you rather be on a beach in Greece or somewhere?"

"Already done that," grins Phyllis.

"Nice!" says Bisckits

"Thing is, I come from a place called Waterloo back in Ontario, so I thought it'd be neat to see its namesakes in London and here in Belgium. Since the Ses I was with in Rome had already been to Brussels, we said goodbye and I hopped on a plane up here on my own."

"I love flying! Have you made it to London yet? We were there last November," enthuses Bisckits.

"It's probably going to be my next stop," replies Phyllis. "I'm really looking forward to it, eh. But Brussels was on the way, so it made sense to come here first."

"And how on Earth did you bump into these two trouble makers?" asks Portia, with a mischievous smile.

"Well, there I was minding my own business, having a bit of a siesta under a bush, eh," the Frogses resumes her story, "When I was woken up by that flying freak yelling abuse at someone. I was just going to tell it to shut up, when I saw it attacking Gravee and Jaspa, here. It all seemed a bit unnecessary, so I decided to lend them a hand."

"And we're really grateful, by the way," says Jaspa.

"Reit enough!" agrees Gravee.

A puzzled look crosses the Frogses' face. "You never did say what its beef with you was," she remarks, echoing the question of the day.

"Honestly, we still huvnae got a Scooby," sighs the Dogses. "But he seems tae think Napoleon's aboot tae come gallopin' doon th' hill, so he's clearly a few pieces short o' a picnic."

"That's an understatement!" agrees Jaspa. "I just wish he'd find some-body else to bother!"

**

Chapter Sixteen

The Eagle's Last Battle

They arrive back at the outskirts of Plancenoit a little less than three-quarters of an hour after Ben's dramatic realisation that Jaspa and Gravee were missing. Thankfully, this time everyone is present and correct. In fact, if you include Phyllis, who has decided to tag along for a while, their little band has actually grown.

All the required introductions have been made. And all the necessary explanations have been given, as to why the Greanings have been let in on one of the best kept secrets in history. Even so, it's difficult for any of them to believe all that has happened in the last 40-ish minutes.

Yet there's still a task at hand, as Bisckits the Sensible now reminds them. (You never thought you'd hear him being called that, did you?)

"Here we are again," announces the little Giraffeses, as the brick wall on the eastern side of the Prussian Monument looms into view once more. "So what are looking for?"

Everyone else looks blank.

"Huh?" says Sam, summing up the general feeling.

"The geocache..." Bisckits prompts.

"Oh yeah!" laughs Jaspa. "I'd forgotten about that in all the excitement."

"I bet Gobber hasnae," snarls Gravee.

That sours the otherwise cheerful mood.

"I don't even know who's got the GPS," admits Abi, a slight note of alarm creeping into her voice.

"What's a geocache?" wonders Phyllis.

***

After a brief moment of panic, which has the McRaes and Greanings desperately searching their pockets, Henry finds the GPS unit in his jacket and turns it on. As they wait for it to boot up, Jaspa starts to explain geocaching to Phyllis, with the inevitable help of his brother.

Once the GPS is ready, Henry and Abi study the cache description for their next set of instructions. Leaving them to get on with it, Ben and Sam (accompanied by the Ses) climb the steps to the right of the brick wall, up to the level of the actual monument.

From up here it's clear that the wall is in fact part of the memorial's foundation. The ground on the other three sides is roughly level with the monument's base, a flagstone area—perhaps 25 feet square—completely enclosed by the black iron railings they'd seen from below. The flagstones slope gently up towards a heavy stone pedestal at their centre. Upon this is what looks like the blackened tip of a gothic church spire, with a German inscription in golden letters on one side and an Iron Cross at its apex. In all, the pedestal, spire and cross must be at least 15 feet tall.

"Hey, Henry!" Ben calls down. "Do you know what the deal is with this thing?"

"It's the Prussian Monument," Henry hollers back.

"Yes, I know that," groans Ben, rolling his eyes.

"It was built to honour the Prussian soldiers who died at Waterloo," replies Henry, climbing the steps (followed by his sister) so he doesn't have to keep shouting.

"I guessed that much, too," counters Ben, at a more normal volume. "But why is it all the way out here, instead of over there with the other monuments?" He waves a hand vaguely in the direction of Lion Mound, which is currently hidden from view by the trees surrounding them.

"Oh, there are memorials all over the battlefield, including a lot we probably won't see today," Henry informs his friend. "This one is here because it's where the Prussians did most of their fighting... at least during the actual Battle of Waterloo. People tend to forget they also fought a couple of their own battles against the French in the days leading up to the main event."

"You mean, like Wellington and the Allies did at Quatre Bras?" asks Portia.

"That's right."

Bisckits' mouth drops open in surprise. "How on Earth do you know about a battle at..." he struggles for the name, "At Cattybra—or wherever you just said?"

"It's Quatre Bras, actually," his cousin replies airily. "And I know about it because I was paying attention when Jimmy referred to it yesterday. And when Henry mentioned it again earlier."

"Busted!" hoots Gravee, slapping his own leg.

"Anyway," Henry returns to his story, "When Napoleon learned that Marshall Blücher and his Prussians were approaching, he sent several thousand men here to Plancenoit to protect his right flank. The Prussians attacked at about half past four in the afternoon. Over the next two or three hours, they captured and lost the village twice. During that time, Plancenoit was a hellish scene of heavy fighting and horror."

Jaspa pretends to look around. "I'm sorry," he says. "For a moment there, I thought I heard Jimmy speaking!"

Henry gives his new Giraffeses friend a smile, before concluding, "This monument was built on the site of a French artillery battery, to remember the nearly 7000 Prussians that died that day. Laurel told me it was one of the first memorials erected here at Waterloo, and that it matches monuments at the sites of other Prussian victories from around that time."

Gravee whistles. "Th' laddie has a lot o' stuff floatin' aroond in that greit heid o' his, reit enough," he says.

"And yet he still hasn't told us what information we need off this monument to find the next stage of the geocache," Jaspa observes dryly.

"I never said it was useful stuff," chuckles Gravee.

***

Abi takes a deep breath and exchanges a glance with her brother. The look expresses something along the lines of, *Oh boy! Here we go!*

"Erm... well..." she hesitates. "The thing is, we already have everything we need to find the next stage of the cache."

There's a slight pause, as the implication of Abi's words sinks in. Then Jaspa asks, "You mean, we don't need anything from here?"

"No... I mean, yes... er..."

"What Abi is trying to say, is that we didn't need to come here in order to find the actual geocache," Henry clarifies. "And we don't need to visit the next two waypoints either, for that matter."

"What?!" erupts Ben, his face turning red. "So Jaspa and Gravee were nearly killed, and the rest of us went through all that misery, for nothing?!" he demands.

"That depends," replies Henry, raising his hands in a calming gesture. "If all we want to do is find the final geocache, then no, we didn't need to come here. But the purpose of the route we're following is about more than that. It's also designed to guide us to the important places on the battlefield, like this monument."

"This is another dot for us to join up, you mean?" asks Sam.

"Kind of," agrees Henry with a sad smile. "But this dot is much more than just another waypoint.

"Think about it... Napoleon had to commit thousands of men to defend this spot, like I said before. So if the Prussians hadn't attacked here, the Emperor would have been able to throw all those soldiers at Welling-ton." As he speaks, Henry's voice becomes evermore intense. "Who knows, perhaps that would have made the difference between the French losing the Battle of Waterloo and winning it. Which means this place isn't just crucial to the story of the battle. What happened here may have also changed the history of Europe, and even the World."

"Wow," breathes Bisckits. "You really do sound more and more like Jimmy."

The older boy looks Ben in the eye. "I really am sorry for the grief you went through," he sympathises. "And I'm sorry that Jaspa and Gravee were in danger. But since everything turned out okay in the end, I'm also incredibly glad I got to see this place."

"And me," agrees Abi. "I might have never learned about the Ses if we hadn't come here."

"Och! I huv a feelin' ye wud huv foond oot sooner or later," chuckles Gravee.

For his part, Jaspa is amazed by Henry's speech. Over the last couple of days, he's learned so much about the terror and bravery that occurred on these fields two centuries ago. Yet he's never considered the enormous impact this one bloody battle had on World history.

It seems that Ben feels much the same. By way of an apology for los-ing his temper, the younger boy grins awkwardly. "I suppose we did all get to meet Phyllis, too," he says.

"I guess that means I'm the only loser in all this then, eh?" laughs the Frogses.

***

"You know, your voice sounds really familiar," Abi tells Gravee, as they head northwest on Chemin du Lanternier through the nowadays peaceful village of Plancenoit.

"Aye, well I get that a lot," he admits. "I'm in the movies, ye ken."

Bisckits sniggers.

"No, seriously," insists Abi. "I mean it."

"Well, o' coorse mah voice is familiar," says the Dogses. "Ye've heard it hundreds o' times afore."

"But I've only just met you," Abi disagrees.

"Mebbe so," Gravee concedes. "But ye've been aroond me loads o' times afore. Ye jist dinnae realise it."

"I get that," Abi persists. "But you were always blending from me before."

"Och! Jist because ye couldnae see me, disnae mean ye couldnae hear me," counters Gravee, cryptically.

"Of course I couldn't!" retorts Abi, beginning to get frustrated. "I wouldn't just ignore a mystery voice coming from nowhere, would I?"

"Ah-ha! But that's exactly whit ye did."

"Don't mind him," interrupts Ben, coming to Abi's rescue. "He's just trying to be funny."

The Dogses chuckles roguishly.

"What Gravee's getting at, is that blending actually only works on your eyes, not your ears," Ben explains. "But hearing voices when no one's there is normally considered a bad sign, right?"

"I guess," she concedes.

"So, although technically you could still hear Ses when they were blending, your brain basically ignored their voices, for the sake of your sanity."

"Oh..."

"But now that you know Ses exist, your brain doesn't have to pretend it can't hear them anymore," Ben continues. "But I reckon, on some level, you remember hearing Gravee in the past, and that's why his voice sounds so familiar. What do you think, Gravee?"

"I think I'm in trouble if she starts rememberin' whit I actually said," the Dogses laughs.

***

At the northwestern edge of Plancenoit, the unlikely bunch of friends come across a three-way road junction. Here they merge right, heading back out into open countryside on Chemin de la Belle Alliance.

"Where are we going now?" wonders Ben aloud.

"That sort of depends," replies Henry, sounding a little uneasy. "We're basically heading towards the next stage of the geocache."

"But?" Ben prompts.

"There are a couple of places we could stop at along the way," the older boy reveals, almost reluctantly. "But we don't have to, if people don't want to," he adds hurriedly.

"Dinnae be daft, laddie," Gravee declares. "O' coorse we'll be stoppin'. Isnae that reit, Ben?"

"Yeah, of course," Ben replies, awkwardly. He puts his hand on Henry's shoulder. "Look, just ignore what I said before, okay. I was upset and being stupid."

"Okay," agrees Henry, although his tone seems far from certain.

***

The road passes between earthen banks and hedgerows, with the ground generally higher on the left than on the right. After perhaps 250 yards, they come across a flight of concrete steps that head up to the level of the field on the left—south, that is—side of the road. Near the base of the steps is an interpretive sign. Following Henry's lead, the group scales the steps.

141

"Nineteen!" Sam declares upon reaching the top. Up here they discover a roughly semi-circular area, perhaps 10 yards across, paved with cobblestones and surrounded by a hedge, approximately three feet high.

Sam glances back towards Plancenoit, looks away, and then quickly stares back again. "Huh," she says with a frown.

"What is it?" asks Ben.

"I thought I just saw the lady in the blue coat," his sister replies. "Back there, near the edge of the village. But when I looked again, she was gone."

"Hmmm!" mutters Jaspa, thoughtfully.

"I'd forgotten about her," admits Abi, her curiosity awakened. "But now Sam comes to mention it, isn't it weird we didn't bump into her when we went back for Gravee and Jaspa?"

"That's right," agrees Portia. "I didn't see her after Sam called to her at the stone cross."

The muttered consensus is that Portia's correct.

"Perhaps she got the information off the cross, realised she didn't have to carry on to Plancenoit, and turned back," suggests Bisckits.

"So what's she doing here now, then?" Abi points out.

"Are ye sure it wis th' same person we saw afore, lassie?" asks Gravee, voicing what they're all thinking, including Sam.

"I think so," replies the girl, although with a touch of uncertainty.

"Weird," says Ben.

***

"Speaking of the stone cross where we saw Sam's mystery woman, we've basically been deep in French territory ever since," Henry resumes his story of the battle, although with a bit less excitement than before. "But now we've made it back to Napoleon's front line, with the battlefield in front of us."

Standing on the crest once held by an Emperor's troops, Jaspa and his companions stare silently north across the rolling fields towards the far ridge. On the horizon off to the left, almost a mile distant, is Lion Mound, a squat, heavy reminder of the all the men that died here 200 years earlier. Yet looking down on the green, peaceful farmland, it's impossible to imagine the true horror of that infamous day so long ago.

"Is this one of the waypoints you wanted to visit?" Jaspa asks Henry, breaking the broody silence.

"That's right," the boy confirms. "Legend claims that Napoleon watched the battle from here, which is why it's become known as *Napoleon's Observatory* or *Observation Post*."

"Wow," says Bisckits, looking down at the ground from Sam's hood, almost as if he expects to see the Emperor's footprints.

"Actually, several of my books say that most historians reckon he didn't come here until late in the afternoon. After the big parade before the start of the fighting, he spent most of the day a ways back down the main road."

"How come?" asks Ben. "I'm no soldier, but it seems to me this would be the perfect place to watch the battle."

"From what I can tell, most historians agree with you," replies Henry, his enthusiasm slowly returning. "But the story goes that Napoleon had terrible stomach pains on the day of the battle. And Marshal Ney, who was his second-in-command, spent the whole day down in the valley, fighting beside his men, being brave as usual. Which meant neither of them could really see exactly how the battle was going. Again, perhaps the result would have been different if one of them had stayed here."

"Hey!" Abi accidentally interrupts the boys' historical discussion. "Oops, sorry!" she apologises, putting her hand to her mouth.

"Och, dinnae keep us in suspense, lassie," declares Gravee. "Whit's ye shriekin' all aboot?"

"Um, well, I was playing with the GPS while Henry was talking. Not that I wasn't interesting in what you were saying, though. Honest!" This last is directed at her brother.

"Will ye nae get on wi' it?" groans Gravee, making speeding-up gestures with his hand.

Abi grimaces, but does as instructed. "Well, I got a bit carried-away, is all. Because I just realised there's another geocache right here!"

The resulting chorus of excitement is all that's needed to completely restore Henry's good spirits.

"You knew about this already, didn't you?" Jaspa asks the elder Greaning, knowingly.

Henry admits he did with a shy smile and a slight nod of his head.

"Well what are we waiting for?" exclaims Phyllis. "Now you can show me what this geocaching is all about!"

***

"Do you want to do the honours, Sammie?" asks Abi.

The younger girl grins eagerly and proudly takes the offered GPS unit. She clears her throat as if about to make an important speech, resulting in a gentle round of well-meant laughter from her friends.

"*The Eagle's Last Battle*," Sam reads slowly and clearly.

The mention of eagles has Gravee briefly looking around nervously for signs of the unhinged Falconses.

"*The coordinates are those of what is believed to be Napoleon Bonaparte's last observatory, during the Battle of Waterloo, on June 18th, 1815.*"

"That's just what Henry said," observes Bisckits.

"*At the given coordinates, you will find NNN and EEE. The cache is located at N 50° 39.NNN, E 4° 24.EEE,*" Sam continues.

"*NNN* and *EEE*?" complains Gravee, still staring at the sky. "Whit sort o' gibberish is that?"

"It's another multicache," guesses Ben. "The final must be hidden at 50 degrees and 39 point something minutes north, four degrees and 24 point something minutes east."

"Exactly," agrees Abi. "And so *NNN* and *EEE* are obviously two three-digit numbers we have to find, and then plug into those coordinates."

"But how do we know which numbers we need?" wonders Jaspa. "The main cache we've been doing always explains that very clearly."

"Does it say anything else in the description, Sam?" asks Portia.

"Nothing helpful. Just that we should come up here and imagine tens of thousands of soldiers fighting in the valley."

"Been there, done that," mutters Gravee.

"What about hints?" wonders Bisckits.

"Hold on," says Sam, pressing some icons on the screen. "It says, *WP1: At the back of the sign. WP2: In a hole at the foot of an oak.*"

"Well, *WP* obviously stands for waypoint," Jaspa translates. "Which means this is *WP1*. So the sign mentioned must be the one down at the bottom of the steps, by the road."

The four humans rush down the stairs, carrying the five Ses with them. At the bottom they gather around the sign. But after several minutes pondering over the information presented, they're still no closer to solving the mystery of *NNN* and *EEE*.

"Oh! This is so frustrating!" objects Bisckits.

"Wait a minute," says Phyllis, thoughtfully touching her lips with a finger. "Didn't the hint say the *back* of the sign?"

"Duh!" exclaims Ben, smacking his forehead with the palm of his hand. He darts around behind the sign, crouches down, and immediately announces, "I've found it!"

Jaspa nods approvingly at Phyllis. "Good catch," he compliments her.

***

Written on a piece of tape stuck to the back of the sign is: *NNN = 982, EEE = 954*. Abi takes the GPS back from Sam and makes the necessary adjustments to the cache coordinates.

"It's just over a hundred yards south of us, across this field," she announces.

"I think I remember passing a farm track heading off that way, as we came along the road," Jaspa informs them.

"I saw it too," agrees Henry.

The band of friends backtrack excitedly towards Plancenoit and soon locate the track Jaspa and Henry had noticed as they passed the first time. It heads almost directly west between two fields, with a high earth bank on its right side and a tall grain-like crop on its left.

Abi counts down the distance as they bustle along the track. "50 yards... 40... 25... 10..."

"Aren't they oaks?" asks Phyllis, pointing at a pair of tall trees growing near the top of the bank.

"Maybe," replies Jaspa uncertainly. "I'm not too good with trees here, to be honest. Back home I can tell a flat-topped acacia from a sausage tree a mile away, but European trees still have me a bit stumped."

"Nae pun intended," laughs Gravee.

Ben starts to head up the bank towards the trees Phyllis has indicated, but Abi surprises him by putting her arm across his path. "That bank looks awfully unstable for someone as heavy as you, Ben," she says, giving him a wink. "Perhaps someone lighter should go."

"Er, yeah," he agrees, catching on fast.

"I'll go!" cries Sam, her arm shooting up into the air as if she were answering a question in school.

"I don't know..." replies her brother, with a dramatic shake of his head. "Maybe we should send Bisckits up first instead. Just to be on the safe side. He's the smallest, after all."

"Erm... I'm not sure that's a good idea," Bisckits pretends to object, playing along. "That bank looks pretty steep to me. I don't know if I could climb it."

"I can do it!" declares Sam, bouncing up and down on the spot.

Ben lets out a long sigh, as if wrestling with a difficult decision. "OK, Sammie," he says finally. "I guess it's up to you, then."

Like a sprinter released by a starting pistol, Sam is up the bank in less than two seconds. She peers into a hole near the base of the first tree's trunk, and squeals. Pushing aside a pile of leaves and sticks with one hand, she triumphantly raises the clear, plastic cache container above her head with the other.

Jaspa gives Phyllis a nudge. "Two for two," he grins. "Looks like you're a natural at this geocaching thing."

"Thanks," she smiles back. Then a look of doubt crosses her face. "But you were joking about the sausage tree, eh...?"

***

Chapter Seventeen

Infantry, Cavalry, Artillery

The four Young Adventures retrace their steps back to Napoleon's Observatory, where they share the lunch they've brought along with the Ses. The early summer sun is now high in the sky, and the McRaes and Greanings all take off their jackets—even Abi—to use as cushions. Jaspa and the other Ses perch on a stone bench beside the girls, while the boys sprawl on the cobblestones.

"At least my sandwiches haven't been banerminated today," jokes Ben.

"My feet are sore," grumbles Sam. "We must have walked 10 miles!"

"Actually, it's more like three and a half," Abi corrects her, after consulting the GPS. "Although we can probably add another mile or so on to that, what with backtracking to rescue Jaspa and Gravee..."

"For which we're reit grateful, by th' way," says the Dogses for the umpteenth time.

"... And to get the final of *The Eagle's Last Battle*," Abi finishes.

"Are you sure you're working that thing right?" objects Sam. "I bet it's at least 10 miles. Probably more!"

"You know, I think we should count *The Eagle's Last Battle* as our first proper geocache," Abi announces. "After all, it's the first one we did all by ourselves, without any help or supervision."

"Sounds about right to me," agrees Ben.

A thought occurs to Portia. "What's the name of the big cache we're doing, again?" she asks.

"*Waterloo 1815*," Henry provides.

"So, maybe finding *The Eagle's Last Battle* without too much trouble is a good omen that..."

"Dinnae say it!" commands Gravee.

"...We'll find *Waterloo 1815* easily, too," Portia finishes.

"Oh!" groans everyone else.

"What?" asks the Giraffeses, confused by the others' reaction. "What did I say?"

"You had to say it, didn't you?" Ben complains, but with a mischievous twinkle in his eye.

Jaspa chuckles. "Thankfully, Phyllis seems to have a knack for geocaching," he says. "Hopefully she can be our good luck charm, to cancel out my cousin's big mouth!"

"What did I say?" Portia repeats.

***

A thought returns to Ben as he lazily stares north across the former battlefield towards the Allies' ridge. It's something that initially bothered him yesterday as they'd watched pretend French horsemen charge make-believe British infantry during the recreation of Napoleon's second attack.

"You know, the French cavalry can't have been much good," he says out loud.

"How so?" asks Henry, clearly not agreeing.

"It's obvious," replies the elder McRae. "A bunch of guys on foot doesn't stand a chance against a load of men on horses. You said yourself that after the first French attack, the British cavalry smashed the French infantry to pieces."

"I can see where you're going with this," admits Henry.

"But during the second French attack, the French cavalry was beaten by the Allied infantry. So like I said, they can't have been much good."

"Hmmm..." says Henry, chewing the inside of his lip. "Do you remember when we used to play *rock, paper, scissors*?"

"Of course," replies Ben, puzzled by the sudden subject change.

"Well, during Wellington's time, battles were like huge, deadly games of rock, paper, scissors, played with units of infantry, cavalry and artillery."

Sam's brother looks sceptical.

"Okay, pretend you're an artillery gunner," says Henry, seeing the doubt in Ben's face. "At a distance, you obviously beat both infantry and cavalry, right?"

"Right," repeats Ben.

"But if the enemy gets past the barrel of your cannon you're in big trouble. So at close quarters, cavalry and infantry actually beat artillery."

"Okay," says Ben, acknowledging his friend's point.

"Now pretend you're in the infantry," Henry instructs. "French infantry usually attacked in tightly-packed masses of men called *columns*. But Wellington preferred to arrange his infantry in line when defending, often only two ranks deep. At first glance, the columns appear unstoppable battering-rams—and in fact they won the French countless victories all over Europe—whereas the line looks frighteningly weak.

"But the problem with columns is that only the front two or three ranks can fire their muskets. Yet every single soldier in the fragile-looking line can use theirs. So, although the line appears weaker, if the defenders keep their nerve and continue loading and firing, infantry in line should beat infantry in column. Which is one of the reasons Wellington never lost a battle."

"That all makes sense," concedes Ben. "But what about the cavalry?"

"I'm getting to that," replies Henry, "First, you have to remember that muskets are very slow to load. Even the best soldiers can only load and fire three times a minute, four at the absolute maximum."

"That's not very much," says Ben.

"Exactly! So if you're in a fast-moving cavalry charge you only need to soak up one volley of musket fire and you're upon your enemy."

"As lang as ye're nae one of th' puir saps soakin' up a musket ball," Gravee interjects.

"The point is," sighs Henry, "That not even the best foot soldier can load and fire a musket with cavalry swords buzzing around his ears. So cavalry beats infantry in line."

"There you go, then," says Ben, as if Henry has finally made his point for him. "If the French cavalry had been any good, the Allied infantry wouldn't have stood a chance."

"Ah-ha!" exclaims Henry, wagging a finger. "But infantry has a secret weapon against cavalry!"

"What secret weapon?" scoffs Ben.

"Actually, it all comes down to horses being far smarter than us humans," answers Henry.

"Ha!" barks Gravee.

"You see, bayonets are essentially big metal spikes, and it's impossible to train a horse to run at them," Abi's brother explains. "They just won't do it. Because their survival instincts are too strong. A cavalryman can charge a mass of bayonets, but his horse will always swerve away at the last second because..."

"...Horses are smarter than humans!" grins Bisckits, finishing the boy's sentence.

"But a second ago you said cavalry beats infantry," objects Ben.

"Actually, I said cavalry beats infantry *in line*," Henry corrects him. "Because the problem with lines is that they have to end somewhere. So all the enemy has to do is use some their cavalry to keep your infantry busy in front, while the rest ride around those ends and attack you from the rear. At that point, life gets very interesting—and very short—for a foot soldier."

"So what's the infantry's secret weapon?" asks Ben, feeling utterly confused.

"Squares!" declares Henry.

"What do you mean, *squares?*" demands Ben.

"Simple," replies Henry. "You arrange your infantry into hollow squares, three or four ranks deep on each side. That way there are no ends for the enemy cavalry to ride around.

"Your front rank kneels, their muskets braced on ground, so their bayonets form a hedge of metal thorns. No horse in the World will charge an obstacle like that, and enemy swords can't reach you over the top of it. Then your other ranks take turns to fire at the cavalry stuck outside.

"So although cavalry beats infantry in line, infantry in square beats cavalry any day of the week," Henry concludes.

"Clever," acknowledges Ben. "So during the second attack, the Allies made themselves into squares, and the French couldn't do anything about it."

"More or less," Henry agrees. "Each time the French charged they were slaughtered by musket and cannon fire, and then counter-attacked by the Allies' own cavalry. After an hour and a half of this punishment, they finally called it a day. By that time, there were so many dead and wounded men and horses surrounding the squares, any more charges would have been impossible in any case."

"So how come the British cavalry were able to beat the French infantry after the first attack?" asks Bisckits.

"I was wondering that, too," says Ben.

"The thing is, forming into squares is a precise manoeuvre, which takes a relatively long time to complete," replies Henry. "But after their first attack, the French infantry was already in retreat and so didn't have the order or time to make squares before the British cavalry slammed into them, so..."

"...Cavalry beat infantry," supplies Jaspa, gloomily.

"Exactly," Henry confirms.

"One more question about the second attack," says Ben. "Why did the French cavalry keep on charging, if they knew it was useless?"

"Dunno," his friend admits. "Maybe Marshal Ney was just too brave and stubborn to stop. Although I should say, the Allies didn't have it all their own way. Because there's one final rule in a game of infantry, cavalry, artillery."

"What's that?"

"Well, squares might be great against cavalry, but like I said, they take a long time to form," Henry replies. "So unless you want to end up like the infantry from the first French attack, you have to stay in squares between cavalry charges.

"Unfortunately, squares provide big, easy targets for artillery. And during the second attack, the French gunners took full advantage of this each time their cavalry galloped out of the way, down the hill to regroup."

Ben instantly sees where his friend is going with this line of reasoning. "So artillery beats infantry in squares, then?"

"Big time," confirms Henry. "So you see what I mean? The Battle of Waterloo was like a massive, deadly game of rock, paper, scissors. The lives of the pieces—the soldiers, in other words—and the fate of Europe were the stakes. And it was up to Wellington and Napoleon to decide which plays to make and when."

***

Chapter Eighteen

Ups and Downs

"We should probably calculate the coordinates for the next stage of *Waterloo 1815* while we're sitting here," suggests Bisckits, once more showing his sensible side.

"That's a good idea," says Abi. "It'll be easier doing it now, instead of as we walk along."

"I'll do it," offers Ben. "Hand me the GPS will you, Henry?"

The older boy fumbles with the jacket he's sitting on. He can feel the device in there somewhere, but it takes him a few frustrating seconds to identify the correct pocket. Once he manages to get his hands on the GPS, he stretches out across the cobbles to pass it to his pal, pressing the *on* button as he does so.

Ben takes the unit and sits up, resting his back against the stone bench. As he begins to study the cache description he's joined by Jaspa, Bisckits and Phyllis, who scramble up his back to peer at the screen from his shoulder.

"Sweet," says Phyllis, who hasn't yet had a chance to see the GPS close up.

"That's exactly what I said," grins Bisckits. He holds up his right hand, and the Frogses rewards him with a high-five. "Sweet!"

"Don't encourage him," groans Jaspa.

"Right," mutters Ben, as he scans through the text. "*The coordinates are those of the Lion Hill...* that's where we started. *At the chapel...* been there too. *Follow the path for about 1.6 km, until you arrive at the Prussian Monument...* probably best to forget all about that bit!"

"Hey!" objects Phyllis.

"Sorry," laughs Ben, before continuing to scroll through the cache description. *"Go northwest towards Napoleon's supposed last observatory...* that's where we are now. *Continue to the 'Belle Alliance' at North 50 degrees..."*

"Those coordinates are already programmed into the GPS," Abi interrupts. "They're a waypoint the cache owner suggests you visit, just for interest's sake."

"We don't actually need anything from there," Henry admits. "But as we're going to pass the spot anyway, I wouldn't mind having a look."

"Sounds fair enough," says Ben, before moving on. *"French visitors may want to go quickly to the 'Aigle Blessé' monument..."*

"That means the *Wounded Eagle*," Abi supplies.

"I think that's where the Imperial Guard made their last stand after the third attack, at the end of the battle," says Henry. "But we don't need anything from there either. And since it's a bit out of the way, we should probably give it a miss today."

Ben scrolls down a little more, until Jaspa declares, "That's what we're looking for. Where it says *Calculate MNO*."

"You're right," agrees Ben. "Hmmm... Seems like we just need to plug some of the numbers we've already collected today into this formula. Doesn't look too hard."

"Here's the list," says Abi, handing Ben a scruffy sheet of paper with a few muddy fingerprints on it. A column of letters, from *A* to *L*, runs down the left side of the page. Each letter is paired with a number, corresponding to the value they've collected by following the geocache's various instructions.

"Okay, let's see," mumbles Ben, starting to scribble calculations on the paper beside the list.

"*MNO* is 770," Jaspa announces after less than five seconds.

Ben throws down his pencil in disgust.

"Wow! That was quick," says Phyllis.

"Not you, too," complains Jaspa.

"Never mind them," Abi sooths the exasperated Giraffeses.

"Where does that put the next stage of the cache?" Portia asks Ben, who has already begun typing the new coordinates into the GPS.

"Just a second..." the boy stalls. "It puts it... I don't believe it!"

"Whit's th' matter?" asks Gravee, suddenly concerned.

"It puts it right back where we started," Ben replies. "Back at the visitor centre!"

"Crivens!" declares the Dogses. "Is that all? I thought it wis somethin' serious!"

"Sorry," Ben apologises.

***

Wrapping up their lazy lunch, Jaspa and the others set out again. The sun is still bright and warm overhead. But leaving the shelter provided by the hedge surrounding Napoleon's Observatory, they instantly notice the gentle but chilly wind that has started up while they've been relaxing. The breeze is no doubt associated with the ominous black clouds building to the west, which were hidden from their view by the hedge while they were resting.

By the time they reach the junction with the busy Chaussée de Charleroi, the main road that cuts the battlefield in half, the human members of the group are all wearing their jackets again. In the southeast angle of the crossroads is an unremarkable group of white-painted farm buildings, a couple of which seem to contain some kind of club, called *Le Retro*.

"This is La Belle Alliance," Henry tells them over the noise of the main road's traffic.

"Napoleon's headquarters!" proclaims Bisckits.

"More or less," replies Henry, a little vaguely.

Portia gives her cousin a surprised look.

"See, I was listening earlier," Bisckits retorts smugly. "Most of the time, anyway," he quietly whispers to Sam.

Ben's little sister giggles.

"La Belle Alliance was at the centre of the French lines during the battle and is often referred to as Napoleon's headquarters," Henry continues the story he's been telling off and on for most of the day. "But like I said before, the Emperor actually spent most of the battle about three-quarters of a mile south of here, at another farm called Rossomme.

"That being said, this is where he watched his army parade in their dress uniforms before the battle began. This is where he made his last stand with what was left of the Imperial Guard after their failed attack that evening. And this is where one of the greatest military leaders in history fled from his last ever battlefield."

"I guess this is another of those places that changed the World," comments Ben.

"Definitely," agrees Henry. "If Napoleon had managed to turn back the Allies and Prussians, we'd probably all be speaking French now."

"An' wearin' Napoleon boots in th' rain and not Wellies," suggests Gravee.

"And instead of the Battle of Waterloo, we'd be saying *la bataille de Mont-Saint-Jean*, which is what Napoleon called it, after a small hamlet that lies between the battlefield and the village of Waterloo," adds Henry.

"Really?" asks Jaspa.

"Yeah, really," Henry confirms. "Actually Blücher, the Prussian commander, gave it a third name: *Battle of La Belle Alliance*—although in German, of course. He called it that because he thought *Beautiful Alliance* was a fitting name, and also because he and Wellington happened to meet near here that night after the battle, or so the legend goes. But since the Duke was considered the real victor that day, he got to name it what he wanted: Waterloo."

***

"All this historical stuff's reit interestin'," says Gravee sincerely. "But we should prob'ly be gettin' a shift on, ye ken."

"He's right," Abi agrees, zipping up her coat. "We really shouldn't have taken so long over lunch. And we don't want to get all this way and then run out of time."

"Okay," says Jaspa. "So, which way do we go now, Ben?"

The McRae boy studies the map on the screen. "Well...." he replies, drawing the word out to again buy himself a little time. "We can either follow the main road north to the crossroads by Wellington's elm and the picnic area, and from there head back west along Route du Lion. Or we can go northwest across the fields, up that farm track on the other side of the road there, and then come at Lion Mound and the visitor centre from the other side."

"Which is faster?" enquires Abi.

"Erm... I'd say going up the main road is a little over a mile," Ben answers. "And the other way is perhaps a quarter mile further."

"I know it'd certainly be a lot nicer walking up a quiet farm track between fields than alongside this noisy road," observes Portia. "But we should probably make up a bit of time and take the quicker route."

"Portia's right," says Jaspa. "Plus those clouds to the west seem to be getting closer and darker by the minute. And the breeze is definitely picking up."

"The road it is then," declares Henry.

"Thank goodness for that," says Sam with a relieved sigh. "For a second there my poor feet thought we were going to have to take the long way around."

***

Trudging alongside the road, down off the French ridge and into the valley bottom, the noise of the traffic makes conversation a bit of an effort. Unsurprisingly then, each member lapses into his or her own private thoughts.

Jaspa mulls over all that has happened since they found the stone cross near Papelotte Farm. In many ways it feels like a lifetime ago. If only they'd read the whole cache description back then, they could have stayed on the northern ridge and saved a whole lot of walking (for the human members of the group, that is).

On the other hand, they wouldn't have seen all the fascinating things here on the French side of the valley, which would have been particularly disappointing for Henry. Nor would they have found *The Eagle's Last Battle* geocache.

On the other other hand, he and Gravee wouldn't have had to endure another attack from that freaky Falconses. What's more, Ben wouldn't have been terrified half-to-death at losing Gravee again. Not to mention the fact that Portia and Bisckits wouldn't have felt the need to reveal themselves to Abi and Henry—goodness knows what trouble that may bring in the future.

On the other other other hand, like Ben said, they wouldn't have met Phyllis, who seems really nice.

Are there always pros and cons to every little thing? wonders Jaspa. *Is anything ever straightforward, black-or-white, right-or-wrong, even with the benefit of hindsight?*

***

As Jaspa and his friends begin to climb the opposite hill, their thoughts inevitably drift back to what it must have been like for a French soldier marching or riding up this slope—which the humans all separately conclude is much steeper than it looks—into the lead teeth of the Allies' cannons and muskets.

Almost without realising it, they draw parallel with La Haye Sainte, the middle of the three 'forts' out in front of Wellington's ridge. Three sides of the farm's courtyard are made up from the farmhouse, barn and several sizable buildings. Yet the side running just a pace or two from the rumbling traffic of Chaussée de Charleroi is a simple, whitewashed brick wall against which a couple of smaller structures have been built (on the inward-facing side, of course).

For most of its length—perhaps 60 or 70 feet—the wall is about nine or 10 feet high. That said, the northern end is actually the two-storey gable wall of the farmhouse itself, while near the opposite end stands a semi-fortified gate tower. The massive, green, wooden gates are purposefully closed, preventing entry of everyone and everything, even the glances of inquisitive tourists.

Affixed to the outside of the wall are several plaques associated with the battle. The largest of these bears a golden Imperial Eagle. Otherwise, La Haye Sainte looks pretty much the same as it did before Wellington, Napoleon, Blücher and their armies arrived to flex their collective muscles.

One by one, the group's gloomy musings drift towards what it must have been like to attack or defend the cluster of farm buildings and walls on that bloody day.

"La Haye Sainte was held by the King's German Legion—or KGL, as they're often called—a British unit made up of soldiers from the Hanover region of what is now northern Germany," Henry raises his voice to be heard over the traffic noise. "They'd spent the previous night in the farm, along with a bunch of other troops. Unfortunately, they hadn't been told they'd have to defend it, so they burned all the wood in the place to keep warm, including the farm's gates."

160

"Oh-oh," Sam grimaces.

"The Legion managed to hold off a major French assault at about 3 o'clock, but used up most of their ammunition doing so. They sent out messages asking for more, but none came. Even after collecting up all the ammunition they could off the dead and wounded, when the French launched their next strike, the KGL only had a handful of cartridges per man.

"Completely outnumbered, and with the last of their ammunition finally gone, the Germans kept fighting with only bayonets and the butts of their rifles and muskets. But the enemy could just hang back and pick them off, one-by-one." Henry mimes a man slowly aiming and firing a musket.

"Eventually the KGL had no choice but to abandon the farm and retreat to the top of the ridge. Of the 370-something defenders, only 43 managed to escape alive."

"Crivens!" exclaims Gravee, neatly summing up how they all feel.

***

Leaving La Haye Sainte behind, they carry on up the hill, passing close to the geocache they'd done with Callum and Davy the previous day.

"See that big monument between us and the road? The one on the other side of the railings, next to where we found the cache yesterday?" Henry asks.

Various nods and noises indicate they all know which monument he's talking about. All except Phyllis, of course.

"That's called the Hanoverian Monument. It was placed in honour of the men of the KGL that died at La Haye Sainte," Abi's brother tells them. "Beneath it is one of the battlefield's graves, the final resting place for around 4000 soldiers."

"I'll never get used to how many men and horses were killed here," says Portia with a heavy sigh, looking back over her shoulder across the battlefield. "And all because one person thought they knew better than everyone else, how other people should live their lives."

"Ye've jist summed up war, lassie," agrees Gravee. "A senseless waste. An' usually started by folk that never grew out o' bein' bullies."

Something suddenly occurs to Abi. "Do Ses have wars?" she asks.

"Not that I've ever heard of," replies Jaspa.

"Then you've got more sense than us humans," grunts Ben.

"Like horses," grins Bisckits.

***

They reach the picnic area and make for the crossroads beside which Wellington's elm once stood. Jaspa looks ahead, west along the length of Route du Lion. The sunlit grass cone of Lion Mound stands out bright green against the looming dark clouds that frame it.

As Jaspa watches, the approaching mass of towering clouds momentarily glows from within. *That's not a good sign!* he thinks.

Phyllis holds out her hand. "Feels like it's going to rain soon," she observes.

"That's weird," says Bisckits.

"Not really," Phyllis disagrees, gesturing towards the clouds Jaspa's still staring at. "Not with a thunderstorm like that coming at us."

"No, I meant that!" The little Giraffeses points back down the hill up which they've just come.

"Where did they come from?" wonders Abi. "And where have they been?"

Gravee looks at the sky nervously, before spying the source of Bisckits and Abi's concern. There, a short distance beyond the white buildings of

La Haye Sainte, is a familiar figure, its blue hood drawn up against the rising wind.

"Och! For a second there, I thought that bloomin' Falconses wis back!" the Dogses confides to Jaspa.

"Thankfully, he seems to have got bored of harassing you," his friend replies with a grin.

"She's following us!" declares Sam, referring to the woman behind them.

"No she's not," scoffs Ben.

"I don't know," Abi disagrees. "Like Bisckits says, it's a bit weird. How come she keeps disappearing and then reappearing? And always roughly the same distance away?"

Ben makes a face that says, *You've got a point.*

"I'm sure it's jist a coincidence, but we should keep an eye on 'em, tae be on th' safe side," says Gravee seriously, having recovered from his brief scare. "Sadly, there are some dodgy scunners aroond. Yers bairns must always keep ye wits aboot ye."

"That's why you should never accept a ride from a stranger," says Sam firmly.

"Well done, lassie," says Gravee, his scowl lifting. "I only wish ye brother had half as much good sense as 'is wee sister."

"Hey!" objects Ben. "I'm standing right here!"

Jaspa scowls slightly, although none of the others notice. While he whole-heartedly agrees with Gravee's advice, he has a feeling that—in this one instance—things are perhaps not quite as sinister as they might first appear.

***

Part 3

Revelations

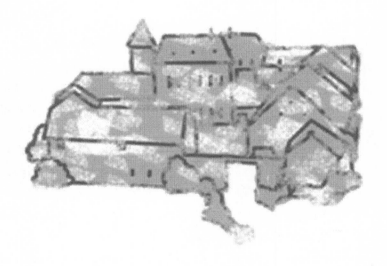

Chapter Nineteen

Sabotage

The GPS unit in Ben's hand beeps urgently. "The next stage is somewhere near here," the boy informs his friends.

"Oh! Is that what that beeping means?" asks Abi, acting surprised. "I've been wondering about that all day."

Ben laughs, feeling slightly foolish.

In front of them is a barrier linking the battlefield's visitor centre and the circular Panorama. Twelve red brick posts, each about five feet tall, support a series of 11 large, dramatic photographs taken at a previous re-enactment. The images are mounted on a metal framework, to form a kind of pictorial fence that prevents access to Lion Mound, behind the Panorama. A vehicle-sized gate spans the gap between the final brick post and the visitor centre.

"We made it!" proclaims Bisckits. "For a while back there, I was beginning to think we'd never get here."

"Now all we have to do is find the numbers that tell us where the next stage of the cache is," says Sam

"Easy!" declares Portia. "Oops!"

They stare at her.

"Umm... I didn't say anything," she assures them. "You're all hearing things."

Jaspa gives his cousin a wink, and then asks, "Do we know exactly what we're looking for?"

Once again, Ben scans through the cache description. "*Here you will find 'NNN' and 'EEE'...*" he reads after a moment.

"Och! Nae that agin," groans Gravee.

"... *To complete the final coordinates to the cache*!" finishes Ben.

"The final coordinates?!" repeats Jaspa.

"That's what is says," Ben confirms.

"Then this is the penultimate stage?" asks Abi.

"Looks like it," agrees Ben.

"Woo-hoo!" cries Bisckits. "The penny-ultimate stage!"

"Gravee's right, though," says Henry. "The *NNN* and *EEE* format is the same as the cache we did at Napoleon's Observatory. Are they hidden by the same person?"

It takes Ben a minute or two to figure it out, but he eventually he confirms that both caches are hidden by the same geocacher. "Someone called Jiheffe," he tells them.

"Which hopefully means we've got an idea of what to look for this time," says Phyllis.

"Hmmm," ponders the Dogses. "The lassie has a point, ye ken."

***

"I don't think they're here," Jaspa finally says out loud what they're all thinking.

"But they have to be!" Ben declares forcefully. "We must have tried at least six times between us: the GPS brings us back to the middle of this wall-thingy every time."

"I get that," replies Jaspa, trying to sound supportive. "But that doesn't change the fact the coordinates are almost certainly missing."

For 20 long minutes, they've searched for the numbers that will lead them to the final of the cache they've been working on since first thing this morning. Each member of the team has carefully examined the wall/fence indicated by the GPS numerous times, while trying not to attract too much attention from passers-by. The humans have pawed over every inch of the metal and brick structure they can reach. And the Ses have climbed all over it, inspecting it from both sides.

But so far, it's all been for nothing.

"What was the hint again," asks Henry.

"We've already been through this," sighs Abi in exasperation.

"*Look for a large oak with a GCAC68 tag,*" Gravee, Sam, Bisckits and Phyllis chorus.

"Sorry, I keep forgetting," Henry apologises.

"What does *GCAC68* mean, anyway?" asks Bisckits.

"It's kind of like the serial number for the cache," replies Abi, trying to calm down. "Every geocache has a unique *GC number*, as they're called."

"Like we said before, the hint must be for the final," says Jaspa, trying to defuse the irritation that's thick in the air. "There aren't any oaks anywhere near here, and it doesn't fit any of the other places we've been either."

With desperation growing, they expand their search to include every possible hiding spot within 30 or 40 yards. They investigate anything and everything: the flower planters on both sides of the street; the signs, flagpoles and shrubs in front of the visitor centre; the bicycle rack; and even the red post box beside the entrance to the Panorama.

Yet they're still no closer to finding what they need.

"Can I have another go with the GPS?" asks Henry.

"It'll just bring you right back here again," snaps Ben, practically throwing the device at him. "But knock yourself out!"

"Come on, Ben," Portia gently scolds her friend. "There's no need to take it out on Henry. It's not his fault, is it?"

"I'm sorry," replies the boy in a slightly calmer tone. "But this is so frustrating!"

"I know," says Portia, sympathetically.

"And I've rechecked your calculations three times already," growls Abi, also getting annoyed again. "I'm *certain* we're in the right place."

While the others were talking, Henry has walked about 50 feet away along Route du Lion. Now he allows himself to be guided by the large red arrow on the GPS's display screen. It brings him unerringly back to the centre-most of the enlarged photographs—showing a group of infantry advancing through thigh-high crops—which Sam is fruitlessly searching yet again.

***

A pall of gloom settles over the group. The previous stages of *Waterloo 1815* have been a breeze. So why is this one giving them so much trouble? The fact that this is the next to last stage just adds to the frustration. If they can only find these numbers, they're off to the final!

All they need to do is find some sort of small container with some numbers inside. Maybe attached with a magnet, or hanging from the branch of a bush, or hidden under a stone. Or perhaps the numbers are written on something, like a metal tag, or even a piece of tape, as was the case with *The Eagle's Last Battle*.

Two numbers that will complete the mystery coordinates and send them on their way to the cache's final hiding place. Two, three-digit numbers and they'll be able to put Gobber firmly in his place. For a little while, at least.

But if those numbers are hidden on, or anywhere near, the wall of images, they're eluding Jaspa and his friends. Not that any of the group truly believes the numbers are still here. Like Jaspa, they're all totally convinced the six digits they so desperately need are no longer here.

***

"I can't believe we can't find them," moans Henry despondently, summing up how they all feel. "Not after we've come so far. We must have walked well over five miles by now."

"Closer to six actually, according to this thing," his sister corrects him, brandishing the GPS device. "If you include going back to rescue Gravee and Jaspa, that is."

"I still think we must have walked at least 10 miles," says Sam. "Probably 15 by now."

"Come on," mutters Phyllis under her breath. "I need a Signal!"

"You mean a sign," Bisckits automatically corrects her, temporarily distracted by the strange plea.

"No," she disagrees. "Frogses always ask for a Signal."

"Why?" wonders Bisckits.

"Oh, erm…" stutters Phyllis, a bit taken aback by the little Giraffeses' bluntness. "Well, Signal is a famous Frogses explorer from Alaska. Late one fall, many decades ago, he was on an expedition in the Wrangell Mountains. During a fierce storm he got separated from his party."

"I ken hoo that feels," murmurs Gravee.

"For days the other members of the expedition tried to find him. But eventually the bad weather forced them to reluctantly abandon their search. Everyone assumed Signal must have died."

"Oh no!" gasps Portia.

"Then one day, over a year later, Signal walked into his village, safe and sound," Phyllis continues. "He told a terrifying story of how he'd become completely disoriented during the storm in which he went missing. After wandering around for days, he'd finally staggered off a ledge and tumbled into a ravine. Having broken both his legs in the fall, Signal had lain there for what must have been several days, unable to move, drifting in and out of consciousness, waiting to die.

"But by pure chance, he was saved by a strange old Ses, who stumbled upon him during a brief break in the weather. By that time, Signal was suffering from malnutrition, hypothermia and frostbite, not to mention his broken bones. Fortunately, the ancient hermit was extremely knowledgeable when it came to mountaincraft, and over the remainder of the winter he slowly nursed Signal back to health."

"Sounds like he had a lucky escape," observes Jaspa.

"That's for sure, eh?" agrees Phyllis. "During that first winter in the mountains, Signal had a lot of time to think. He realised that if he hadn't fallen and broken his legs, it was likely the hermit Ses would never have found him, and that he probably wouldn't have survived. Ironically, breaking his legs so he couldn't move almost certainly saved his life.

"Signal came to understand how important it was to grasp the opportunity to learn from his rescuer. So when the spring arrived, instead of going home, Signal asked if he could stay, as the hermit's apprentice. For another whole year, the old Ses taught Signal everything he knew, training him in the ways of the mountains.

"When Signal eventually returned home, he continued his studies, researching and compiling hundreds of years worth of Ses and human folklore, mostly passed down by word-of-mouth, on how to survive and find your way in the wild. Goodness knows how old he is now, but to this day Signal continues to instruct young Ses—Frogses mostly—on how to survive in untamed and inhospitable places. I met him once myself, although I was only a tadpole, and don't really remember it."

"Were you really a tadpole?" asks Sam, eyes wide.

"Not in the way you're thinking," laughs Phyllis. "Frogses don't have a true tadpole stage, like frogs and toads do, but that's still what we call our children.

"Anyway, many believe that Signal's teachings are his attempt to prevent anyone else getting into the same sort of trouble he did, all those years ago. Whatever the reason, it's become a kind of tradition for Frogses to ask for a *Signal* if ever they're lost or in need of guidance. It reminds us of how bad things looked for Signal, lost and dying in the Wrangell Mountains, but how he not only managed to survive, but eventually turned his misfortune to his advantage."

***

Despite Phyllis's uplifting story about Signal, the group's search becomes increasingly hopeless and frantic.

"I don't believe it!" Ben suddenly exclaims, so loudly that several nearby tourists turn to stare at him. He begins to laugh, slightly manically.

Shocked by Ben's strange behaviour, his friends abandon their own searching and return to his side.

"What is it?" asks Abi softly, attempting to quieten things down so that the passers-by will lose interest. "Are you all right?"

"How could I have been so stupid?" declares Ben.

"What?" asks Jaspa. "Have you found the numbers at last?"

"Of course not," replies the boy in a resigned tone. "They're not here."

"I think we decided 10 minutes ago that they're probably missing," Jaspa points out.

"Oh, they're definitely gone," agrees Ben. "But they're not missing."

"Whit are ye blatherin' on aboot, laddie?" says Gravee. "Yer talkin' in riddles."

"I'm certain the numbers to complete the final coordinates aren't here. But they haven't just gone missing," Ben explains. "Somebody took them!"

"Who?" wonders Portia. But even as she's asking, the answer comes to her. "Not Gobber?"

"Exactly!" confirms Ben. "We saw him looking suspicious right by here, yesterday. I didn't think much of it at the time. You know Gobber, he's always doing something suspicious."

"But he was stealing the coordinates for the final stage of the cache!" says Jaspa, grasping the boy's point.

"That's right. Oh, how could I have been so stupid?!" Ben chides himself again, gently thumping his temples with the heels of his hands. "Gobber played me right from the start. He must have known his parents were going to introduce us to geocaching, and he decided to have some fun with me. He manipulated the whole situation. And I took the bait, like a greedy fish swallowing an angler's worm, hook and all."

"Who's Gobber?" asks Phyllis.

***

"It's useless," sighs Ben. "We might as well accept it. I've lost the bet."

"We can't just give up," Abi protests half-heartedly. "Perhaps Gobber didn't steal the clue, after all. Maybe it was just a coincidence, him being by here yesterday."

"And Dennis won't be back to pick us up for a couple of hours yet," adds Sam, with surprising urgency. "We might as well keep looking," she almost pleads.

"Nah," says Ben, exhaling explosively. "It's time to face facts. It doesn't matter how long we look, we're not going to find the numbers, because they're gone. I shouldn't have made that stupid bet with Gobber. Now I'm just going to have to pay the price."

"You're really going to give him the 50 quid?" asks Henry incredulously. "Even though we know he cheated?"

"What choice do I have?" replies Ben, sounding increasingly resigned. "Gobber will never let me live it down if I don't honour the bet. And we don't have any proof he took the numbers. He'll just tell everyone I'm a sore loser."

Even though Ben has no idea how he's going to come up with the £50, it's not really the money that bothers him. It's not even the associated

172

gloating, sniggering and embarrassment he's undoubtedly going to have to endure back at school.

No, the thing that really annoys Ben is knowing that he allowed Gobber to goad him into losing his temper and making the foolish bet in the first place. Especially now he realises that the bully planned the whole thing goodness knows how long in advance.

"It's worse than the £50," says Sam in a strained voice. "Much worse." She stares at her feet, great big tears welling up in her eyes.

"What do you mean?" asks Ben, suddenly confused.

"Och, lassie," groans Gravee, the first to catch on. "Whit huv ye done?"

"I didn't mean to!" sobs Sam.

"What have you done, Sammie?" Abi asks gently, repeating Gravee's question.

"I made another bet with Gobber," Ben's little sister admits in barely a whisper. "That we'd find the geocache."

When everyone else fails to respond, Portia poses the obvious question, "What did you say you'd give him if we didn't?"

Pause.

"Sam?" Ben softly prompts. "What did you bet?"

Pause.

"Mum's smartphone."

The little girl continues to stare at her shoes in the shocked silence that follows. And then words and tears start flooding out of her in great, heaving sobs.

"It was just he was being so mean to you," she tells her brother, desperately. "And it wasn't right. And I couldn't let him get away with it. So I told him. And he laughed at me. He said you were an even bigger baby than he thought, because you needed your little sister to stick up for you. And I knew that you'd be mad at me. So I got even more mad at him.

And the next thing I knew, I'd bet him Mum's smartphone that we'd find the stupid cache."

Weeping uncontrollably, as if the World's about to end, Sam throws herself into her brother's arms. He strokes her hair and murmurs things like, "Shhh!" and "It's all right!" in an attempt to comfort her.

Some nearby tourists are again openly staring at them, curious as to what's upset Sam so much. As he continues to soothe his sister, Ben smiles at them in what he hopes is a *Nothing to worry about* kind of way.

Slowly—very slowly—the little girl's misery subsides into those barely audible, hiccup-like sobs that children make when they're trying to stop crying.

Unexpectedly, Jaspa suddenly clicks his fingers in triumph.

"Don't worry Sam," he declares with a broad grin. "We're not handing your Mum's phone over to Gobber just yet. I think I may have just had a Signal!"

***

Chapter Twenty

A Long Shot

"Yesterday, Laurel said that when someone finds a geocache, they go online and post a log, right?" Jaspa begins to explain his plan.

"That's right," confirms Abi. "In fact, Ben and I set up our usernames and logged our find of *In View of Lion Hill* last night, using Jimmy's laptop."

"And didn't she say that people can include photos with their logs if they want?"

"I think I remember her sayin' somethin' aboot that, aye," agrees Gravee.

"And she also said that sometimes those logs and photos provide unexpected and unintentional hints on how to find the cache," Jaspa continues.

"I see where you're going with this, Waver," declares Portia. "You think there might be something in one of the past logs or photos that will help us find the final."

"Or at least narrow down where we should be looking," her cousin confirms.

"But how's that going to help us win the bets we have with Gobber?" sniffs Sam. "We don't have a laptop to go online."

"You're right, we don't have a laptop," concedes Jaspa. "But we do have the next best thing. In fact, it was you mentioning the bet you made with Gobber that gave me the idea."

"Of course!" exclaims Abi. "Mrs McRae's smartphone!"

"But we're only allowed to use Mum's phone in emergencies," Sam protests.

"I know this probably wasn't what she meant," her brother replies. "But I don't want to have to explain to her how we lost her phone in a bet. Do you?"

Sam shakes her head vigorously. "No."

"Then it seems to me that this is about as big as emergencies get!"

At that, Ben takes out the smartphone and, despite his mum's instructions and his sister's objections, turns on the data roaming.

***

"The cache info looks a lot different on the webpage, doesn't it?" observes Bisckits.

It's taken a few minutes, but they've managed to find the geocaching website and log on using Ben and Sam's username—*Jaspa's Journeyers*. The online version of the *Waterloo 1815* cache description includes several photos not visible on the GPS. The images are of some of the places they've visited along the way, including the stone cross and the roadside chapel.

"They might huv bin useful earlier," says Gravee, peering over Ben's shoulder with everyone else.

Reaching the end of the actual cache description, Ben comes to a bunch of what looks like technical mumbo-jumbo under the heading *Additional Waypoints*. He starts to head back up towards the top of the page, where he's already seen a *View Gallery* link, but Abi stops him.

"That's just a list of all the waypoints we've visited today," she says. "There might be something useful after that."

Without a word, Ben returns to scrolling downwards. Unfamiliar as they are with the world of geocaching and this particular website, much of what comes next doesn't mean very much to any of them. Until...

"I don't believe it!" exclaims Jaspa, his voice full of excitement.

"What?" asks Portia.

Rather than answering his cousin's question, Jaspa instructs Ben to slowly back up a little.

With the tip of his finger, the boy begins to creep upwards once more.

"That's it!" Jaspa cries in triumph, almost immediately. He points towards the bottom of the current screen, where there are two links to self-proclaimed spoiler photos.

"What do they mean by *spoiler?*" wonders Bisckits.

"It basically means *If you want to find the cache without any help, then don't look at these photos,*" Henry informs him.

"But in our situation, they're just what we want!" adds Abi.

***

Ben gingerly selects the upper of the two links, which is labelled *Additional Spoiler.* The image that opens is actually two photos combined into one. The top half shows a small metal plate engraved with *GCAC68*, screwed to the trunk of a tree. Judging from the size of the screw heads and the texture of the bark, the homemade plaque can't be more than perhaps two inches long and less than three quarters of an inch high. The same logic suggests the tree it's attached to is a large, mature specimen.

The lower half of the image is a photo of the cache container itself, an old, olive green ammunition box. On the side of the box is a black, stencilled cartoon of a funny little fat man with electric-shock hair and the name of a website: *geocaching.be.*

"I hope th' other spoiler is mair helpful," says Gravee, summing up the general feeling. "This one's aboot as useful as a chocolate fireguard."

Ben hits the back button to return to the cache page. His finger hovers nervously over the lower of the two photo links. This one reads *SPOILER - The place to be,* which is encouraging. Unfortunately, just below the link it says, *Well, actually, it's not a BIG spoiler,* followed by a winky face made from punctuation *;-).*

The second link leads to a picture of a tall tree. It's taken by someone standing close to the trunk, looking up at a steep angle. The photo is obviously taken in winter (or the tree is dead), because a beautiful blue sky is clearly visible through the network of branches, which are devoid of leaves.

"Mah mistake," says Gravee, again acting as the voice of the whole group. "That's another chocolate fireguard, reit enough."

Hopelessness descends on the group once again.

"That must be the oak tree we're looking for," Jaspa points out, remembering the hint and trying to be positive. "Looking on the bright side, we at least have a chance of recognising it if we see it."

"Bright side?" exclaims Portia, uncharacteristically losing her cool for the second time today. "In case you haven't noticed, we've just walked around an entire battlefield. That tree could be anywhere out there. In fact, we could have already walked straight past it, without realising. We might even have touched it, for goodness sake!"

"No offence, Jaspa, but Portia's right. It's impossible," agrees Abi, although in a slightly calmer tone. "All we have is a photo of a perfectly ordinary-looking tree. It could be an oak, but we're only guessing that because of the hint—although it's likely, I admit. And anyway, how are we supposed to find one particular oak tree, no matter how large it is, and no matter what might be attached to it, on a battlefield this big? It'd be like looking for a needle in a haystack."

"They're right, you know," says Ben gloomily, turning off the phone's data roaming. "It was a good idea, Jaspa, but they're right."

"I know," sighs the Giraffeses.

Sam looks like she's about to burst into tears again.

***

"Not the whole battlefield," murmurs Henry, thoughtfully.

"Sorry?" asks Abi.

"Not the whole battlefield," Henry repeats, more loudly and confidently this time.

"What do you mean?" demands his sister.

"You said just now, *How are we supposed to find one particular oak tree on a battlefield this big?*" says Henry. "But we don't have to search the whole battlefield."

"Why not," asks Sam, desperate for anything that could provide even the slightest chance of finding the cache.

"Our route around the battlefield has taken us everywhere, right," Henry explains. "Even places we didn't need to visit to complete the cache."

"Right," agrees Ben, intrigued to see where his pal is going with this. "Because the cache owner wanted to show us the whole battlefield."

"Exactly!" replies Henry, stabbing a finger at Ben. "Then doesn't it seem funny that there's one part of the battlefield we've not been to yet? A place where some of the most intense and famous fighting occurred."

"Just get on with it!" groans Abi.

"Ooh! Ooh! I know!" interrupts Bisckits the Historian, with a proud grin. "Hoogeemot!"

Henry touches his own nose and then points at the little Giraffeses. "That's right," he laughs. "Hougoumont Château. The final to the cache has to be somewhere between here and there."

"Are you sure?" Sam almost pleads.

"Pretty sure," Henry nods. "I can't guarantee it, of course, but it's the only thing that makes sense to me."

"I think Henry's on to something," agrees Jaspa. "And I think I can narrow it down a bit further."

"How?" asks Sam, intently.

"Look at the photo of the tree..." Jaspa tells Sam and the others. "Doesn't it look like it's surrounded by other trees?"

"I see where ye're goin' wi' this," says Gravee. "Ye reckon we're after a wood. Or at least somethin' bigger than jist a wee hedgerow or a tree by itself."

"I do," replies Jaspa. "And if I remember rightly, when Laurel pointed out Hougoumont from the top of Lion Mound yesterday, there was a small wood just this side of the château."

"There is," confirms Phyllis. "I was out that way yesterday morning. Some of the people pretending to be soldiers had campsites over there."

"You didn't happen see this tree, did you?" asks Ben excitedly, getting ahead of himself.

Phyllis treats the boy to her best *You've got to be kidding me* stare. It evidently works, because Ben's face turns bright red.

"So what do we think?" Abi asks, looking around the group. "Should we give it a try?"

"It's still a long shot," admits Henry.

"But what have we got to lose?" counters Jaspa.

"What the heck!" declares Ben. "Let's kick this pig!"

***

Filled with nervous optimism, the geocachers head down Chemin des Vertes Bornes, a cobbled lane that meets Route du Lion beside the Panorama. By the time they leave behind Lion Mound and the tiny hamlet that has grown up around it, the cobblestones have been replaced by asphalt, although in places the surface is so badly potholed it's practically a mud track.

Out among the fields once more, the children and Ses realise how much the buildings and mound have been sheltering them from the wind. Their route is now taking them southwest, straight into the rising storm. The gusting wind seems determined to make them turn around and go back the way they've come.

Something elusive has been trying to get Jaspa's attention ever since he and Gravee were rescued from that ridiculous Falconses. And as they walk along, he finally figures out what it is.

"I was impressed earlier with how calm you were when Bisckits and Portia turned up with four humans," he tells Phyllis.

"Thanks," she replies distractedly, her attention focused on the sky ahead.

During the confrontation with the Falconses, there'd barely been time to exchange much more than names. They certainly hadn't been able to warn the Frogses to expect a Seer and three of his friends at any moment.

"And you didn't seem that surprised to learn Sam could see and hear you, either."

"I suppose not," says the Frogses, after a moment's consideration.

"I'm just curious..." Jaspa admits. "Don't take this the wrong way, but most Ses I've met don't even believe Seers exist—although, actually, Ben is the only true Seer here. Yet you seemed to take it all in your stride..." He leaves the end of the statement open. An invitation for an explanation, without actually asking for one.

Several seconds pass, and Jaspa is beginning to think he must have offended Phyllis. He's about to apologise, when the Frogses finally responds.

"I met a Seer. Not long ago, actually," Phyllis says simply. She pauses, before adding, "It didn't end well."

"What happened?" asks Jaspa, fascinated. He can sense the sudden attention of his friends, Ses and human alike.

"Maybe I'll tell you about it sometime," replies Phyllis, evasively.

***

Sensing Phyllis's discomfort, Portia attempts to divert the conversation. "So is this where the Allied squares beat the enemy cavalry during the second French attack?" she asks Henry.

"Yeah," confirms the boy. "We'd have been pretty much in the heart of the action right here."

"Except it happened above where our heads are now," Ben amends.

"Actually, no," Henry corrects his friend. "Like I think I said before, historians reckon the only part of the ridge crest altered to build Lion Mound was between the monument itself and the Brussels road. So like most of the battlefield, this part of the ridge looks exactly as it would have done during the fighting. Even the road we're walking on was here, although at that time it was actually part of the Ohain Road and just a mud track."

Once past the fence and hedge that run around the base of Lion Mound, a single small tree is the only cover on either side of the lane for almost half a mile. At a muddy 'T' junction, the gang reaches a farm track that cuts diagonally across the fields to La Belle Alliance.

Up ahead, Chemin des Vertes Bornes appears to be lined on both sides by hedges and the odd tree. Although the vegetation doesn't look anywhere near substantial enough to conceal the tree for which they're hunting, it should at least offer some protection from the wind. Hopefully.

"She's back there again," Bisckits announces.

Everyone turns around to look back down the track. Sure enough, the familiar figure with the dark blue jacket is just emerging from the hamlet beside Lion Mound.

"That's it!" declares Ben, starting back down the lane. "I've had enough of this."

"Where do you think you're going?" asks Abi.

Ben stops and turns around. "I'm going to see what her deal is."

"You know, those storm clouds are going to open up before too long," Jaspa notes. "And I for one would rather be back at the visitor centre when that happens, if at all possible. But first, we've got to find a single tree hidden somewhere in a wood full of other trees. So perhaps we should concentrate on that for the moment."

"Ye ken, I dinnae think Ben's idea is that bad..." begins Gravee. But Jaspa cuts him off with a gesture, which the Dogses correctly interprets as a combination of *Back me up here* and *Trust me*.

"I mean, mebbe Jaspa has a point," Gravee starts over. "Mebbe we should find oor tree first, an' worry aboot oor mystery woman later."

***

"That sounds like a lot of traffic," says Portia.

"It's noisy, eh?" agrees Phyllis.

Less than 150 yards past the muddy track from La Belle Alliance, Jaspa and his friends unexpectedly stumble upon a road junction that would be more at home in the middle of a town—if it weren't for the fact it's surrounded by trees instead of buildings. Unfortunately none of the trees appear to be the one they're after.

The large asphalt clearing seems totally out of scale with the lane they've just come along, or the one that carries on in front of them, for that matter. The inappropriateness of the junction and sudden traffic noise is explained by the Frogses.

"There's a bridge, about 50 yards that way, crossing the main Brussels ring road," she says, pointing down the third road, which goes off to the right. "The lane in front of us runs parallel to the highway for about a quarter of a mile, before turning south towards Hougoumont Château. There are some trees between the lane and the Highway, but the main part of Jaspa's wood is to the left of the lane."

"Before we get carried away and blunder off blindly into the woods, perhaps we should try walking along the track towards the château," Portia suggests. "Maybe we'll get lucky and see our tree without having to go bushwhacking."

"Good idea," agrees Abi.

***

Less than five minutes later they emerge from the wood, the full force of the wind blowing directly into their faces takes their collective breath away. They've come about 300 yards west from the strange junction where they entered the wood. To their left they can see the western edge of the woodlot, which measures roughly half that distance.

"It was worth a try," says Bisckits, over the noise of the wind. "But I knew it wouldn't be that easy." He gives Portia a meaningful look.

"You don't really think this is my fault, do you?" Portia asks in disbelief. "Just because I said finding *The Eagle's Last Battle* so quickly was a good sign?"

Bisckits manages to hold his poker face for perhaps three seconds, before a huge impish smile practically splits his head in two.

His cousin gives him a well-practiced scowl in return.

In reality, none of them are surprised that their walk along Chemin du Goumont—as the lane down to Hougoumont Château is called—didn't lead them past the oak they're looking for. At least, they hope it didn't. Because if they have just passed the tree, they completely failed to recognise it.

Henry is oblivious to the blast of the wind and the light-hearted banter of the two Giraffeses. All his attention is focussed on Hougoumont, only 200 yards away across a pasture. Having learned so much about the heroics and sacrifice that occurred in and around those fortified farm buildings, he'd hoped for the chance to see them. And there they are.

"Would anyone mind if I went and had a closer look?"

Ben sneaks a glance at his watch and then at the still-darkening sky. He shrugs, and to Henry's surprise, answers, "Of course not. In fact, we'll all come along."

"Um, I'd prefer to keep looking for the tree," Sam admits, sounding a little panicky.

"But Sam..." her brother begins.

"Sam's right," Henry relents, although the disappointment is clear in his voice. "We should focus on finding the cache. I can see the farm fine from here."

"Don't be silly," says Abi, firmly. "Ben, give me the phone."

Ben does as he's told. "The lock code is 2009," he says.

Abi taps in the sequence of numbers, and the phone unlocks to reveal the image of the tree they're seeking still on the screen. "Right," she says, with a business-like attitude that forbids argument. "We've got a wood that's roughly 200 yards square. You boys go and see your farm, while us girls go and start the search. Come and help us when you're finished."

Despite his sister's commanding tone, Henry is about to object. But Ben beats him to it. "Thanks," he says quickly. "We won't be long."

"I know," smiles Abi. She and Sam turn around, and are about to head back up the lane into the wood, when Ben calls them back.

"Hey! If it's going be boys and girls, Bisckits best come with us," Ben suggests.

"Wicked," grins the little Giraffeses from his customary place with Portia in Sam's hood.

"In that case, I'd best swap with him," laughs Phyllis, who's sitting on Ben's shoulder with Gravee and Jaspa. "I have to stick with my sisters, eh?"

The McRae siblings gently exchange Ses.

"Okay then, ladies," declares Abi. "Let's show the boys how it's done. We'll find this tree while they're off playing soldiers!"

Chapter Twenty-One

Needle in a Haystack

Jaspa and 'the Boys' stand in Hougoumont's cobblestone courtyard, surveying the structures that surround them. For the most part, the buildings along southern and western perimeters are still intact. They include a solid, cream-painted farmhouse with an impressive two story gatehouse to the south, and two massive barns to the west. At the heart of the complex, which measures approximately 50 by 80 yards, is a small, brick chapel. A few fragments of wall and foundation are all that's left of the eastern and northern ranges.

Over the last couple of days, Jaspa has heard Hougoumont alternately referred to as a château or a farm. To his ears, the former conjures images of grandeur, aristocracy and opulence, whereas the latter sounds much more commonplace and mundane. Standing in courtyard of the famous collection of buildings, with their shabby, rundown air, he decides that the term *farm* is far more appropriate these days.

"Before the battle, the farmhouse there was just the gardener's house," Henry tells them. "The actual château stood in the empty area where the bits of wall are now. But sadly it was damaged beyond repair during the fighting."

"That explains it," says Jaspa. "I thought *château* seemed a bit impressive for what's here."

"In fact, there used to be a walled, formal garden to the east of the inner courtyard," Henry expands. "You can still see most of the wall. And beyond that was an orchard to the east and a large wood to the south, but they're gone now, too."

Sure enough, Jaspa can see the wall Henry is talking about. Standing seven or eight feet tall, it borders the south and east sides of what now looks like a pasture, about 200 yards long and 100 yards wide.

If that used to be a garden, no wonder they needed a full-time gardener with his own house, Jaspa thinks. *Before Napoleon decided to invade this part of Europe, and Wellington chose here as the place to stop him, that is.*

***

"The fighting here at Hougoumont began almost as soon as Napoleon's guns fired their first cannonball," says Henry, turning once more to the story of the battle itself. "When the French released their first attack against Wellington's main lines—on the far side of the main Brussels road, over where we were this morning—the battle for Hougoumont was already two hours old.

"All day the French launched one offensive after another against this fortress-like farm. For over seven hours a total of about 3500 defenders kept roughly 14,000 enemy at bay, thanks to the protection offered by the château's buildings and walls. The southern woods and the orchard were both lost and retaken several times, but the château courtyard and the walled garden were never captured.

Ben and the Ses look out over the former garden, almost as if expecting to see French soldiers come swarming over its walls.

"At one point, a group of French soldiers did manage to get in through the north gate, the only one not completely barricaded. It became one of the most famous stories of the entire battle.

"A gigantic French Sergeant named Legros managed to smash through the gate with an axe. Together with about 30 other soldiers, he charged into the courtyard. The fate of the battle hung on the desperate, vicious skirmish that followed. If the French could only keep the gate open long enough for reinforcements to arrive, they could take Hougoumont, and the Allied right flank would be dangerously exposed."

Wide-eyed, Ben and the three Ses all hold their breath, as Henry tells his exciting tale.

"But somehow, the commander of the farm's defenders, Lieutenant-Colonel James Macdonnell of the Coldstream Guards, and three of his men managed to shut and bar the gates. Wellington later named one of those men, Corporal James Graham, the *bravest man at Waterloo*. The Duke also said *the outcome of the battle of Waterloo turned on the closing of the gates at Hougoumont*, or something like that."

"So what happened to the French soldiers?" wonders Bisckits, although he has a feeling he already knows the answer.

"They were all killed, including Legros, here in this courtyard," Henry replies bleakly, looking around. "All except a young drummer boy, who the British spared.

"Later in the afternoon, French artillery set the château and barn alight. A lot of wounded, from both sides, died in the barn, and the château was destroyed in the fire. In all, about 10,000 men were lost in the fight for Hougoumont alone. Over three quarters of them were French."

"Crivens!" breathes Gravee.

"But the saddest thing for me," Henry concludes, "Is that despite all the men that were killed or wounded in and around Hougoumont, the offensive against the farm was basically a diversion for the main attacks against Wellington's ridge."

"It's been said before," states Jaspa. "But you really do have a gift for storytelling, Henry."

The boy blushes slightly.

"Jaspa's right," agrees Ben, earnestly. "But we'd best be getting back to help the girls. Otherwise Abi will have some storytelling of her own to do... while bending our ears!"

***

Ben cups his hands around his mouth and calls, "Abi! Sam! Can you hear me?"

"Yes!" comes back Abi's reply a few moments later, muffled slightly by the gusting wind and the distance. "We're coming to meet you!"

They continue to yell back and forth every five or 10 seconds, each time their voices sounding louder to the other.

"I can hear them coming," says Bisckits.

A few moments later Jaspa also hears the crack of twigs from the girls' approach. It reminds him of the crackle of musket fire from yesterday's re-enactment. That, combined with an acute awareness of where he is and how many men died nearby, sends a violent shiver down his spine.

"Are ye all reit, laddie?" asks Gravee.

"Just thinking about what happened here again," Jaspa responds. "It felt like someone walked on my grave."

"I ken whit ye mean."

Sam and Abi come into view, zigzagging between the trees.

"Any luck?" enquires Henry.

"None at all," confesses Abi. "We decided to start at the southern edge of the wood, but we didn't see many oaks down there."

"We've been looking for oak leaves on the ground first," Sam informs the new arrivals. "That helps us find the right type of tree. Then we compare them with the one in the photo."

"That's a good plan," acknowledges Ben.

"Actually, it was Phyllis's idea," Sam admits.

"Well done Phyllis," grins Jaspa.

***

After a brief discussion, they decide to try and cover the area as systematically as possible. Starting at the north end of the wood, the four children form a line, roughly 20 feet apart, and attempt to walk more-or-less parallel to Chemin du Goumont. The Ses perch on their friends' shoulders, acting as spotters.

Unfortunately, they all fail to properly account for how much slower progress through the wood is compared to walking along the lane, even if you're not continually stopping to look for oak leaves and stare at trees. Combine that with the fact that the spoiler photo was taken in winter, with no leaves on the trees, and it's now the middle of summer, and the task at hand becomes even more of a challenge. The wind flailing the branches around, and whipping up fallen leaves, doesn't help either.

Unsurprisingly then, while it took them less than five minutes to hike from one side of the wood to the other along the track, after 20 minutes among the trees, they've still not finished their second traverse.

"This is going to take forever," groans Ben, as they stop to examine yet another potential contender for what will be the most beautiful tree ever, if they manage to find it.

"Or perhaps even longer!" adds Bisckits, dryly.

"I cannae see any other option," says Gravee. "We've nae way o' knowin' whether it's hidden near th' edges or in th' middle."

"If we're realistic, we don't even know for sure that it's in this wood at all," Bisckits points out.

"That's true. But this is definitely our best bet," counters Jaspa. "What other choice do we have but to keep looking?"

***

Another fruitless half hour of fraught stumbling through the underbrush goes by. They're all on the verge of despair, and Ben is about to call it a day.

When a squeal echoes through the trees.

"Ben!" cries Sam

"What's the matter?" Ben calls back, looking across at his sister, understandably worried that something bad has happened to her.

Thankfully, it's immediately clear that Sam is fine. She waves impatiently at her big brother. "Bring the photo here!" she yells, her voice high and tight with excitement.

Ben rushes over, joined by the Greanings.

"What is it?" asks Abi, breathlessly.

Sam, Portia and Phyllis are almost buzzing with nervous energy, as the little girl reveals, "We think we might have found the tree!"

***

Sam's excitement is contagious, and Ben fumbles as he tries to hurriedly get his mum's phone out of his pocket. His over-eagerness again slows him down as he tries to unlock the device. Twice he inputs the wrong number sequence.

"Och! Mair haste, less speed, laddie," Gravee quotes the old proverb unhelpfully.

Finally, the phone unlocks with an artificial click and the crucial photo reappears. All eyes flick backwards and forwards between the image on the screen and the real tree in front of them.

"It could be the right tree," reasons Henry. "The trunk splits into two, like in the photo, then one of the limbs splits again."

"We should try walking around the tree," suggests Phyllis. "See if we can try and find the same view as shown in the image."

Ben holds the phone slightly above head height in his left hand and begins to slowly circle the oak. The others move in unison with him, pressed close to his back. They all stare repeatedly up at the tree, then at the photo on the phone, then back at the tree.

191

"Stop," demands Portia. "Move a bit closer in."

"That's our tree!" whoops Jaspa.

"It certainly looks like it," agrees Abi. "The shape seems right and..."

"No! That's definitely our tree," insists Jaspa once again, pointing at the trunk. "The metal tag's right there!"

***

Eight pairs of eyes focus on Jaspa's finger and then track along the imaginary line that sprouts from its tip. At the other end of that line is a small, silver-coloured tag, attached to the tree about 5½ feet off the ground with two screws. Engraved on the tag between the screw heads is a string of four letters and two numbers: *GCAC68*.

"We found it," breathes Henry. He starts to chuckle. "I can't believe we actually found it!"

"What do you mean?" asks Ben, also laughing. "It was your idea that got us here. Yours and Jaspa's."

"Well... I know..." stutters the older boy. "But I guess I didn't really think it would work. Not until right now."

"Me neither," confesses Jaspa. "It was a bit of a long shot, to say the least!"

"So you two had us crashing around in the woods based on a plan that neither of you really believed would work?" asks Portia in disbelief, although still smiling.

"I was confident our ideas made sense," replies Jaspa, a little defensively. Henry also looks a bit disappointed. "But there was no guarantee we were right. We admitted that before we started. I thought everyone was clear on that."

"Hey! I'm not criticising!" his cousin assures him. "Far from it. Thanks to you and Henry we just managed to find one particular tree, in a wood, on a battlefield covering a couple of square miles, with only a vague photo on a cell phone screen to go on. I think you both deserve medals!"

"Hear, hear!" cries Abi.

***

After a lot of congratulations and slapping each other on the back, Gravee returns them slightly closer to Earth. "We'd better sign th' logbook an' be on oor way, dinnae yers think?" he suggests. "Time's gettin' on, an' its gonnae start rainin' sooner or later, ye ken."

Still full of beans after their improbable success, the friends nonetheless see the sense in the Dogses' advice and set about locating the actual cache. After five minutes, however, their jovial mood has once more been shattered.

"This is ridiculous!" rants Ben, irritably. "We know exactly what the cache container looks like from the spoiler photo. We know it's hidden by the tree with the tag. And against all the odds, we even know where the tree with the tag is!"

Yet they still can't find the cache itself!

***

"Crivens, Henry, ye greit galoot!" calls Gravee. "Will ye nae watch where yer puttin' them stonkin' greit boats o' yers! Ye'll dae a Ses a mischief, if yer nae careful."

With the hunt for the elusive cache container clearly hitting another speed bump, the Ses have joined in the hunt at ground level. Literally.

"Sorry," apologises Henry. "I'm still not used to having to watch out for little creatures around my feet." Realising that perhaps that wasn't the best choice of words, he quickly adds, "No offence meant."

"Och! None taken," the Dogses assures him. "Although I cannae promise that won't change if ye step on me!"

"Fair enough," Henry concedes.

***

A sudden gust of wind knocks Portia onto her bottom. "Well, that was undignified," she protests.

Phyllis leans over and offers her new friend a hand. Portia accepts the Frogses' help with a wry smile and stands back up again. "Thanks," she says, brushing some dirt off her behind.

"Is geocaching always this difficult?" wonders Phyllis.

"I don't think so," replies Portia. "Although, to be honest, this is only our third cache."

Another squall funnels between the tree trunks, but this time Portia is ready for it. The latest gust is accompanied by a dull rat-a-tat-tat high up in the canopy.

"That doesn't sound promising," notes Phyllis.

Although, so far they're protected down here beneath the leaves and branches, some intermittent rain has clearly started to fall outside the wood.

***

They've exhausted everywhere they can think of. They've looked all around the tree. Twice. Three times.

They expanded their search all the neighbouring bushes, shrubs and trees.

Nothing!

"This is so unfair!" whines Sam.

Ben begins scouring through the cache's photo gallery, in the hope there might be another clue to the container's whereabouts.

"Could it be up the tree itself?" wonders Bisckits.

"Maybe," admits Henry. "My gut says it isn't, but the cache does have a terrain rating of 3½ stars, so I guess it might be."

"If you give me a lift up, I can go and take a look," the little Giraffeses offers.

Jaspa, Portia and Gravee exchange glances. "I'm not so sure that's a good idea," says Jaspa.

Bisckits opens his mouth to object, but the words freeze on his tongue, as he spies a small shape flashing towards them through trees. Its speed and path instantly give away the fact this is no leaf on a breeze. It's moving way too fast and with too much purpose.

Bisckits rapidly rearranges the words he was about to say into something more useful. "Gravee! Get down" he yells.

Instinctively, the Dogses instantly follows his young friend's advice. He throws himself to the ground, but not quickly enough to prevent two sets of talons from raking up his back, ripping out large clumps of fur along the way.

"*Vive L'Empereur!*"

***

Chapter Twenty-Two

Crash

"Owww!" Gravee screams, although more in shock and anger than actual pain. "That hurt, ye wee scunner!"

The Falconses banks through the trees like a tiny, enraged fighter jet. He turns fast and tight, his flight muscles straining from the effort and g-forces he inflicts upon them. Staying so low his wingtips almost brush the ground, he skilfully avoids the numerous obstacles in his path and sets up his next run.

The second assault comes from the side. Gravee again drops to the ground, but not fast enough to avoid losing another clump of white fur.

"I'm gettin' reit tired o' this," he snarls, but the Falconses has already disappeared.

***

The Birdses has clearly upped his game since their last encounter. No longer does he waste energy shouting useless threats as he approaches.

On the plus side, at least this means Gravee doesn't have to put up with any verbal abuse this time around. Unfortunately, it also means the Falconses is much more focused on the task at hand. What's worse, the silent attacks mean it's almost impossible for Gravee and his friends to hear their adversary coming until he's literally on top of them. Especially over the noise of the wind.

It also soon becomes obvious that Ben managing to land a blow on the Birdses this morning was a total fluke. The new and improved Falconses makes his attacks and is gone long before any of the four humans can even react. Although they continue to try.

Time and again the Birdses presses home his hit and run strategy, with intense efficiency. All Gravee can do is try and dodge the worst of the onslaught, while his friends are more-or-less forced to watch helplessly.

"I'm gonnae be bald as a coot if this carries on much longer," complains the Dogses. He's lost count how many flybys his adversary has made already, but he's pretty sure he could figure it out by totalling up his cuts, scrapes and patches of missing fur.

***

Yet again the Falconses approaches low and fast, this time from behind. But instead of simply lashing out at his enemy on the way past, as he's done up until now, he decides to attempt something more daring.

A split-second before crashing into Gravee, the Falconses pulls his taloned feet up in front of himself and gives his tail a flick. At the speed he's travelling, the subtle movement rockets him upwards.

He misses the Dogses back by a hair's breadth, reaching out with both feet as he passes. Eight razor-sharp talons bite into Gravee's shoulders, gripping like anchors, as the Birdses lifts him bodily off the ground.

"Owww!" Gravee screams again. But this time he really means it!

Unfortunately (or fortunately), the Falconses doesn't seem to have thought his latest plan through properly. Most significantly, he's apparently completely ignored the fact that Gravee is a least twice as big as he is.

Instead of soaring off into the wild blue yonder with his prey gripped firmly in his talons, the additional weight drags the Birdses back down, pitching him suddenly forwards. He immediately releases his captive, but it's too late. With an odd thump, hunter and hunted both collide violently with the ground.

In a blur of limbs, fur and feathers, the pair half-tumble, half-slide, through the leaf litter. They finally come to rest against the trunk of the oak with the metal plate screwed to it.

***

Gravee's friends rush over to the crash site, where the Dogses is already pulling himself up into sitting position.

"Are you alright?" frets Jaspa.

"Aye, I'm fine," he replies crossly. "Nae thanks tae this bampot!"

To be truthful, the Dogses looks in desperate need of a good bath and brush, and has tiny rivulets of blood running from each of the eight small puncture wounds in his shoulders. But otherwise, considering what he's been through, he doesn't seem too badly off. At least not physically.

Gravee's mental state is another story. He's quite obviously—and understandably—furious. "Whit on Earth is ye problem?" he yells at the Falconses, who has yet to get up. "Whit huv I done tae deserve this? Ye dinnae even ken who I am!"

Still the Birdses lies still, unmoving.

"Is he all reit?" wonders Gravee, his anger rapidly melting into concern.

Phyllis quickly crossed to the prone Birdses, who is lying face down against the tree. She gently checks around his neck, before carefully turning him onto his back.

The Falconses' feathers are ruffled and dirty after his skid across the ground, and there are some fresh, deep scratches on his hooked beak. The wound Jaspa and Gravee had noticed above his right eye this morning has reopened and is oozing blood. A bump is already coming up in the same place. Thankfully though, his chest is rising and falling regularly beneath his feathers.

"I think he's just unconscious," Phyllis announces after a few moment. "He may have a slight concussion from hitting his head. But other than that he seems to be all right, as far as I can tell. I expect he'll wake up on his own before too long. In the meantime, I should try and clean that cut. Does anyone have any water left? And perhaps a paper tissue?" she asks.

"I've got some water," Sam replies, taking a plastic bottle out of her pocket.

"And here's a tissue," says Abi, handing one to the Frogses.

"Could you poor a little water into the cap for me, Sam?" Phyllis asks, ripping a corner off the tissue.

"*Tubby*," says Portia suddenly, tapping the side of her mouth thoughtfully. "Or perhaps *Hefty*."

"Sorry?" asks Abi.

"I give people nicknames," Portia explains. "It's kinda my thing. So Bisckits is Bizzee, and Jaspa is Waver. But after all this time I still haven't found one for Gravee that I'm happy with."

"Well, it isnae goin' tae be Tubby!" Gravee declares.

"I don't know," the Giraffeses jokes, much to the amusement of everyone else. "Luckily for you, you're clearly packing a bit of extra weight. Otherwise our Falconses friend here would have carried you away to who-knows-where."

"Hey!" Gravee objects. "I'll huv ye know, I've lost over half an ounce since New Year!"

***

Now he knows Gravee and the Falconses are both unharmed, Jaspa decides to investigate something he thought was strange about their initial

199

impact. He grabs a stick and heads towards the spot where the two Ses first smashed into the ground.

"What are you doing?" wonders Bisckits the Inquisitive, following along.

"The ground's pretty solid around here, isn't it?" asks Jaspa in return.

"Yeah," his brother replies, rolling his eyes. "Ground is usually like that."

"Not always," Jaspa contradicts. "Some ground can be quite loose and soft... Like a marsh... Or the Shifting Sands back home."

"Fair enough," Bisckits concedes. "I guess the ground here is pretty solid, when you put it like that."

"So, did you hear the noise Gravee and that Birdses made when they hit the ground?"

"Not really," admits Bisckits. "I was too busy wincing."

"It sounded strange," Jaspa tells his brother.

"What do you mean?"

Jaspa takes the stick he's carrying and drives its end into the earth as hard as he can. The result is a dull thud that immediately dies away. "That's the sound you'd expect to hear, right?"

"I suppose so," agrees Bisckits, still unsure of what his older brother is getting at.

Jaspa walks the last few inches to the start of the trail ploughed through the leaf litter by the colliding Dogses and Falconses. He lifts his stick up high and once again brings it down with all his strength.

The noise the staff and ground make this time is altogether different. Instead of a flat thud that cuts off instantly, this sound is a rounder, thrumming note that lingers for a second or two.

"It's hollow!" exclaims Bisckits.

***

The brothers brush away some more leaves, and discover a flat piece of wood beneath.

"Can we get some help over here?" calls Jaspa, excitedly.

The McRaes and Greanings come to see what the fuss is all about, leaving Portia, Gravee and Phyllis with the still-unconscious Falconses.

"What have you found?" asks Ben curiously.

Sam takes a more practical approach. She kneels down behind the two Giraffeses and takes over their leaf-removal duties. In a matter of moments she's uncovered a rectangular piece of plywood, approximately 15 inches long and six inches wide.

"Is that what I think it is?" enquires Abi, her hand nervously covering her mouth.

Sam digs her fingernails under one end of the wood and prises it up. Underneath is a wood-lined hole, slightly smaller than the cover plate, and about nine inches deep.

Snugly nestled in the buried compartment is an green metal case. Grasping the handle on top, Sam extracts an ammunition box, instantly recognisable as the one from the spoiler photo.

Ben punches the air. "Take that, Anakev!" he yells triumphantly.

***

Even before the cache container is out of the ground, the difference in everyone's mood is like night and day. They're all ecstatic to have found the cache, especially after Gobber's deceitful cheating. The change in Sam is particularly striking. Gone is the nervous little girl on the verge of tears, replaced by the bubbly Sam they all know and love.

With a grunt of effort, Henry levers open the handle of the box and peers inside. As with the other two caches they've found, it contains an assortment of odds and ends.

"Anything good in there?" wonders Biscuits.

201

"Nah," replies Henry, passing the blue logbook to his sister. "Looks like mostly junk to me."

Abi takes the offered book and flicks through it, glancing at the previous logs. Most appear to be written in either Dutch or French—the official languages of Belgium—but there are quite a few in English.

The entries indicate that, in addition to a lot of native Belgians, geocachers from as far afield as France, the Netherlands, Germany, the UK and Austria have found the cache. One odd-sounding family calling themselves Geddorna seem to have travelled all the way down from Sweden. There's even a couple with the caching name Ußtastic, from Phyllis's homeland, Canada.

"Hey! I've found Jimmy and Laurel's log," declares Abi. "Thanks for a fantastic adventure, *JKL*," she reads.

"What does Gobber's log say?" wonders Jaspa.

"*I'm a complete pain in the neck, love and hugs, Anakev*," Bisckits suggests.

Abi flicks back and forth through the logbook. "I can't find a log by *Anakev Skywalker*," she says eventually, with a frown.

"Oh well," says Henry. "So long as our names are in the book."

In response, Abi accepts a pen from Ben and proceeds to date and sign the logbook on behalf of *HenAb* and *Jaspa's Journeyers*. "Now it's official," she grins.

***

Leaving the humans to do the paperwork, the two brothers return to the tree. "Any change with our uninvited guest?" enquires Jaspa as they approach.

"His pulse seems stronger," replies Phyllis, who is in the process of placing another piece of moistened tissue on the Falconses' forehead. "I expect he'll wake up before too long."

"How do you know so much about this stuff?" wonders Bisckits, impressed.

"It's all thanks to Signal," Phyllis shrugs. "These days, all Frogses parents use the knowledge he collected to teach their tadpoles how to look after themselves and others."

***

Chapter Twenty-Three

François

Unlike on TV or in the movies, there's no fake groan, or cough, or eye rubbing to warn them that the Falconses is about to wake up. He simply opens his eyes slowly and nervously looks around. The sight of five Ses standing over him registers as confusion and a touch of fear. He instinctively attempts to push himself up to sitting and scrabble away using his wings like arms.

"It's okay," Phyllis reassures him. "No one's going to hurt you."

The Birdses relaxes slightly, but still seems wary. He tries to say something, but it comes out as a dry croak.

Phyllis offers the Falconses a drink from the plastic bottle cap, which is as big as a bowl to the Ses. He dips his hooked beak to the water and a small, pink tongue laps thirstily at the liquid.

"*Merci*," he says. "Zank you."

"You're welcome," the Frogses replies. "My name is Phyllis, by the way. And this are my friends: Portia, Gravee, Jaspa and Bisckits."

"*Je m'appelle*... er... I mean, I am called François," the Falconses introduces himself. "Where am I?"

"You're in a wood near Hougoumont Château," Portia informs him. "Do you remember what happened?"

François thinks for a moment before answering slowly, as if it's coming back to him as he speaks. "I was flying over zee battle, admiring zee wonderful French cavalry wiz zee magnificent golden eagles. Zen zere was zee big bang and many smoke..."

Obviously trying to remember, François touches the wound above his right eye with his wingtip. The resulting tenderness causes him to flinch.

"An' zen I woke up 'ere."

***

"He is the Falconses we were watching at the re-enactment," declares Bisckits. "I knew it!"

"Ye ken it wisnae th' real Battle of Waterloo, reit?" Gravee asks the Birdses, warily.

"But of course!" François looks at the Dogses as if he's just sprouted a second head. "Everyone knows zee Battle of Waterloo was happening 200 yearz ago."

"Thank goodness we finally agree on that," says Gravee, breathing out heavily.

"The bang and smoke you remember were from a volley of musket fire," Jaspa tells François. "Bisckits saw you fly into the smoke cloud, but you never came out. We went looking for you, but all we found was a patch of blood, probably from that cut on your head, I'm guessing."

The Falconses touches the wound on his temple one more. "You came to 'elp me?" he asks, sounding surprised.

"Imagine that," replies Gravee, with more than a touch of sarcasm.

François stares at the Dogses for a long moment, a hint of recognition dawning. "You zeem veree familiar to me," he says finally.

"I should hope I would," declares Gravee hotly. "Ye've been trying tae kill me all day!"

***

François looks horrified. "But zat is reediculous!" he exclaims. "Why on Earth would I want to 'urt you?"

"I huvnae got a Scooby," admits Gravee. "Ye tell me."

"Eet eez nonsense!" says the Falconses stubbornly. "I do not beelieve eet!"

"Are ye callin' me a liar?" Gravee growls.

The Falconses attempts to stand up in order to confront his accuser. Unfortunately, the effort brings on a wave of dizziness. His head spins, his eyes start to roll upwards in their sockets, and he tips sideways. Ironically, it's the Dogses who catches his fall.

"I'm afraid what Gravee says is true, François," says Portia, gently. "We've all seen it."

The others nod their heads, as Portia tells the Falconses about the attacks throughout the day. First near the Inniskilling Memorial. Then on the way to the Prussian Monument. And most recently here in these woods, just a short while ago.

"But why would I want to 'urt you?" François asks again, almost pleading. "I am not a violent Ses."

"I might have an idea about that, eh," replies Phyllis. "I reckon it's to do with that gash and lump above your eye. Perhaps you got confused in the musket smoke, or perhaps the sudden blast of air was the problem. In any case, I'm guessing you ended up colliding with a musket, or a soldier, or even the ground. That's how you ended up with that nasty cut."

"But zat does not explain why I would suddenly start attacking zee people," the Birdses objects.

"Not on its own, no," Phyllis agrees. "But the impact also caused a bump on your head. If there was swelling on the inside as well, it might explain why you've been acting so strangely."

"If I'd known it were all in his heid, I'd huv lobbed Mrs McRae's cell phone at him," Gravee whispers to Jaspa.

François doesn't hear the Dogses' joke. He just stares at Phyllis, astonished by what she and the others are suggesting. He finds the whole thing impossible to believe. And yet he's unable to come up with a better reason for the black gap in his memory.

"But why would François think he was back at the real Battle of Waterloo," wonders Bisckits.

"Possibly, because of what he was doing when he was injured," suggests Phyllis, "But I think there's more to it than that. Would you mind me asking when you were born, François?"

The Falconses looks at her warily, obviously trying to see the trap in the question. "1797," he answers slowly.

"But that's impossible!" declares Ben. "That'd make you more than 200 years old!"

"*Mon dieu!*" exclaims the shocked Birdses, again trying to thrust himself backwards. "They can see and hear us?"

***

François is already having trouble accepting what Phyllis, Gravee and the others are telling him. And then suddenly things take an even more bizarre and frightening turn.

Ses are used to being around humans. Yet for the most part they don't pay them very much attention, except to keep out of the way of their clumsy feet. So although the Falconses had noticed the four children standing close by, he'd pretty much ignored them.

Until now!

"It's all right," Portia assures the terrified Birdses. "They're our friends." She tries to place a comforting hand on his shoulder, but he shies rapidly away.

Jaspa had been surprised when Phyllis had calmly accepted that the McRaes and Greanings could see her when they first met. But François's reaction is much closer to what he expects. Clearly the Falconses had no clue that Seers really exist. Imagine a cow in a field you're walking through suddenly starts speaking to you, and you'll have some idea how he feels.

"I'm guessing you grew up around here," says Phyllis, speaking gently, in an attempt to calm the Falconses.

"*Oui*," he confirms distractedly, as he continues to stare unblinkingly at the humans.

"And I bet you saw the battle, didn't you?" Phyllis persists. "The real one, I mean."

"But, of course," Francois agrees, dragging his attention back to the Frogses. "Alzough I was still veree young at ze time."

"But there's no way he's 200," repeats Ben. "It's impossible!"

The Falconses flinches, almost as if he's been struck, wrenched back to this strange new world when humans can see and talk to Ses.

"Two hundred is gettin' up there, I'll grant ye," says Gravee, addressing Ben's objection. "But some Ses can live a lot langer than whit ye might call 'regular animals'. A lot langer."

"But over 200 years?" protests Ben.

"Actually, I met a Leopard Tortoises on my Journey who was almost 350," Portia puts in.

Bisckits whistles, impressed.

"Wow!" breathes Jaspa. "Imagine how much of the World you could see in 350 years!"

"Not very much at the speed she travelled," chuckles Portia.

"In François's case, it could explain a lot, if you think about it," says Phyllis, bringing the Giraffeses' conversation back on track. "He'd been watching the re-enactment and got a nasty bump on the head. Somehow in his confusion, he thought he was back watching the real battle. But this time believed he had some part to play in it."

"So why was he focussed on Gravee, instead of the rest of us?" asks Jaspa.

"This is all just guesswork," Phyllis admits, "But if François did believe he was taking part in the Battle of Waterloo, then naturally the British became the enemy. And Gravee was the only Ses with a British accent in the neighbourhood."

"Lucky me!" observes Gravee.

"Thankfully, this latest tumble seems to have knocked you back to your senses," Phyllis consoles the Falconses.

***

"I'm sorry, but we really need to be leaving soon," Abi apologises.

Phyllis shakes her head. "François can't be left alone yet," she informs them.

"*Non!*" the Falconses disagrees forcefully. "I will bee fine."

"He needs someone to keep an eye on him for the next couple of hours, at least," the Frogses declares firmly, ignoring her patient. "Preferably overnight."

"*Non!*" François almost begs. "Pleeze go!"

"Changed his tune, hasn't he?" chuckles Gravee. "He's been chasin' after us all day, an' suddenly he wants rid o' us!"

"Overnight?" says Henry, shaking his head. "There's no way we'll get away with a couple of hours, let alone overnight."

"He's right," agrees Abi. "We're probably already in a heap of trouble after Ben's little deception this morning. We can't afford to get into any more by being late."

Not for the first time today, Ben looks sheepish.

"It's not a problem," says Jaspa. "You head back to the visitor centre and we'll stay with François."

"We're not leaving you behind," Sam argues.

"Och! We'll be fine, lassie," Gravee assures her. "We'll make sure this wee bampot is okay, and then find oor own way back to th' Eurostar Station."

"Or we could go to the airport," Bisckits the Aviator suggests eagerly.

"Aye," agrees Gravee. "Or we could dae that."

"But..." begins Ben.

"Crivens, laddie!" exclaims the Dogses. "It wudnae be th' first time we've made oor own way hame." His voice softens, "Ye'll see... We'll be back in Edinburgh afore ye can say *Greyfriars' Bobby.*"

Ben sighs, realising the battle is already lost.

***

"You know, there's no need for any of you to stay really, eh," says Phyllis. "I can handle this just fine on my own."

"We know," replies Jaspa. "But it doesn't seem fair to leave you alone."

"Seriously?" laughs Phyllis. "I've been travelling on my own for most of the last six months. Besides, I get the feeling François could use the space right now."

"*Oui!*" agrees the Falconses urgently. "I will bee no trouble pour Mademoiselle Frogses."

"What do you think?" Jaspa asks the other Ses.

Portia looks unconvinced.

"You're heading back to Scotland tomorrow, anyway," adds Phyllis. "And I've still got unfinished business in Brussels. So we'd be going our separate ways in the morning in any case."

"I'd feel better if the four of you came home with us," admits Sam, quietly.

"There you go then!" grins Phyllis. "It's agreed!"

***

Ben, Sam, Abi and Henry say their goodbyes to Phyllis, then walk a short distance away to allow the Ses to say theirs. François relaxes noticeably.

Following the traditional Ses method of greeting and parting, Jaspa goes to clasps arms with Phyllis, but she surprises him by giving him a big hug instead. One by one, Gravee, Portia and Bisckits also hug the Frogses.

François doesn't seem the hugging type. At least not today.

"I guess this is it, then," shrugs Jaspa. "It was great meeting you."

"Likewise," replies Phyllis.

"Thanks for comin' tae oor rescue against ye ken who," says Gravee, nodding in François's direction.

"No problem."

"An' if ye're ever in Scotland, Edinburgh's a bonnie wee toon," Gravee adds.

"I'll be sure to stop by Greyfriars Kirkyard if I visit," Phyllis promises.

"I only wish we could have spent longer together," says Portia.

"Yeah!" agrees Bisckits. "We could have had some real fun!"

"Another time, perhaps."

"I'm going to hold you to that," says Jaspa, pointing a warning finger at Phyllis. "And I haven't forgotten that you never did tell me your story about meeting a Seer."

"Next time," she grins. "I promise."

Jaspa and his friends are about to walk away when, to their surprise, François stops them. "Zank you for everything," he says shyly. "Zank you for trying to 'elp me at the battle. And zank you for beeing so understanding about evereething since."

Portia treats him a big smile. "You're very welcome."

The Falconses sighs and looks directly at Gravee. "I am sorree for all zee trouble I made you."

"Dinnae be daft, laddie," the Dogses replies. "I'll be a greit story when we get back hame!"

***

211

The four Ses make their way over to the children. Jaspa and Gravee take their usual place on Ben's shoulder, while Sam helps Portia and Bisckits into her hood.

Looking backwards, Jaspa continues to wave goodbye to Phyllis and François, until they're lost from sight among the trees.

***

Chapter Twenty-Four

End of an Empire

"I still can't believe we found the cache!" declares Ben happily, as they make their way through the trees back to Chemin du Goumont. "Gobber's going to be furious. Especially after all the effort he put into making sure we wouldn't."

"Don't you mean Anakev?" grins Bisckits.

Something occurs to Jaspa. "What if doesn't believe you found it?" he asks.

"Henry thought of that already," the boy replies. He reaches into his pocket, takes out his mum's smartphone, and types in the unlock code. Ben selects the *Photos* app, which opens to reveal a picture of himself, Sam and Abi holding the cache above their heads, looking victorious.

"Nice one," Gravee compliments him.

"I photographed the logbook, too," Henry informs them. "After we signed it, of course."

"It had a rocky start," says Abi. "But it turned out to be an incredible day, didn't it?"

"And it didn't even rain," adds Sam, as a gust of chill wind makes her shiver.

"Oh-oh!" laughs Portia. "Now you've said it!"

"Thanks Sam!" Henry pretends to complain. "Now it'll definitely start raining on the way back to the visitor centre."

Ben suddenly sprints off towards the road. "Then we'd better get a shift on, if we want to outrun it," he calls cheerfully over his shoulder.

"In ye dreams!" exclaims Gravee. "Ye might be a Seer, laddie, but ye'll never be a Ses!"

Laughing and joking, the four children and their Ses passengers race each other to the edge of the woods. They tumble recklessly out onto the windy lane that leads down to Hougoumont.

And almost knock over the person in the blue rain jacket.

***

"Watch where you're going!" a familiar voice protests.

"We're sorry," Abi quickly apologises. "We didn't see you."

"Well perhaps you should pay more attention to where you're going, Abi Greaning," says the woman, removing her hood.

"You?" gasps Sam.

"I knew it!" says Jaspa.

***

"You've been following us all day?" asks Ben.

"Of course," scoffs Diane. "You didn't really think we'd let you go wandering about the Belgian countryside without keeping an eye on you, did you? How incompetent do you think we are?"

"We?" wonders Abi. "Laurel and Jimmy know about this?"

"It was their idea," Diane confirms. "You all seemed so desperate last night to do this alone, that Jimmy guessed you might pull some kind of stunt this morning."

"Yeah, about that," says Ben, awkwardly. "I'm really sorry about what I said. I didn't mean it."

"I know," replies Diane, mussing his hair. "No hard feelings."

"I'm not sure Dennis will agree," sighs Ben.

"Oh, Dennis is fine," the young woman disagrees. "He was in on the whole thing."

Ben looks greatly relieved.

214

"Actually, I thought you'd figured out our little trick at one point."

"When?" Henry enquires.

"Going across the fields between Papelotte and Plancenoit," Diane replies. "Just after Sam waved to me."

"I thought you were another geocacher," Sam admits. "I was just trying to help."

"I got that," says Diane. "But you nearly gave me a heart attack after you got to the Prussian Monument and then started coming back."

"Ben dropped his mum's smartphone," explains Abi. She looks around at her friends, none of whom can meet her eye.

"Well, lucky for me he didn't lose it any earlier," replies Diane, believing the recycled white lie. "I hid behind some bushes beside the track, less than 50 yards from where you must have found it. If you'd had to backtrack any further, you would have caught me for sure."

"That was lucky," Jaspa says to Gravee.

"Nae kiddin'."

"And I was starting to worry again just now," Diane continues, unaware of the Ses. "Laurel had told me the final of the geocache was in these woods, but you seemed to be in there an awfully long time."

"We had trouble finding it," Henry confesses.

"Well, I've been walking up and down this lane for the last half an hour. I was afraid I'd missed you, and that you'd somehow slipped past me and were already on your way back to the visitor centre. But without a GPS to lead me to the cache location, I didn't want to come into the woods after you, in case I missed you in there."

***

They leave the trees behind and head out into the fields, backtracking via Chemin des Vertes Bornes along the Allies' ridge towards Lion Mound.

Sporadic gusts of wind deliver the occasional spatter of rain, producing infrequent concentric rings in pothole puddles.

Diane looks at Ben, who has become increasingly quiet and withdrawn over the last ten minutes. "What's wrong, Ben?" she asks.

"Nothing," he replies, although this is clearly not true.

"You found the cache didn't you?"

"Yes," he answers with a sigh. "Not that it matters anymore."

"Why not?"

"Oh no!" exclaims Abi. "Gobber!"

"Oh no!" groans Sam, turning white.

"What about Gobber?" asks Diane, confused.

"The thing is, Ben made a bet with Gobber that we'd find the cache," answers Abi. She doesn't mention that Sam also made a bet with the bully. "But it had to be on our own. With no adult help."

"But I didn't help you," Diane points out.

"Yes, but Gobber won't believe that," replies Ben with a resigned shrug. "And even if he does, it won't stop him telling everyone what a little kid I was and how you had to help me."

"But I didn't help you!" repeats Diane adamantly.

"I doesn't matter," says Abi. "Gobber has it in for Ben. He won't let a little thing like the truth get in the way. He'll have a field day embarrassing Ben at school."

"I'm sorry, Ben," Diane apologises. "But we didn't know. And even if we had, what would your parents have said if we'd really let you go off completely unsupervised?

"I guess they wouldn't have been very happy," Ben concedes.

"Jimmy and Laurel tried to give you as much freedom as they could," says Diane. "But ultimately, your safety is their responsibility, so they had no choice but to have me keep an eye on you."

"And Gobber no doubt knew that when he pushed you into making that bet," concludes Henry with a grimace. "We already know he cheated by removing the final coordinates."

"He didn't!" gasps Diane.

"Yeah," replies Abi. "He really did."

***

Halfway back to Lion Mound hamlet, Henry stops to get one final look down the slope of Wellington's ridge and across the battlefield.

"Go on, then," Ben encourages him (mainly to take his mind off his upcoming confrontation with Gobber). "Tell us how the battle ended."

Henry looks at his friend, checking that he really wants to hear this. Ben gives him a small grin and nod.

"Well... It's just after 7 o'clock in the evening and we've reached the turning point of the battle," Henry begins. "The French cavalry attacks have failed and retreated, and Napoleon's forces have more-or-less abandoned their unsuccessful offensive on Hougoumont. But the fall of La Haye Sainte sets the scene for the Emperor's final play.

"Through death, injury and desertion, Wellington's main line has shrunk to something like 35,000 troops, by this point. It now stretches from Hougoumont to just east of the Brussels road. One more assault and Napoleon will smash through these abused Allied defences. One more push and he'll shatter the Duke's exhausted and battered army to pieces and send it sprinting for the English Channel.

"And the Emperor has saved his best troops for just this moment. It's time for him to unleash his beloved Imperial Guard.

"To victory!"

***

"The French artillery redouble their bombardment of the ridge we're now standing on. Again the Allied infantry are ordered to lie down behind the crest." Henry points to the gentle northern slope of the ridge, away from the valley where most of the bloodshed occurred.

"The soldiers stay as low as they can, hoping and praying they'll survive the hail of shells and cannonballs. So only Wellington's officers see more than 5000 infantrymen of the Imperial Guard form into column and begin their advance across the valley, beneath the protective canopy of flying metal.

"The Imperial Guard is Napoleon's elite bodyguard. Each man is hand-picked. The Best!" Henry tells them with a flourish. "And the Best of the Best are the veterans of the Old Guard.

"The rest of the French army are in awe of the Guard, calling them *The Immortals*. Now, on the spot where the cavalry failed, the infantry of the Imperial Guard will hammer their way through the Allies' lines and give victory to their Emperor."

***

"Three columns of Imperial Guard approach the crest of the ridge. When they're only 30 yards away, Wellington commands his infantry to stand up and fire," Henry continues his timeless tale.

"The French are taken completely by surprise. One minute there's a clear path to glory. And the next, thousands of Allied soldiers seem to rise up out of the ground and start punishing them with musket and cannon fire.

"Those men from the decimated front ranks of the French columns still alive and able to walk try to halt. But the momentum and weight of those behind continues to push them forwards.

"In the meantime, British, German and Dutch-Belgian troops wrap around their flanks and savage them with musket fire from three sides at close range. The defenders' efficient gunmanship takes a terrible toll on the French infantry.

"Until now, the Guard have never been defeated. But all that is about to change. With almost half their number already down, the unthinkable happens... The Emperor's invincible Imperial Guard stops.

"Then begins to fall back.

"And while some of the Guard retreat in good order, others break and flee. The message to the rest of the French army is clear:

"The Immortals have been beaten. All is lost. Run for your lives!"

***

"The enemy is broken and on the run," Henry winds-up his story. "But Wellington doesn't want to give them any opportunity to change their minds. So he releases his army to charge the retreating French and drive them from his battlefield.

"For the last four days, a portion of Napoleon's forces has fought the Prussians in a series of battles and smaller skirmishes to the east of Waterloo, in an effort to keep Blücher's soldiers from joining those commanded by Wellington. Now, in the dying moments of the Battle of Waterloo, the Allied and Prussian armies finally come together, to clinch victory and pursue the French all the way back to Paris.

"Less than a month later, Napoleon surrenders to the captain of a British ship, marking the end of the French Empire. And bringing to a close over 20 years of war that had engulfed the whole of Europe."

"Crivens!" says Gravee, not for the first time today.

***

Chapter Twenty-Five

What Goes Around. . .

In the end, they get back to Lion Mound with twenty minutes to spare before their prearranged pick-up time. A steady, persistent drizzle has set in, so at Diane's suggestion, they take shelter in the Wellington Café, beside the visitor centre. With an order of hot chocolate all round, they invade one of the tables by the window to keep an eye out for their ride.

The mood around the table is a strange one, a mixture of excitement and gloominess. On the positive side, they're all still thrilled to have found the cache, especially given what they were up against. And Abi and Henry, now they again have time to think about it, are still trying to wrap their heads around the existence of the Ses.

On the not so positive side, for their part, Jaspa and the other Ses are sad at having to say goodbye to Phyllis (and even François) so soon. And then there's the dark cloud hanging over the whole group, but particularly Ben and Sam, thanks to the inevitable upcoming confrontation.

"Gobber's going to try every dirty trick he can think of to get you to pay up, you know," Henry tells the McRaes. "He's going to say you broke the terms of the bet."

"But Diane didn't help us!" objects Sam. "And Gobber cheated, anyway."

"It doesn't matter," Henry replies. "Whatever you say, he's going to claim that Diane did help us, and that the pair of you backed out on the bet because you lost. Face it: he's going to try and embarrass you into paying."

"Henry's right," Jaspa reluctantly agrees.

"I can have a word with the wee scunner," offers Diane, who has been quietly listening to the human part of the conversation.

"I couldnae huv said it better mahself," Gravee approves.

"Or I could speak to Jimmy and Laurel for you."

"Thanks," replies Ben. "But it wouldn't do any good. In fact, Gobber would just give us more grief when you weren't around."

Diane makes a face, accepting the truth of Ben's statement.

"I don't believe Gobber even found the cache himself," says Sam. "There was definitely no Anakev Skywalker in the logbook."

"It doesn't matter," counters her brother. "He'll just have some cockamamie excuse why it's not there. Like the page must be missing, or his mum signed the book and forgot to write his name. In any case, the bet was to do with us finding the cache, not him."

"Still, you can't be thinking of paying him," declares Abi. "You might as well admit Diane did help us."

"But Diane didn't help us!" Sam repeats.

"We know that, obviously," says Henry. "But Gobber's going to say she did, and if you cave in and pay, everyone else is going to believe him."

"Don't worry," Ben assures them all. "There's no way Sam and I are going to pay Gobber. What's the point? He's going to have a field day with me anyway. Handing over the cash and Mum's phone isn't going to change that. So why give him the satisfaction?"

"But that's not fair!" cries Sam.

"Fair's got nothing to do with it," snorts Bisckits the Wise.

***

"Where are they?" mutters Diane, looking at her watch. She holds it up to her ear, to check it's working. "They should have been here ages ago."

"How many times is she going to ask that?" complains Bisckits. "That must have been at least the 20th time."

221

"Leave her alone," Portia defends Diane. "She's worried. Dennis should have been here half an hour ago."

Another five minutes pass before Dennis finally pulls up outside the visitor centre. The minibus has hardly come to a stop before Diane is out of the cafe's door and hurrying down the street towards it. Ben and his friends unenthusiastically follow on behind.

"You're late," Diane accuses Dennis, as she pulls open the front door.

"Sorry. We got stuck at the waterpark," he apologises. "No prizes for guessing whose fault it was... But you're never going to believe why!" A huge grin splits Dennis's face as he makes this last proclamation.

Diane ushers Ben and the others into the back of the minibus before climbing into the passenger seat herself. Unsurprisingly, Gobber has the rear seat to himself. Equally unsurprisingly, the two other kids in the van have occupied the forward-most seat, as far from the bully as possible.

With a large exhalation of breath, Ben slumps down into the seat immediately in front of his enemy's. In his mind, he imagines Gobber's eyes burning holes into the back of his neck.

***

Dennis looks over his shoulder at his passengers. "Everyone comfy?" he asks cheerfully.

A series of nods and grunts indicates they are.

"So what happened?" Diane asks her friend.

"Well, I'd just..." But as they pull away from the visitor centre, the noise of the engine masks the rest of Dennis's softly-spoken answer from those in the back of the minibus.

Dennis heads down Route Du Lion and turns left on Chaussée de Charleroi, towards the village of Waterloo itself. After a few hundred metres, however, he bears right onto the ramp that feeds the anticlockwise side of the main Brussels ring road.

"You're joking!" exclaims Diane as they descend the ramp. Jaspa spots her looking in the rearview mirror, seemingly at Gobber.

***

They've been driving for almost ten minutes, when the pressure becomes too much for Ben. He turns around in his seat to confront Gobber.

Ben had expected to find his rival grinning smugly at him. In fact, he's shocked that Gobber didn't launch into his tormenting straight away. So Ben is even more surprised to discover his nemesis staring out of the side window, paying him no attention whatsoever.

Thinking this is some ploy to make him squirm even more, Ben decides to go on the offensive. "C'mon then," he says bluntly. "Let's get it over with."

Gobber doesn't reply. Instead he continues to gaze at the passing trees with unfocused eyes.

"We know you cheated," declares Sam.

Gobber slowly fixes her with an expression of contempt. "Whatever!" he growls, before turning to stare out of the window once more.

***

"What was all that about?" asks Jaspa, as soon as they're alone. "I expected Gobber to start into Ben as soon as we got in the minibus, but he didn't seem the slightest bit interested."

They've returned to the hotel and have congregated in the room shared by Ben and Henry. They boys are lying on their beds, Abi and Sam are slouched in a couple of armchairs, and the Ses are sitting on a small dressing table.

"Me too," Ben admits. "I can't believe he just sat there looking out the window."

"It must have something to do with whatever happened at the water-park," Abi points out. "If only we knew what it was."

"Diane was clearly shocked when Dennis told her about it," says Jaspa.

"An' jist as clearly, Dennis finds whitever it is reit funny," Gravee agrees.

"Couldn't you hear what the two of them were saying, Bizzee?" asks Sam.

"Sorry, but I wasn't paying attention," Bisckits apologises. "I was too focused on what Gobber was about to do."

"And then he didn't do anything!" Jaspa brings the conversation full circle.

"Oh, it's coming," Ben assures him. "Gobber's just playing with me. Just wait and see."

"Well, something weird's definitely going on," says Portia. "Did you see Gobber's eyes? They were all red."

"Aye," Gravee concurs. "Mebbe the wee jessie has bin greetin'."

A vindictive smile plays around the corners of Ben's mouth. "If that's true, no wonder Dennis found it funny."

"Ben McRae!" Portia scolds him. "You're better than that."

"Anyway, I'm not convinced," says Abi. "I thought Gobber looked more furious than sad."

"Nothing new there, then," observes Jaspa.

***

Still none the wiser regarding Gobber's uncharacteristic silence, the gang heads down to the hotel dining room. On the way, Abi tries quizzing the two Adventures who'd been at Océade with Gobber and Dennis, but they've seemingly been sworn to silence by Jimmy.

The McRaes and Greanings take their places at their usual table and are soon joined by Callum and Davy.

"Did you hear?" asks Callum in a hoarse whisper. "Gobber got into some kind of trouble at the waterpark."

"Do you know what he did?" enquires Henry.

"Not really," answers Davy. "Lily says someone spotted him peeing in the water."

"Eeeew!" exclaims Bisckits. "I must have accidentally drunk half the pool when we were there the other day."

"You and everyone else," agrees his brother.

"But Tommy reckons Gobber got caught shoplifting in the gift shop," Callum puts in.

Davy shrugs. "To be honest, we don't know if either of them is right," he admits. "We figured you'd know more than us, seeing as how you were on the same minibus."

"'Fraid not," says Henry. "Nobody will tell us anything."

The loud, animated buzz in the room suggests they're not the only ones discussing Gobber's latest misbehaviour.

Diane catches Ben's eye as she makes her way towards the leaders' table. She gives him a wink. Abi urgently waves the young woman over.

"Did Dennis tell you about what happened with Gobber at the water-park?" Abi asks.

"Oh, I don't want to spoil the surprise," Diane replies with a mischie-vous grin. "But trust me, it'll be worth the wait."

Laurel enters the dining room. She's closely followed by Jimmy, who is gripping their son gently but firmly by the upper left arm.

Suddenly, you could hear a pin drop.

Obviously reluctant, Gobber nevertheless allows himself to be guided to his chair at the leaders' table. He sits slack faced, staring at the place mat in front of him. Whereas he would normally seek out someone at whom to scowl (Ben, more often than not), this evening Gobber seems determined to avoid eye contact with anyone.

**

During the meal, the volume of the excited speculation grows ever louder. Through it all, Gobber keeps his attention firmly fixed on his plate. He pushes his food around, but doesn't actually eat anything.

The feverish chatter builds to a crescendo...

Until a squeal from Jimmy's chair being pushed back across the wooden floor silences it instantly.

Jimmy stands up and looks over at Laurel, who gives him a slight nod. He breathes out heavily before addressing the room.

"Everything we do has consequences," Jimmy begins. "Sometimes to ourselves, sometimes to others. If I jump into a pool, I'll get wet. If I give a friend a nice present, I'll make them happy. If I kick them, I'll make them sad.

"Sometimes consequences are good and sometimes bad. Sometimes they're significant and sometimes barely noticeable. Sometimes they're intended and sometimes accidental.

"We should always try to consider the consequences of our actions, to ourselves and other people. Admittedly, this isn't always easy. And we all make mistakes. But if we try to avoid doing things that hurt others, hopefully we won't be hurt too often ourselves.

"However..." Jimmy pauses for emphasis. "If you go out of your way to upset other people, sooner or later the consequences will come back to bite you. Sadly, this is what happened to Kevin today.

"And one of those consequences, is that his mother and I have decided that he himself should be the one to tell you all what happened."

Jimmy's announcement is greeted by a moment of stunned silence. This is immediately followed by a runaway outbreak of impatient conversation among the Young Adventurers: *What could Gobber have possibly done? Finally he's getting what's coming to him. Couldn't have happened to a nicer guy.*

For his part, Gobber looks like he wishes the floor would open up beneath him and swallow him whole.

"I cannae wait tae hear this," declares Gravee, voicing the overall feeling in the room.

***

Jimmy sits back down, and indicates to Gobber that he should stand up instead. The boy gets to his feet. His face glowing red as the setting sun, he begins to mutter something inaudible.

"No one can hear you, Kevin," Laurel patiently informs him. "Please speak up."

Gobber shoots his mother a look of disdain, but nonetheless starts again, this time in a louder voice. "We were at the waterpark," he tells his spellbound audience. "And I accidentally knocked some kid down one of the slides."

"That's not quite true, is it?" Laurel suggests.

"So what?" barks Gobber, the familiar defiance flaring up. "He was in my way and taking forever. He shouldn't have been up there if he was that scared."

"What happened next?" asks Laurel calmly.

"Nothing," insists her son, in a more composed tone. "I went down the slide."

"But that wasn't the end of it, was it?"

"No," Gobber grudgingly admits.

"Why?"

Gobber sighs sharply. "Because some big-mouthed staff member went and told security I'd pushed the kid down the slide."

"And what did they do?"

"Told the manager."

"And what did she do?"

For a few seconds, it seems that Gobber isn't going to answer. Then he suddenly snarls, "She made me spend the rest of the afternoon cleaning the changing rooms."

A collective gasp comes from the Adventurers listening to the unfortunate tale. But it's not quite over.

"Including...?" Laurel prompts.

"The shower drains."

At a table in the corner, someone sniggers.

"And...?"

Jaspa notices the bully has begun to shake, although whether it's from embarrassment or anger, he can't tell. Most likely a combination of the two.

The initial snigger is proving contagious. And the air in now thick with the tension of people trying not to giggle.

Laurel fixes her son with a firm gaze, until Gobber hangs his head and mumbles, "And the toilets."

The room erupts into uncontrollable laughter.

***

Epilogue

"That! Was! Classic!" proclaims Ben, as he leaps Superman-style onto his bed.

"I wish I could have been in one of those changing rooms to see it," grins Bisckits.

"Eeeew!" giggles Sam. "Gross!"

"What I'd like to know, is how on Earth they made him do it?" says Henry. "I mean, it's not like Gobber normally does what people tell him to. And anyway, the manager at the waterpark didn't really have the authority to make him do it, did they?"

"Actually, I was just speaking to Diane," Abi replies. "She told me that the manager called Gobber's parents and the three of them came up with the plan together. And then Jimmy and Laurel threatened to give Gobber's Playstation to Davy and Callum's foster home, if he didn't do whatever the waterpark staff told him to do."

"Good for them!" says Jaspa.

"They used the same threat to make him stand up in front of us all and admit what had happened," Abi adds. "Apparently, they've decided the only way to help Gobber is by being tougher with him."

"Wow," says Henry. "That's some really tough love!"

"If ye cannae dae th' time, dinnae commit th' crime," declares Gravee, staunchly.

"I don't know," says Portia. "Part of me feels a little sorry for Gobber."

"What?" exclaims Ben. "You can't be serious. After what he put us through today? After what he always puts people through every day?"

"I get how you feel, Ben. But I sort of know what Portia means, too," admits Abi. "Diane also told me that Dennis found Gobber crying in a corner of the men's changing room. It sounded really pitiful."

"That's so sad!" sighs Portia, compassionately.

Jaspa feels torn. Gobber has done nothing to justify his sympathy, yet he too can't help feeling a little sorry for the boy.

Even Ben seems a little taken aback.

"Everyone deserves a second chance, I suppose," Jaspa suggests after a few moments. "Who knows, perhaps he'll see the error of his ways after this."

"Mebbe," Gravee concedes doubtfully. "But dinnae hold ye breath."

"One thing's for sure," says Henry, trying to lighten the mood again. "Gobber's not going to be in a position to make fun of anyone else for quite a while."

"And I doubt he'll say anything more about the bets he made with Ben and Sam," adds Abi.

***

Since it's their last night in Belgium before returning home, the Young Adventurers are treated to one last expedition into central Brussels. As the sun goes down, Ben and the others find themselves sitting outside a crowded café in the fashionable Place du Grand Sablon, enjoying their second dessert of the evening. The occasional car slowly rumbles past along the pretty, cobblestone street.

"Life really is sweet," says Bisckits contentedly, as he scoops a large dollop of chocolate-flavoured whipped cream (from Abi's enormous slice of chocolate cake) off the end of his nose.

As if to prove the little Giraffeses wrong, Gobber suddenly appears from nowhere and slumps down into the only spare seat at the McRaes' and Greanings' table. "Well, if it isn't my two favourite debtors!" he ex-claims, feigning surprise at seeing them there.

Jaspa's heart drops in his chest, as he realises that Gobber's trademark smirk is firmly back in place. It seems that Bisckits wasn't the only one to speak too soon. They were all clearly mistaken (except perhaps Gravee) about the chances of Gobber keeping a low profile and forgetting the bets he'd made with Ben and Sam.

Jaspa's worst fears are confirmed, when Gobber leans forward and threateningly whispers, "Time to pay up McRaes!"

"Go boil your haggis!" retorts Sam.

"Now, now, Sammie," replies Gobber, pretending to be hurt. "If you play nicely and pay up straight away, I won't have to tell everyone what a loser your brother is." The bully pauses, as if considering this last state-ment. "I won't have to," he adds, with a malicious grin, "But I still will, of course. I'm a giving kind of person!"

"We're not paying you anything, Kevin," declares Ben, with as much self-confidence as he can muster.

"Oh, I think you are, tough guy!" Gobber contradicts, his smile grow-ing wider with each syllable. "After all, we all know you always follow the rules, McRae. And the rules of the bet were simple: you find the cache, on your own, or you pay me £50." He transfers his glare to Sam. "And one smartphone."

"Och, th' devious, arrogant wee scunner!" fumes Gravee.

***

"We did find the cache, and on our own. So why should Ben and Sam have to pay you?" demands Abi. "Especially when you haven't even found it yourself!"

"It doesn't matter whether I found the cache or not," snorts Gobber. "And anyway, I did find it. Unlike you bunch of losers. Even with that cretin Diane helping you."

Jaspa can't help notice the middle-aged couple sitting at the table directly behind Gobber are becoming increasingly distracted by the children's quiet but heated discussion. In fact, their own conversation has all but stopped, as they eavesdrop on what Ben and the others are saying.

"We know for a fact you didn't find it," says Henry. "JKL signed the logbook, alright. But there's no mention of Anakev Skywalker in it."

"You lot are just guessing. There's no way you've seen that logbook," replies Gobber. "And anyway, I bet my Dad already told you I stopped using that stupid geocaching name years ago," he adds, perhaps a little too defensively.

"Show him the photos!" yells Bisckits the Infuriated. "That'll shut him up!"

Ben begins reaching for his mum's phone, about to follow his small friend's advice. He stops, however, when Abi places a hand on his arm and gives him the slightest shake of her head.

"How come you're so sure we didn't see the logbook?" Abi enquires. "Maybe Diane really did help us find it."

"But she didn't help us!" complains Sam.

"It wouldn't matter, even if she had," Gobber sneers.

"But we followed the cache description all around the battlefield," says Abi. "From the visitor centre to the Inniskilling Memorial, to the chapel, to the cross. And then over the fields to the Prussian Monument, Napoleon's Observatory and La Belle Alliance. And then all the way back to the visitor centre."

As Abi catalogues the places they'd visited, Gobber sits arms folded, with a smug grin on his face. But his superior smirk melts off his face, as the younger Greaning concludes, "And eventually to the woods by

Hougoumont, where we found the final cache, hidden in a wood-lined hole in the ground, beside the oak tree with the metal tag on it."

"How on Earth...?" demands Gobber, incredulously. "There's no way!"

"Why not?" scoffs Abi, dismissively. "You claim you did."

"Is that steam comin' oot o' his lugs?" laughs Gravee, enjoying himself immensely.

"There's no way you found it!" Gobber erupts. "Because I took the final coordinates off the fence by the visitor centre yesterday morning before the re-enactment! So you must be lying!"

"Oh, don't worry. We know you took the final coordinates, Anakev." Abi says the name slowly and sarcastically. "But we found the cache anyway. Because despite what you think, we can do anything you can. And so much more."

"We can even show you a photo of the us holding the cache, if you don't believe us," Henry goads the bully further.

***

"Excuse me," interrupts the middle aged man behind Gobber. "You're talking about the *Waterloo 1815* geocache, aren't you? The one that takes you around the Waterloo battlefield."

"Er... yeah," replies Henry. "That's right."

The man fixes Gobber with a look that would melt titanium. "Why you thoughtless little... so-and-so!" he says angrily, shaking his head in disbelief. "My wife and I spent all yesterday afternoon and evening trying to complete that cache. We were at the visitor centre for over an hour alone, failing to find the final coordinates. And now we learn that they weren't even there, because of your stupid, selfish little prank."

"I never did noth..."

"There's no point lying, sonny," the man snaps. "I just heard you admit to taking the coordinates. Tell me you still have them, at least."

Gobber's silence strongly implies he doesn't.

Getting a grip of himself, the man turns to his attention back to the other children. "I don't suppose you still have the final coordinates, do you?" he asks in a pleasant tone.

"Sorry," replies Henry. "We never found them. In the end, we just used the spoiler photos and the hint to find the cache."

"You *übercached* the final, from only the spoilers?" asks the man's wife. "Wow! That's impressive!"

"Or just plain stubborn," replies Abi, with a shy grin.

"Gobber knew where to steal the penny-ultimate stage from, because he did the cache with his mum and dad last year," Sam informs the couple, helpfully. "They're right over there. Perhaps they can help you with the final coordinates," she suggests.

"Really?" replies the man. "Well, I'd love to have a word them about them about their son's antisocial behaviour, in any case. Come with me, you," he instructs an unusually timid Gobber.

Ben smiles broadly as the stranger marches Gobber over to his parents, while lecturing the bully on why people like him spoil geocaching for everyone else.

"So, I guess Gobber's actions had some unintentional positive consequences, after all," grins Jaspa.

"Reit enough," chuckles Gravee. "But dinnae tell him that!"

###

Keep up to date with Jaspa's ongoing adventures through his website and social media pages...

Website: *www.jaspasjourney.com*

Travel Blog: *jaspasjourney.wordpress.com*

Facebook: *facebook.com/jaspasjourney*

Instagram: *@JaspasJourney*

Twitter: *@JaspaJ*

If you enjoy the ***Jaspa's Journey*** books, please review them on *Goodreads.com*.

Watch for

Jaspa's Journey

Book 4

The Hermit
of
Kennecott

by

Rich Meyrick

As Ben and Sam McRae head out on an Alaskan adventure, Jaspa and
the gang can't resist tagging along. But when Portia comes down with a
mysterious illness, this trip of a lifetime rapidly becomes a life and death
race to find a cure.

Their pursuit leads them ever deeper into the Alaskan wilderness. To
ghost town abandoned almost a hundred years ago. And the one person
who can save her… An elusive Ses known simply as *the Hermit*.

Now Available

Now Available